FALLING IN LOVE

and Other Misadventures

SHORT STORIES BY

L. WADE POWERS

LUMINARE PRESS

WWW.LUMINAREPRESS.COM

"Redemption" was first published in the 2017 NIWA anthology
*Bridges: A Collection of Short Fiction by Members of the Northwest
Independent Writers Association,* edited by Lee French.

"With This Ring" was first published in the 2018 anthology
A Linkville Press New Year, edited by Amanda Marie.

"Lawnmower Ted" was published, in a modified form, as a chapter of
The Party House, by Luminare Press (Eugene, OR) in 2019.

Printed in the United States of America

Cover Design: Claire Flint Last
Cover illustration: Roslyn McFarland, Farlands Publishing.
(www.RoslynMcFarland.com), based on "Sparkle."

Luminare Press
442 Charnelton St.
Eugene, OR 97401
www.luminarepress.com

LCCN: 2019937623
ISBN: 978-1-64388-106-5

For those who seek, laugh at, cry over,
and eventually find that most elusive human relationship.
Been there and done that, friend.

The women always look better at closing time.

—AN OLD BARROOM PROVERB

The men never do.

—AN OBSERVATION BY BARROOM WOMEN

For Alla Vichurina Powers:
My wife and partner,
who looks better all the time.

For Erik and Leslie:
They never stopped believing and
I never stopped dancing.

TABLE OF CONTENTS

Falling in Love at the Dixie Hotel 1

Redemption 22

Sweet Dreams 33

Only a Pile of Leaves 55

Safety Pin 62

With This Ring 80

Interlude I: Pandora's Secret 91

Death Is a Man I Know 94

Autumn Cats 115

A Night on Big Rat Island 119

Interlude II: Six-Word Stories 137

Lawnmower Ted 138

Sparkle 146

Odometer Moments 182

Another Cup of Coffee To Go 192

Ghost Birds 199

Under the Porch 214

I Am Not a Well-Qualified Buyer 218

The Omaha Two-Step 225

Reception 237

Health Fair 244

Door-to-Door 255

Afterword 285

Acknowledgments 286

About the Author 287

FALLING IN LOVE AT THE DIXIE HOTEL

One experience that many males, but not all, have to look forward to,
or not, is their first intimate sexual encounter. Often it is with someone
they know, a girl or young woman from school or their neighborhood.
For some, it is a professional transaction, a pay-to-play and learn.
Sometimes, it seems like you just don't have a better choice.

Melvin wasn't kidding. No jokes, no smile, not this time. Charlie and I had never seen him that serious and he commanded our complete attention. He sat across the table from us, his right hand clasped firmly around a not-so-frosty mug of root beer. He had finished a third of it, another indication of important things on his mind.

At two in the afternoon, it was slack time and we had the corner diner mostly to ourselves. It was early summer in Montgomery, Alabama, a few weeks before all hell would break loose with Freedom Riders, martial law, and the ugly events of the Civil Rights Movement in 1961. That day in the city, however, was one of tranquility and business as usual—outside the restaurant. Inside, the three of us were quietly consulting on matters of life altering consequence.

Melvin was in love. It had happened suddenly and, for all of us, unexpectedly. Melvin was twenty-six and a quiet, shy guy for whom romantic notions and intimacy were yet to be realized. He was an artist, a sensitive Jewish guy who liked fine books and classical music. The opposite sex was still a blissful mystery—in other words, he was a virgin. He wasn't the only one in our little group, but Charlie was twenty and I had not yet turned nineteen, so we believed we still had a legitimate excuse for our failure to fulfill the manly rites of passage. The three of us were stationed at a nearby Air Force base undergoing technical training. We were many hundreds of miles away from home and had known each other as barracks mates for only a few months. Like most young guys in college, in the military, or working for a living, we talked a lot about girls-women-females. Most of us dreamt about them, desired them, and fantasized endless scenarios of encounters involving introductions, conclusions, and all of the steps in between. From romantic interludes to purely physical bouts of lust, our conquests occurred mainly in our imaginations and dreams. But, some of the dreams weren't bad.

Melvin was a bit different. He rarely discussed women, saying it was a topic that gentlemen didn't share with others. The truth was he didn't have anything to share. While other guys were bragging about their exploits and conquests, real or imagined, Melvin would sit off to the side with a disgusted look on his face. Often he would find some other place to go. A few of the guys at the base commented that he might be "one of those." In those days, "one of those" was taken a lot more seriously, especially in the military. Most guys didn't want to share a barracks with someone whose sexual proclivities were radically different from their own. We not only didn't want to tell, we really didn't want to know.

But Melvin wasn't gay. He was merely inexperienced and at his advancing age he was becoming increasingly depressed about it. On the base, we were all old enough to drink beer and Melvin was also peculiar in this regard. There are a hundred different ways to react to alcohol and Melvin had his. First, he became withdrawn, quiet, and moody. Then he became very aggressive, his belligerence spilling out at the slightest provocation or opportunity. After the first few unfortunate incidents, Charlie and I cut him off after a couple of beers, insisting he drink a soda instead. He usually finished the night with root beer. He stayed calm and we stayed happy. Melvin's alcoholic arousal was such that he also lost all discrimination. He was just as likely to punch the biggest, meanest son of a bitch in the bar as he was to choose the smallest. As fate would have it, his fervor for a fight was not matched by requisite skill in the manly arts and he usually finished the night on the floor or heaped in a corner. We were wise to monitor his libations.

On this day, however, Melvin was sober. He was in love and he needed our help. Actually, what he needed was our money. Airmen in training didn't make much per month and he had already spent his allotment. He needed a loan and he needed to convince us his cause was just. We were skeptical.

His need actually started a few nights earlier, at the same diner. The three of us had been in town, hanging around, fantasizing about romance and adventure as usual. The local women knew all about airmen, especially those with only one stripe on their sleeve. That meant we were still early in our careers and that as soon as our training was finished, we would be transferred elsewhere. Not good candidates for developing a long-term relationship, nor did we have the money to entertain them in the short run. Can you spell L-O-S-E-R? The smart girls avoided us and the not so smart girls were in heavy demand. We were eating White Castle hamburgers, the square ones you could buy for one dollar a bag. A bag contained eight sandwiches consisting of white bread and a very thin slab of meat. We were never sure what the meat was, but if you added enough mustard, catsup, and relish, it didn't matter. It matched our pocketbooks if not our gastronomic sensibilities.

Melvin ate silently that night, lost in thought. As the oldest, he usually sat across from Charlie and me. I'm not sure why. Perhaps it was so we could receive the full benefit of his wisdom or maybe so he could keep an eye on both of us at the same time—we weren't beyond playing an occasional prank. The diner was on a downtown corner and he kept staring out the window at a large building located kitty-corner from us. It was a once fashionable hotel, built in the late nineteenth century. It shared an increasingly decadent ambiance with much of the rest of downtown Montgomery, a city that had seen better days. We had never been inside it, but we knew a few things about it. The Dixie Hotel, it was rumored on base, was where you went to find yourself a lady of the night. Charlie and I had never inquired further, but apparently Melvin had.

"I know how to do it," he said between mouthfuls of greasy meat and doughy bread.

"Do what?" Charlie and I said together, thinking he had discovered a new way to consume cheap hamburgers.

He looked up at us, pausing significantly, swallowed, and reached for the root beer. We waited. He put the glass down, looked each of us in the eye and said, "Get laid."

"Congratulations," answered Charlie. "If I had known you were still ignorant about the birds and bees, I would have found a sex manual for you."

"I don't mean that, I mean I know where to get laid and who to talk to." He was obviously not in the mood for us to take him any other way than serious, so Charlie and I sat up in the booth and leaned forward so we could talk quietly, if not seriously.

"One of the older guys that works in the base exchange told me what to do," he continued. "It's across the street, at the Dixie Hotel."

"You're going over there to get a piece?" I asked. "You sure you wanna do that?"

"Yeah Walt, it's time. I need to get this over with, get it behind me." He folded his hands in front of him on the table, as if he was discussing paying off a loan or going to college. He kept looking at each of us, waiting for a reaction.

We had also heard the gossip: a guy could go to the hotel, talk to one of the black shoeshine guys or one of the janitors, and he would make the arrangements. We had also heard the cost could be anywhere from ten dollars for a quickie to a hundred dollars or more for a classier woman for the night.

"Do you know what you want?" asked Charlie, fighting hard to keep a grin off his face. He knew as well as I did that Melvin wouldn't appreciate his flippant sense of humor at this pivotal moment. Besides, we weren't sure if Melvin had any idea of what he wanted.

"I want to get laid. I want to be able to say I slept with a woman, you know, had intercourse. I need to do it tonight, now, while I'm here and thinking about it." He stated it with the determination of a corporate CEO reporting to his board of directors.

Only Melvin would use the word "intercourse" as if he was a medical student or social worker. We had shorter and more colorful terms for the grand deed but it wasn't the moment to correct him.

"Do you want one or both of us to come with you, you

know, to sort of watch out and make sure nothing bad happens?" I asked. I wasn't sure what "bad" might entail, and my experience in these matters was exactly the same as Melvin's. That is, nada.

"Thanks, but unless you're gonna get a woman of your own, I don't think that's allowed. The guy at the base told me not to worry. They depend on airmen for most of their business and they're not going to mess anybody up. They're afraid the MPs would close them down or something."

Charlie and I were transfixed, amazed that our buddy was going to make this move, a step we had all talked about but seemed ill prepared to take.

"I still don't know, Melvin. You don't know what'cher getting—she could be old, fat, diseased—I mean you could end up with something real disgusting." I was trying to picture myself walking across the street, doing what he was about to do.

Melvin looked at me, speaking slowly, very deliberately, as if he had been asking and answering the same questions. "He told me I can ask for what I want and they would tell me what was available. And, he said, the women don't have any diseases. They're clean. Another reason why they don't get in trouble with the base."

Charlie looked at him, then at me, and picked up his Coke. "Wow, I guess this is it, old boy. It's been good to know your virgin ass." He gave his patented laugh, a nasal snort of amusement that most people found disgusting, particularly right after he had a drink of something.

"We'll wait for you here. How long do you think it'll take?" I asked.

"Probably not long, maybe a half hour to an hour. Depends on whether what I want is available or I have to wait."

"Yeah, sloppy seconds," I said.

"Or thirds or fourths," added Charlie.

Somehow this didn't reassure Melvin and he finished his next three sandwiches in silence. Charlie and I commenced to speculate on what kind of women might be available: long hair, short hair, blonde or red head, young and naive (surely not), experienced, maybe even a grandmother.

"Yeah, but can she bake an apple pie?" said Charlie.

"She can bake something else," I retorted.

Melvin broke out of his meditation. "Do either one of you guys have a rubber?"

Condoms were available in almost every men's room in Montgomery. You had choices between luminescent ones, French ticklers, oh-so-smooths, and many others. Most of us carried one in our wallet, "just in case." The problem was that most of us had been carrying them for some time. Charlie pulled his out. The aluminum foil wrapper looked like it had been aging for decades. Melvin politely declined and told us there were probably some available at the hotel. We could also tell that, despite his determination, he was very anxious about the pending encounter. We knew if we delayed him further, he might easily talk himself out of it or find an excuse for putting it off.

In many ways, his courage was our own and we were waiting to vicariously experience that first time through his encounter, without the risk of failure of course. The risk was real—failure was the demon that haunted our own vulnerable inner recesses. What if we entered that room and we didn't know what to do. What do you say to your intended partner? Suppose something went wrong? It wasn't like asking someone to dance, was it? Worse of all, suppose you couldn't? She was ready, waiting, all you had to do was step up and be a man, and…you COULDN'T. We didn't voice these fears to Melvin. We hardly wanted to express them to ourselves. Instead we smiled, patted him on the shoulder, and told him to "go for it," "make us all proud," "do it for the glory of the United States Air Force," and "don't leave any essential body parts behind."

Melvin stood up, a look of grim resignation on his face. He had thin lips anyway, and they seemed even thinner, as if he was tightening his jaws and preparing for battle. We again reassured him we would be right here waiting for him. The diner was open all night and we could drink coffee until the wee hours if necessary. Actually, we had to be back by midnight, but it was only three p.m., so that would give Mighty Melvin more than enough time to show the women of Montgomery what it was all about and still enlighten and entertain us for the rest of the evening.

Melvin walked out the door and across the street without once looking back. We watched him approach a side door to the hotel where a shoeshine stand was located. He walked up to an elderly black man we had passed on the street any number of times. We could see them talking and the black man nodding. Melvin started to reach for his wallet, but the shine man shook his head and Melvin put the wallet back. They entered the side door, the black man leading. Our wait started.

Charlie and I spent most of the time speculating on what Melvin was doing at each moment. We fully expected to get a blow-by-blow (Charlie snorted) account of what happened. We expressed a mixture of envy, worry, and sarcastic dismissal.

"Do you think that's something you wanna do?" Charlie asked.

I hesitated. I wasn't sure. "Maybe, but not here. I don't know about the Dixie. I'd like to see what I'd get before I give anyone any money. I don't want to give up a lot for some old whore. What about you?"

"I don't want a whore. I want my first experience to be with somebody I know. You know, the girl next door or a schoolmate, someone like that."

"Yeah, I guess so. I had a chance once when I was in high school to join my friends when they went up to some woman's apartment. She was a fat old nympho named Ophelia. The guys took turns with her and they each paid five dollars."

"Did they say they liked it?"

"A couple of them did, but one of my friends said that she was so disgusting that he walked right out of her bedroom. A couple of others said they only went in because they didn't want to back down in front of the older guy that had brought them there. I was glad I didn't go."

<hr>

THE TIME PASSED AS WE DRANK COFFEE AND ATE PIE, constantly glancing at the clock. About forty-five minutes later, Melvin walked through the door of the diner and sat down. The look of triumph and relief was visible, as if a billboard had been erected on his forehead in bright neon lights, flashing to the world, "LOOK AT ME. I DID IT! I'M A MAN AT LAST."

"Are you a man, at last?" I asked.

Melvin looked at me, then at Charlie. "Yep." He paused, looked over at the counter. "Boys, think I'll have some of that pie." He got up, serving notice that Charlie and I would have to wait a few minutes longer to learn the exquisite details. We watched him order at the counter. He stood on one foot, his right hip jutting outward, his head held at an angle to his body and tilted upward, as if he was communicating with heaven. Offering thanks and receiving congratulations, no doubt.

Charlie nudged me. "What a difference an hour makes."

I agreed. "A different guy. I wonder how long we're gonna have to live with this." Melvin returned with a root beer and a piece of pie and started eating.

"Well?" Charlie asked.

"Good pie. Did you try their peach pie? This is pretty good stuff."

"Fuck the pie," Charlie said, in a voice loud enough to attract the attention of people in the adjacent booths. "What the hell happened?"

Melvin smiled at last, noting with satisfaction our irritation. Now he was as anxious to tell his tale as we were to hear it. He took a sip of root beer, cleared his throat, and related to us the "most significant forty-five minutes of my life."

"I almost turned back, at least twice before I got to the other side of the street," he began. "I was so damned nervous, wondering if I was about to make the biggest mistake of my life. As I got nearer to the shoeshine stand, I figured, what the hell, it won't be any big deal to ask. The man looked up at me, put his paper down and smiled. 'Help yuh, sir,' he asked. I blurted it out pretty fast, telling him that I had heard I might be able to get a girl at the hotel, but I wasn't sure who to talk to. He told me I was talking to the right person. I asked him how much it would be and started to get my wallet out, to let him know I had some money, but he told me to put it away, that they didn't do business out on the street where everyone can see. 'Some folks might not appreciate their business,' he said. He told me to follow him inside and I'd be taken care of there."

Melvin took another sip of root beer. Charlie and I said nothing. We didn't twitch a muscle.

"We went down a corridor and down a few stairs. There was a large bathroom in the basement. There was another shoeshine guy in the bathroom, a middle-aged black guy. The first man told him I needed some help. That was all, just that I needed some help. He turned to me, said that Grover would take care of me, and left. Grover was having a smoke and looking at me, sort of like he was sizing me up. He said, 'What'cha have in mind, son?' I told him I just wanted one of the women. 'Anyone special?' he asked. I told him no, maybe someone young, not too experienced. He kept looking at me, as if he could read my mind. It was starting to give me the creeps. He took another drag and asked me if it was my first time. I didn't know whether to say yes or try to bluff it, to pretend that I had done it lots of times. I figured they might not take advantage of someone who was more experienced. So I told him I had done it lots of times. 'No,' he says, 'I mean here. Is this your first time in the Dixie?'"

"Shit," interrupted Charlie, "they're about to have your young Jewish butt."

"Shut up, Charlie," I said, "let him go on."

"I told him that it was and I wasn't too sure about the procedure. He told me I was to pay him and he would take me up to the room and pick me up later. He asked me for thirty dollars."

"Thirty dollars!" I said, a lot louder than intended. Again a few people in the next booth stopped talking and looked our way. One of the guys was grinning at us, as if he knew exactly what we were talking about. I leaned forward and lowered my voice. "I thought you said it would only be ten or twenty dollars."

"Yeah, I was surprised too. When I asked him about it, he told me I wouldn't want no ten dollar pussy. He said it wasn't for a nice white boy like me. He said he would fix me up with a real sweet one for thirty, that she'd be worth it."

"Was she?" I asked. Melvin ignored me and continued.

"I asked him about rubbers, if I could get some there in the bathroom. He told me 'the lady will provide every-thing yuh need, all included.' He finished his smoke, then stood up and asked me if I was ready. I said I was. He held out his hand and then I remembered I had to pay him first, so I got out thirty dollars and gave it to him. He folded it and stuck in his pocket, then turned and walked out the door. I followed several feet behind him. We walked up another long corridor and came to a freight elevator. 'Our special way,' he told me. We got in and went up three or four floors, I'm not sure, then the elevator stopped and we got out.

"What was it like there?" asked Charlie. He seemed completely mesmerized by Melvin's account.

"Where?" replied Melvin.

"In the hallway. Did it look like a whorehouse or like a regular hotel? I mean, were there fancy things on the walls… you know, nude paintings and red lights, that kinda stuff?"

"No. I don't think so. It was just regular lights, yellow bulbs, not real bright. It just looked like any other hotel. Kind of old, a little cheap looking, worn carpet…"

"Get on with it," I said. "Who cares about the decor? Tell us what happened, in the room." Both of them looked at me.

Melvin grinned. "You should have been there. Maybe

both of you should go next." We didn't say anything.

"I followed the man about half way down the hall, then he stopped at a door and knocked twice. Someone opened the door, but I couldn't see who it was from where I was standing. He just nodded then stepped aside and waved me toward the door. I froze for just a second, not sure of what to do, but he stood there, gave me a smile and said 'this is your place, son, have a good time.' So I entered the room and he closed the door behind me."

Charlie put both hands on the table. "Man, I gotta take a leak. All this coffee." We both looked at him as he started to get up from the booth.

"*Now*, you gotta go? *Now*?" I said. "Can't you wait just five damn more minutes? I want to hear this."

"Let him go," Melvin told me. "It'll wait. I'm going to have another piece of pie." He looked at me like a salesman who knows he has what you need and want. "Damn good pie." With that, he also got up and walked back to the counter. Charlie strode quickly to the men's room and I was left alone in the booth. I glanced over at the Dixie, but the shoeshine man was gone.

A few minutes later, both of them returned and Melvin continued his story.

"She was young and pretty, with reddish-blonde hair and a few freckles. She was wearing a bright red negligee, one of those silky short ones. Her legs were very pretty." He paused, lost in thought while we tried to imagine what he had seen, what he was seeing.

"What did she say?" I asked.

"She said 'hi' like we were old friends, meeting at school for lunch. She asked me if I was from the base and I told her I was. I told her my name. She sat on the edge of the bed and put her legs up, holding her knees together with her arms. Just like some schoolgirl, I swear. I didn't expect that."

"So what did you do, besides tell her your name?" asked Charlie.

"At first I just stood there, but she told me to come closer so she could see me better. I was standing in the shadow by the door. I moved over by the bed and she asked me if I wanted to sit down. So, I sat next to her. Then she asked me if there was anything special I wanted to do. I wasn't sure what to say, what to ask for." Melvin hesitated, as if reliving each moment.

"And…?" I prompted.

Melvin looked a little sheepish and his face became noticeably pinker in the harsh white lights of the diner. "Well, I told her I just wanted the usual. 'The usual what?' she asked. She was smiling at me, but I didn't feel like she was making fun of me. It was more like she was having fun, enjoying herself. I told her I would do whatever she wanted to do. Then she asked me to take off my clothes. I stood up and took off everything but my skivvies. She got up and dimmed the lights, pulled back the covers, then slid out of her nightgown. I could see she was really beautiful. She climbed in the bed and asked me to join her." Again, Melvin paused, lost in thought.

"And…?" I said.

"And I did. I got in the bed with her and it was…it was great. I never realized how much I've been missing. I can't explain it."

"Sure you can, Melvin, give it your best shot," said Charlie. "We're all ears. What did you do to her? What did she do to you?"

Melvin looked down at his empty plate, his hands folded in front of him. "We had sex. She took care of me. That's all I really want to say about that. Exactly what we did isn't important." He looked up at us. His demeanor had changed. The cockiness was gone and we could tell he meant what he was saying and was reluctant to elaborate further.

"Okay, fair enough," I told him, "but what happened afterwards?"

"We laid in the bed together for a few minutes, then she told me she had other customers and she had to get ready for them. She told me I could wash up at the sink but I needed to be dressed and ready to go in a few minutes. She got up and washed too."

"What about the rubber?" asked Charlie. "You didn't say you used a rubber."

"Oh yeah, she had one in a drawer by the bed. She made me put it on after I got ready. You know, stiff."

"Did she get you stiff…?" Charlie didn't finish. The look from Melvin told him that it was off limits and he wasn't going to provide any additional details. Except one.

Melvin coughed then looked at each of us in turn. "I know you may not believe this, but I think she might have been a virgin."

"What?" said Charlie and I in synchrony.

"You're shitting us," I said. Charlie just sat there with his mouth open, not knowing whether to laugh or not.

"I'm serious. When we were both really worked up, you know, ready to have a climax, she started panting and grabbing me. I could tell she was really coming, that she wasn't faking it like we had always believed whores do. And then…afterwards, when we were lying there, I could see she had some tears in her eyes. One of them was rolling down her cheek."

"No shit, Melvin. Do you really think they have virgins at the Dixie Hotel, just waiting for you to have your first time?" Charlie wasn't trying to be insulting, but I could tell Melvin was convinced about the innocence of his "lover" and he wasn't going to entertain any contradictions on the subject.

"Hey, maybe he's right Charlie," I said, trying to be conciliatory. "Everyone is a virgin at some time in their life, even whores. How do you know she wasn't?"

Melvin didn't say anything and Charlie didn't answer. After a few moments of silence I reminded them that we needed to be on our way home. Not because it was getting late, but I had eaten all of the cheap mystery meat I could handle that weekend. We left the diner and walked to a nearby bus stop where locals often picked up airmen and gave them rides into the base. Charlie and I kept looking at each other—Melvin was lost in a world of his own. We couldn't blame him.

ONE WEEK LATER WE SAT AT THE SAME DINER, WATCHING Melvin. We hadn't asked him anything more about his experiences and he didn't volunteer further insights, but Charlie and I could tell he had been doing a lot of hard thinking. We had just started our usual bag of burgers and some greasy fries when Melvin announced that he was going back to the Dixie to see his girlfriend.

"And which girlfriend would that be?" asked Charlie, thinking Melvin might know someone else who worked at the hotel.

"You know, my lover. My redhead from a few nights ago." Melvin seemed a bit tense as he answered.

I had a burger in my hand, about half way up to my mouth. I froze, looking at Melvin. "You mean you're ready to pay another thirty dollars for another go at her?" I knew that the first thirty dollars had probably exhausted his bankroll for the month.

He answered carefully and slowly, "If I have to. But I don't think I'll have to. If I can get to see her and tell her how I feel about her, then I know she'll want to be with me. I don't want to meet her in the hotel like last time. In fact, I don't want her to do that kind of work anymore."

Charlie leaned closer to Melvin. "Hey man, you better think this through. They're not going to let you go up to her room without paying. She works there. It ain't a social club." He looked over at me for support.

"Charlie's right, Melvin. You no pay, you no play." I felt strange talking to him this way. He was seven years older than I, Charlie and I were still virgins, Melvin wasn't, and here we were telling him the rules of the game.

We might as well have been talking to a concrete bunker. Melvin just shook his head and said he knew she was just starting out. If she wasn't a virgin, then she was close to it. All she needed was someone to care, to rescue her from a horrible life.

"Do you even know her name?" I asked. I didn't remember him mentioning it a week ago.

He shook his head. He was sure the man in the basement would tell him, perhaps if he gave him a few dollars. Charlie and I looked at each other. Charlie shrugged and continued eating, pretending to be extremely interested in what was in the burger bag. I put my sandwich down and tried to reason with Melvin, but he wasn't having it.

"What I need from you guys is twenty dollars, just in

case I have to pay to see her. I have ten, so let me borrow the rest until payday."

I had never heard him plead before. It was pathetic and neither Charlie nor I knew how to deal with it. In the few months we had known each other, we had become very tight, willing to share our good times and bad and every dime that any of us had. How could we turn him down?

"I love her," he said. "I know it's sudden and seems impossible, but I know it's the real thing. If you could have been there, seen her and heard her, you'd know what I mean."

Charlie opened his wallet and gave him ten. I did the same. Melvin grinned from ear to ear as he stood up, adding our money to his. "I'm forever in your debt, guys, I can never repay you for this."

"Oh, yes you can," replied Charlie. "Forever means until payday, two weeks from now. You will repay us."

I was thinking as hard as I could. Melvin had the money and I knew he was about to make a fool of himself or worse. In desperation, I pushed my lunch away and stood up. "Tell you what, let me go over and see if I can find a way for you to meet her without dealing with the pimps."

Melvin looked at me uncertainly, considering the idea. "I don't know. What will you do?" he asked.

"I'll talk with them, describe her and tell them that I heard she had been really great to a friend of mine and I might be interested in her. I'll see if I can't find out her name or room number, or something about her before I give them any money."

Charlie kept eating but looking at me as if I had lost it completely. Melvin wasn't convinced, but he was thinking. It was obvious he didn't have a better plan and he didn't want to spend the money if he could avoid it. Fortunately, neither of them thought to ask how I had managed to possess an additional thirty dollars.

He finally relented. "Okay, but don't mess it up. Find out what you can and come right back." Then he added in a grim voice. "And that doesn't include seeing her or trying her out yourself."

I thought Charlie was going to choke on his food and I had to reach over and pound his back. There were tears in his eyes, but Melvin was on his way to the rest room. Still unable to speak, Charlie gave me that I-hope-you-know-what-the-hell-you're-doing look. I merely told him to wish me luck and I left the diner and crossed the street before Melvin returned and had second thoughts.

I approached the shine man near the side door, trying to think of the right words to say, anything that didn't make me sound like the biggest fool in Alabama. As I neared, he asked me if I wanted a shine. I told him no but that I could really use a favor from him, one that would help me, my friend, and probably his "business." I told him about Melvin and that he was a well-meaning guy but he had become infatuated with a young woman at the hotel and he was planning to return and claim her. The shine man grinned and nodded. He remembered Melvin and knew that he was a first timer. He had seen it all before with young airmen and their first-time women. Would he help me? "Maybe," he said, "it depends."

I pressed a ten, my last one, in his hand. I told him all he had to do was to lie to Melvin when he came over. Tell him his lady was somewhere else—no longer available. I told him that no matter how much my friend offered to pay for her, that he was to say he was sorry, she was gone to Mississippi or someplace.

"I'll do what I can," he said. He sat down and picked up his paper as I walked away, wondering if I had done the right thing.

I crossed the street to the diner, thinking I had probably just thrown away ten dollars for nothing. They were waiting at the table, Charlie sitting back against the wall, Melvin on the edge of his seat. I didn't waste any time.

"I couldn't get much information, but the shoe shine man said if you talked to him yourself, he'd answer your questions." I looked Melvin in the eyes, giving him my best swear-to-God stare.

Melvin got up. "Right. Okay. Thanks Walt, I'll go over and see." He spun on his heels and was out of the diner before we could give him any last parting advice. I could only hope the shine man would come through and not take him for another thirty dollars.

We watched through the window as Melvin and the shine man talked. Melvin climbed up in the chair and the shine man got out his rags and polish and started slapping leather, working on Melvin's black-laced dress shoes. We watched them talking while he worked. About ten minutes later, Melvin stood up, handed some money to the man, said a few more words, and walked back toward the diner. We watched him carefully as he approached the table and sat down. He seemed to be neither disturbed nor anxious. In fact, he was more like his old self than he had been since the night of his magical hotel visit. Charlie and I waited.

"You guys ready to go?" Melvin asked. "Let's go find something to do in this town."

"What did he tell you?" I quietly inquired.

"I asked him about the girl I had visited on Wednesday. He remembered me and said he knew which one I had been with, that he and his inside friend kept track of everyone's guests. He said she had been transferred to another place, somewhere in Louisiana, he wasn't sure where. 'It happens all the time,' he said, 'Keeps the customers coming back for something new.' I asked him if he knew exactly where she was and he told me that only her husband knew that. Imagine that! She's married! And, her husband knows what she's doing. She works for him."

Charlie and I stood up and left the booth, agreeing we should make the best of the time we had left that evening. Melvin gave us our money back and thanked me for my trouble. We weren't sure exactly where we were going or what we'd be doing, but two things we did know. Charlie and I were sure we could wait a while longer for our first ladies and that they wouldn't be found at the Dixie Hotel. And secondly, we wouldn't be eating any more of those thin square greasy burgers on doughy white bread for the next several days.

REDEMPTION

Love and loyalty are partners entwined in a complex dance.
Are they interdependent? Does one require the other?
For those growing up, before they reach the enlightenment
tagged "puppy love," loyalty to peers presents an expression of
love, complicated and challenged by what is right and wrong.

Brad Wilkins could have squished me like a bug. Flat, lifeless, a cockroach spread across a sidewalk to rot in the sun. That's how I thought it might be when I was ten years old. Mr. Wilkins was tall, with broad shoulders and big hands, the kind that could catch a football and run it past other big men that wanted to stop him. He wasn't mean or anything like that. In fact, most of the kids in our neighborhood thought he was a hero. He always smiled and waved at us when we saw him in the drugstore or walking along the street. My dad said that Brad Wilkins should have been a pro and that he would have been if it hadn't been for some trouble he had in college. We didn't know much about that and the adults didn't think it was important to tell us what they meant by "trouble." What we knew was he was a giant, towering over my friends and me. Our eyes barely came to his belt buckle—he always knelt or bent over to talk to us.

But then I was, like my friends, short for my age. The other kids called us the "sawed-off gang," "the midget express," and other names I'd just as soon forget about. Peter is my real name, according to mom, "a good solid name for a serious young boy who will go to college and be someone important." My dad never called me that. He worked in a factory and had never been to college. He called me "Shorty." He was about an inch shorter than my mom and he thought it was a good nickname, but I hated that. My friends called me "Pete" or "Petey."

My best friend was Gary. He had freckles everywhere and bright red hair. Some of the kids called him "Flame" or "Carrot." He didn't mind those names, but he hated "Red." His dad was nicknamed Red, and he hated being compared to his banker-mister-business-suit-dad. He must have the most boring, the worst job in the world, Gary would tell us. He sat in an office and wrote down numbers, and talked to people about numbers. That's all he did every day.

Mikey, the youngest in our gang, wasn't so sure. He said, "Your dad gets to handle lots of money. That's pretty cool." His eyes grew large and his mouth made a perfect circle when he talked. Mikey was easily impressed. He didn't have a dad. His father was killed in the war, in Korea.

Gary looked at him in disbelief. "Who told you that crap?"

"My mother. She said that bankers are rich. They have lots of money and get to count it everyday and…"

"Your mother don't know diddly squat." Gary walked away, leaving Mikey standing there with his mouth still open, turning to us for support. We sometimes felt sorry for Mikey, for being little, only eight years old, and not having a dad like the rest of us, but we didn't argue with Gary. He knew a lot about parents and we had to respect his judgment. Gary didn't mean to embarrass Mikey or any of us. It was just the way things were.

"It'll help Mikey grow up," Gary told us. "I don't think they want us to get older. They'll keep you kids forever if we let them. My older sister wants to date but dad said no. She can't wear lipstick or tight sweaters and can't go out with anyone and she's already fourteen. But she does anyway, secretly with a guy who has a car. So that's why we got to stick together, make our own rules." Gary said this with an emphatic nod of his head and even Mikey had to agree.

"Yeah, well our rules don't get us a whole bunch, do they?" said Justin, mouthing each word slowly and separately, as if he was talking to someone who needed time to understand him. "All we do is play around. Maybe we ought to do something different." Justin was also ten and the toughest kid in our group. Even though we were small, no one messed with us when Justin was around. We called him our bantam rooster because he scratched and kicked dirt when he fought. He wasn't the smartest, however. He liked things plain and simple. You either liked someone or you didn't. He was your friend or he wasn't. We understood him.

Gary looked at Justin with his patented scowl and red face, never a good sign. "Play around? I've never heard you offer anything to dance about."

That was Gary. He had a temper to match his red hair and he could get excited about almost nothing. He got all worked up one day because a kid was wearing a Yankees jacket. The kid was probably from New York or liked Mickey Mantle or something. But Gary couldn't stand it. It's the Giants, he would remind us. The Giants are the cool team. Only an idiot, a real scuz, doesn't know that. The Giants had just arrived in the Bay Area from New York and Gary was already a rabid fan. He collected baseball trading cards and could quote stats on all the players. Justin stared back but didn't answer. He was tougher and stronger but Gary was the leader and we looked to him for ideas and inspiration. Justin wasn't the creative one.

Most of the time that summer we roamed the neighborhood, climbing over fences to make surprise visits on our buddies. We played with soldiers in the dirt, staging elaborate battles. Gary had a lot of toys, especially tanks and artillery pieces, jeeps, and trucks, earthmovers, and all kinds of model planes and ships. His dad gave him a big allowance, ten dollars a week, and he could buy almost anything he wanted at the hobby store. If it was a big model or toy, he asked his dad and got it. Going to his house and sorting through his stuff was always something to look forward to.

There were large fields and ditches and drainage canals in our neighborhood. We built rafts and poled around the canals, pretending to be pirates or castaways. We played war games in the fields, inviting other kids to join us. We made up teams to take a hill, plant our flag, and hold it against attacks from the other team. Gary usually decided what to do, when to organize a battle or wander around the neighborhood. Justin was our battle leader and enforcer—our protection. Mikey and I were what Justin called the foot soldiers. We usually went along with what Justin and Gary thought up.

August was always hot and sometimes there were days without much to do. Some of the kids left with their families on vacation. One Saturday, Justin, Gary, and I sat along the brick wall outside the hobby store. It had been a long afternoon of "what'cha wanna do's" and "I don't knows." We were in the shade of a small strip mall that included a drug store, a pet shop, and a beauty salon. Gary was throwing and sticking a pocketknife in the dirt between his sprawled legs. Justin was lying back against the wall, chewing a large wad of gum. He liked to do that, letting the wad bulge in one cheek or the other and chomping on it, like a cow chewing her cud.

"It's getting old," he said.

"What, your jokes?" grinned Gary.

"Your face and this gum," replied Justin. He could be sharp in answering Gary. He never let him get away with too much or let him forget who the real boss of the group was. Mikey and I didn't have any doubt, but Gary would get pissed off sometimes. He didn't let Justin forget who had most of the toys.

"Let's get some more gum. Besides, I'm still trying to get an Ernie Banks card." Gary folded the knife and got to his feet.

Justin looked up at him. "You got money?"

It was a frequent question. Justin never had money. His folks were poor and he had a lot of brothers and sisters. I usually had more money than Justin, but that wasn't saying much. My mom did the best she could for my sister and me and we got along okay, but we didn't have a lot extra. My dad drank a lot and it was rare for him to remember to give me anything. Both of us were busted and looked to Gary. The banker's son always had money.

"Yeah, I got enough for all the gum we need. But we won't need any."

We stared at him, waiting.

"I figure that one of us should go into the drug store and ask for help. While she's busy helping, two of us can stuff a bunch of packs in our pants and be out of there before they know we've been there." Gary stopped, grinned, and watched us, as if he had just delivered the boldest and most original plan in the world.

Justin looked at me and then at Gary. "You serious?"

Gary folded his arms and stepped in front of us. "What's the matter, colonel? You wanted something different, something besides playing, didn't ya?" It was always General Gary, Colonel Justin, and Corporal Pete. Mikey was the squad's only private.

I looked at Justin but he just sat there, staring at nothing. "Gary, that's stealing. If they catch you, you'll be in big trouble. Big trouble," I said, getting to my feet. Justin got up slower, standing between us.

Gary dropped his arms. "Pete, don't piss your pants. And this isn't me, this is us. We're gonna do it. Even you can carry a few packs of bubble gum." Gary looked at Justin. He was slowly moving that wad around in his mouth and hadn't made a sound, not even a predictable grunt. "You said you were tired of kid stuff, tough guy. How about it? Do we get you some fresh gum and me some new cards?"

"Gary, if you've got the money for gum, let's just go in and buy some," I pleaded.

Gary looked at me with the kind of disgust he usually reserved for Yankees fans. "Peter, you little yellow belly. Maybe you want to stay in the kiddie pool. Not ready to swim? Afraid someone in the store will catch you? Afraid of Mrs. Henson?"

Justin laughed and I turned crimson. Mrs. Henson was ancient, at least sixty years old, overweight, and very, very slow. She talked slow and moved slow. Justin looked at me without speaking and I knew he was reassessing me as a future warrior on his team.

"Hell no," I blurted, sticking my chest out and shoulders

back. "But this is Saturday and sometimes it's Mr. Wilkins that's in the store."

"Yeah, Pete's right," said Justin, his eyes squinting, like John Wayne thinking up some special tactics before an attack. "He could probably outrun a train and if he caught you he'd hit like one." Brad Wilkins' dad owned the drugstore, but Brad helped out during the summer. He was friendly to everyone in the neighborhood and he knew our parents. None of us were anxious to test his athletic ability.

Gary paused, considering the possibility. "We'll go in and see. Pete, since you're so afraid, we'll let you be the decoy while Justin and I grab the packs." Gary nodded to Justin and he shrugged, spitting his gum out.

I had never stolen anything in my life. Gary told us a couple of times about lifting comic books and even a model airplane kit once. Even with little money to spend, I had never been tempted to take anything. I wasn't sure about Justin because he never talked much about himself. Gary and Justin were both waiting on my decision.

"No, I'll help grab the stuff," I blurted out. "Justin, you be the decoy." As soon as I said it, I knew I had just doomed myself to eternal damnation, like my mother and grandmother always said would happen if I were bad. But, once you cross that bridge, there is no going back.

Justin looked at me and shrugged, like he knew I needed a chance to prove myself, a chance to stay on his team. He nodded to Gary and started walking toward the drugstore.

"Okay, Pete, but don't screw this up." Gary had one hand on my shoulder and I started to protest but he continued. "You know what kind we want? The ones with the orange wrappers. They're in the boxes by the Life Savers, on the front counter." I nodded and he let go.

Justin walked into the store first, with Gary and I trailing several steps behind. Mrs. Henson wasn't in her usual place at the register. We looked down the aisles, trying to locate her. Gary and I looked at each other and moved slowly toward the counter.

Brad Wilkins' voice boomed from the back of the store. "Yeah, I think we have some, but they're in the back. Don't get much call for them at this time of year. Be just a moment."

Justin had scored! We didn't know what he had asked for, but it had worked and the coast was clear. Gary and I stepped over to the gum packs and quickly shoveled several under our shirts. We were careful not to take them all, leaving a few in each box. Gary started for the door and I turned to follow when I caught sight of the Life Savers. Butterscotch, my favorite, within easy reach. I grabbed a roll and started for the door.

"How many do you want?" Wilkins asked Justin. I glanced over my shoulder and saw Brad Wilkins standing in the aisle, talking to Justin but looking straight at me. His eyes were piercing and I knew he had seen me pocket the Life Savers. I turned and moved as casually as I could toward the door.

"None, right now. I was just asking for my mom. I'll be back later," said Justin and followed behind me.

"Yeah, okay, see you later," said Mr. Wilkins. I could feel his eyes as we cleared the door and kept walking. We forced ourselves not to run until we reached the corner of the store where Gary was waiting.

"Oh shit, oh shit, oh shit," I said, panic just a heartbeat away.

"Wilkins probably saw Pete grab some candy on the way out," Justin said, slowly and carefully, as if he was reporting on a routine shopping trip.

"Let's get the hell out of here," Gary said and the three of us raced up the street, making our way back to Gary's backyard tree fort by a number of detours and switchbacks.

Sitting in the fort, we unloaded the gum packs and divvied them up. Justin didn't care about baseball cards, all he wanted was the gum. In fact, Justin was the only person I ever met that liked card pack gum. It was a flat, pink, tasteless sheet, often hard and brittle. We usually just threw it away, but, as I said, Justin wasn't always too quick on the uptake.

I was sure that Mr. Wilkins had seen me grab the Life Savers, but Gary and Justin told me to forget about it. He would've done something then and there, Justin told me. "He can outrun a squirt like you any day," added Gary, as if that was supposed to boost my confidence. I was just about to ask them how any of us could ever go back in the store when a knock on the topside door of the fort froze us in place.

"You guys in there?" came Mikey's voice.

Gary laughed and we relaxed as Mikey climbed down to join us. We told Mikey about our heist, and Gary gave him some of the duplicate cards he didn't want.

"Petey is worried that Brad is gonna get him," Gary said to Mikey. Mikey didn't know what to say, sitting beside Gary with his mouth open, staring at me and then at Justin. Gary had the hard eye on me.

"Like you said, he could've gotten me already. He either didn't see me do it or he doesn't care." I answered with less conviction than I voiced, but it seemed to satisfy Gary as he returned to opening packs and shuffling through cards. I knew that eternal damnation was waiting.

Justin mumbled through a fresh wad of gum. "It'll be

okay, guys. Wilkins don't want to make no trouble. Cops and papers, all that."

"What the hell," Gary said finally. "All these cards and still no Ernie Banks. What a rip-off." Gary looked at Justin and his forehead creased. "What in hell did you ask Wilkins to get you?"

Justin grinned. "Candles. I asked him if he had any Christmas candles."

Gary and I looked at each other. Sometimes Justin just amazed us.

———

That night at home I had trouble falling asleep. At first it was visions of flames consuming me as I wrapped both hands around a circular piece of orange candy with a hole in the middle. Next was the image of a tall man with short hair kneeling beside me. There were no words, but he reached out and put his hand on my shoulder. His eyes were sad but he didn't seem angry. The next morning I wanted to tell mom about my dream and about the store, but I knew she would remind me of my eternal fate and make me pray every night for the rest of my life. Dad's only concern would be if I were caught. No, I had to put out the flames by myself.

———

A week later I walked into the drugstore. I was alone, making sure that Justin and Gary were busy doing something else. Gary had talked about going back for more cards. He probably would have taken every gum pack and still not gotten an Ernie Banks. I was terrified to go back in the store, even with mom. The butterscotch candy hadn't tasted as good as it had before. After the first day, I threw the rest of the roll in a garbage can along with the cards Gary had given me.

When I entered, Brad Wilkins was the only one in the store—I had waited until the last customer left. He towered over the shelves and I approached him slowly, afraid to speak, afraid not to. I had rehearsed what I wanted to say at least a thousand times, afraid that if I didn't, I wouldn't be able to finish it. When I was next to the counter, he stepped into the aisle and knelt down, so that we were eye-to-eye.

"Last week I left here without paying for something," I blurted out. "I forgot to pay for a roll of Life Savers." I held out a nickel and he took it. He had big hands.

"I know," he said, with a softer voice than I thought was possible. "Thank you."

I mumbled something about being sorry and I left the store, thankful that he hadn't mentioned the gum and hoping he hadn't noticed the wetness that was making it hard for me to see. I was especially grateful that he hadn't squished me. I never found out what kind of trouble kept him from becoming a pro, but whatever it was, it didn't matter that day.

I couldn't tell the guys what I had done. For them, it would be a moment of weakness, a question of my resolve and commitment to the gang. I was either on their side or not. Whether by common consent or merely by luck, we never shoplifted again. Safe with my secret and content with my decision, I hoped I had avoided the fiery pits. We continued to fight our heroic battles. Most important, I earned my share of the glory and was promoted to lieutenant. After all, what's so hard about competing with short guys after you've confronted a giant?

———◆———

SWEET DREAMS

How far can love reach? How many miles and for how long? Is it a mutual or unilateral expression of eternal admiration or is it just a convenient indulgence to provide gratification? When all else seems lost and all hope vanishes, can we love what is left? And what can be simpler or more precious than the love of life itself?

This isn't as easy as I thought it would be.

What did I think it would be? Like this? No, not this, not the endless waiting, this confusion. I can't seem to focus on anything, thoughts flashing in random snatches, disconnected memories, no way to…

"Mr. Watson? Can you hear me, Mr. Watson?"

Yes, I hear you. You and the others, coming and going. How can I not hear the noise you make around me? Should I ignore you, like I have been doing for the past several…hours? Days? There's no time sense here. It's difficult to concentrate.

"Mr. Watson?" The same high-pitched but not unpleasant voice, slightly saccharine with a Southern touch.

I wonder what you look like. Do I even care? Does it matter now, your appearance or who you are?

"No, he's not with us, Anna, not responding at all."

A different female voice, older, a bit rougher. I don't remember her. What else don't I remember? Anna? Is that my sweet voice? Did someone touch me? My hand? Yes, my left wrist.

"His breathing changed. Its faster," said the older voice.

"Maybe he felt my hand, but I don't think he can hear us," said the sweet voice.

A touch on my wrist. I could feel it! There was a time when being touched wasn't unusual, but it seems like a long time ago. How long has it been? Maybe I should open my eyes, see what the sweet one looks like. Maybe she's not sweet or pleasant and it would be just another disappointment, one more frustration. Life is like that, throwing curves when you expect a fastball, never what you expect. Like I didn't expect this…waiting in the dark…for what? If I could just open my eyes, see what was going on…

NO! YOU CAN'T.

No? Can't what?

YOU CAN'T OPEN YOUR EYES.

Damn, this voice is new, loud and resonating, like from inside a metal hallway or pipe just large enough to produce an echo. And it answered me, screamed at me. Or did it?

"Did you see that? He flinched. His cheeks, around his eyes, a tremor," announced the older voice. "His status may be changing. We'll need to keep a closer eye on him for the next twenty-four hours. I'll notify Doctor Rao."

Doctor Rao? I must be in a hospital. Something has gone wrong. I must open my eyes. I think I'm trying. How can I know if I am or not? Am I asleep? Is that where I am, in another dream, a long and intense one I can't control? I used to do that so well when I was younger. Tell myself it's a dream. Yell in the dream, force it to let me go, and wake myself. I knew I could control it and it couldn't hurt me.

In the past few years, my wife worried because she would see my nocturnal struggles, hear me moan and argue with myself. Then, suddenly my eyes would open and I'd be back in her world and the dream would recede into thin clouds and finally dissolve, becoming nothing. I was always amused about her concern and I tried to reassure her that this was normal for me. Parasomnia, they call it, a form of REM disorder in which the body is not paralyzed during sleep. For me, it was the gateway to lucid dreaming.

Now, this time, there is a mist, as if I am inside a dense cloud or fog bank. But I don't remember talking to myself in past dreams or remembering about past events within a dream. Nor did I listen to others talking about me, as if I was a voyeur looking in on my own life. What has happened? When did I lose control?

THERE WAS ALWAYS A DIFFERENCE INSIDE MY NOCTURNAL fantasies, something that let me know it wasn't real, that I could enjoy it, laugh at its mock terrors and impossible consequences. I can still recall, even now, many of those virtual excursions, bad ones and good ones. Some of my favorites were about driving a car or riding a bike over a cliff or simply stepping off the edge to begin dropping into a vast, seemingly bottomless chasm. Then somehow, I was never sure why or how, a transformation took place and I would be flying, controlling the action and turning it to my advantage. It seemed to happen because of my own willpower, not some external force. I could stop the dream as if it was a tape recorder. Pause! Examine the story. Don't want to continue falling or to be smashed on the rocks below? Time to soar skyward like a bird, arms outstretched. Punch the play button and the story resumes. I am the writer, the director, the actor, and the audience. It's a very tidy and self-contained world.

Chases sometimes ended this way. When my attacker caught me and I turned on him or it and overpowered the creature with sheer determination, it was merely another manifestation of my will operating the playback. At those times I was not afraid and I faced the danger willingly. From prey to predator, the metamorphosis was both physical and spiritual. There was always a sense of victory, a feeling of exaltation within the dream. Sometimes the fantasy transferred to the real world, especially if it was a morning session just before waking. Drifting in and out of consciousness, I was able to recall those dreams with more detail and, even more important, more emotion. I felt the experience as an active participant, not as a passive voyeur from backstage. Dreams didn't happen to me—I made them happen! I suppose that's what started my…yes, I confess…obsession with dreaming and interacting with the characters and situations buried in my unconsciousness. Always trying to test the boundaries of what is and isn't real, attempting to create new and more powerful dreamscapes that allowed me to confront my fears. It was more than confrontation, wasn't it? My attempts at direction and control became increasingly concerned with creating stories, much like a writer devising and populating a world of characters and relationships. I was the prime character and I wanted no limits on where I could go and what I could do.

The bad dreams decreased with maturity. The worst had been associated with frequent illnesses as a child, especially during attacks of pneumonia that left me in a fever, hallucinating about suffocating clouds, boiling fumes of yellow and gray mist rolling over me, snuffing out everything as I disappeared into the void. I could see, could feel, the clouds gathering. No noise would escape from their billowing masses. They were like a giant, expanding cauliflower composed of gray, enveloping fog. Nothing could live or even exist within the interior of the puffy demons. It was my biggest fear—nothingness. I would wake up drenched and my mother would bring cold washcloths for my forehead. "Another dream?" she would ask. I'd nod yes and she would ask me if it was about tornados.

I sometimes dreamt about tornadoes, especially multiple ones dancing on the horizon. However, I wasn't afraid of the cyclones and the dark storms that gathered in my sleep. Instead, I was fascinated with their wild gyrations, their unpredictability. They were the incarnation of nature's power, and I felt exhilaration as they approached, at my daring, as if I was invulnerable. No matter how close or how fierce, the storm couldn't touch me. And storms were anything but nothingness. Mother said I probably remembered the tornado from *The Wizard of Oz*. Perhaps, but the storms weren't a threat. I also experienced them less often as I got older.

My darkness doesn't seem as intense, as if it was early morning behind heavy curtains, the blue-gray dawn of another day. For what seems like the first time in a long time, I feel a change.

"Am I awake?"

"What? Mr. Watson? What did you say?"

The older voice. Did she hear me? I must have said something. Or, maybe they are now part of my inner world, trapped in my…what? Dream?

"Oh, that's wonderful, he did say something. I heard it too," exclaimed the sweet thing.

She sounds like a cheerleader watching her team cross the goal line. Maybe she's wearing a short skirt and carrying pom-poms. She has to be young. For some inexplicable reason, I would like to see her, if nothing more than to confirm the image of her I created. I can still do that, can't I? What about it? Is the dream over? Am I awake?

YOU ARE NOT AWAKE. THIS IS NOT A DREAM.

Shit! Now what?

"Mrs. Watson! Come in here, please," said sweet voice. "Your husband is showing some small responses. He flinched when I felt his pulse and he just mumbled something, but I couldn't make out what it was."

"I'll get Doctor Rao to come in and examine him," said the older one, her voice fading, fading, and…

Another dream (a real dream?) materialized around me.

STANDING IN A DARK MOIST CAVERN, BARELY ABLE TO make out shapes moving in the distance, dark shadows against icy gray walls. Echoing voices, reverberating through endless chambers, as if chanting but without syncopation. I feel weak and disoriented. The noise is suffocating, rolling over me like my boyhood clouds. Now the clouds of sound become wetter and cold, like thunderous waves of surf, breakers pounding my body, pulling me below the surface, not letting me breathe. I can sense my arms outstretched, flailing in the water, attempting to reach safety, something solid. I am drowning and the chanting is louder, deafening, and I want to scream at them to get in step, to chant together, and to let me breathe, and I can't open my eyes and I scream…

STOP!

Who are you? Where are you? Am I still in the dream?

No, I can't be. I screamed and that should have been enough to wake me. I left the nightmare, but I'm not awake and I'm not in control. Something else is. I can still think and ask myself if this is possible in a dream. I don't think I've done this before. I would remember it. No, this is new. And where or what is this imperious voice that now intrudes? Where is sweet voice? I seem to have lost her. And the other one? She was going to get someone. Where am I? What am I? Why won't my eyes open?

RELAX. IT WON'T BE LONG. THIS WILL SOON END.

Wonderful! Just fucking wonderful! What have I done to myself?

JUDITH ANN WATSON LEANED OVER THE BED AND scanned her husband's face, noticing especially the corners of his eyes. A slim woman, younger looking than her forty-eight years, she brushed her straight blond hair back from a tan, freckled face. She had fine wrinkles, healthy marks of an outdoor life, much of it spent in her beloved garden. When she and Steven were younger, they hiked along ocean beaches for hours at a time, enjoying the fresh air and the numerous delightful discoveries of the Oregon coastline. Steven liked to pick through the tide pools among the shoreline rocks, searching for crabs, anemones, urchins, and other creatures exposed by the receding water. They both loved the sun sparkling off of the white foam as it raced up the shore, then disappeared into the sand, leaving wet arcs that stretched into the distance. At home she cultivated a variety of vegetables and flowers in and out of the house. Steven would tease her about sun wrinkles and how she would age because of dedication to her precious plants. She would smile and tell him that laughter also produced wrinkles and she would gladly age for both. Those were happy days of sunshine and optimism, when it seemed love would answer most problems. Judith looked up at the young nurse standing on the other side of the bed.

"He appears to be resting comfortably, Mrs. Watson," said the nurse. "Nurse Windham is notifying Doctor Rao about his response."

"What did he do?"

"We heard him say something. He may have asked if he was awake, but he said it in a whisper and we weren't expecting it. Also, his eyes blinked when I felt his wrist. It's the first time we've noticed any change in his behavior."

Judith sat down but didn't take her eyes off her husband's face. She thought about their last few years together, his growing restlessness, dissatisfaction with work, and the slow alienation from life. They didn't have children, and he had lost contact with the rest of his family many years earlier. He maintained his job as an accountant for a local bank, but at home he drifted. He was no longer interested in weekend hikes. He spent time reading and resting, often sleeping during the day. She urged him to see a physician, fearing he had become depressed and needed help. Yet Steven seemed to be happy at home. He was gentle with her and he professed to be well. He needed time to think, he said. He also told her about his dreams, like the ones that he had experienced from childhood and how they seemed to be changing, becoming ever more vivid.

Finally, he confessed to her that the dreams had taken on a life of their own. They came to him during the day and filled his sleep at night. "It is as if the world was becoming a black and white movie and my dreams are the only place where color exists," he said. She had nodded while holding his hand, unable to think of anything to help him or her. He told her everything would be all right, he wasn't afraid and she shouldn't be either.

"Afraid?" she had asked. "Afraid of what, Steve? What is happening to you, to us? Are you leaving me behind to… to indulge in a fantasy world? I could understand being left for another woman or if you were addicted to a drug or something else that was real. I could fight that. I could help you overcome whatever it was, but this, this isn't real. It has no substance. It's like…like…"

"Clouds."

"Clouds? Yes, I suppose it is like clouds. They are there but you can't hold onto them, can't push back at them," she replied, mostly to herself.

He looked at her as if she had finally understood, that she now knew what he knew. You can't fight clouds, she had admitted. He knew that resistance wasn't an answer, that acceptance was the only valid option.

He took a leave of absence from his job to, as he put it, "work on some projects at home." As the days passed, he became increasingly lethargic, eating less, spending more time on the living room couch. His naps became longer. They talked less frequently and she became increasingly desperate. She was about to consult with their physician when Steven told her about his 'project.'

It was a bright sunny autumn morning, filled with leaves turning color, migrating birds chirping in the garden, a few puffy clouds in a crisp blue sky. Steven smiled and looked at her across the dining room table. His face was suffused with a pink glow and his eyes radiated with much of their former bright luster. He was alert and talked enthusiastically about coming to a decision. Judith listened with a mix of hope and wariness.

"I think I have discovered a way to enter a hidden world. A place in my mind that has only revealed part of itself to me, but I think I have a path, a way to penetrate deeper and discover what's inside," he said between bites of cereal and toast.

"Inside? What do you mean, Steve?"

"I'm not sure, but it is like walking through a room with curtains and you step through one set and see a room with another set. But they are not curtains of cloth. It's like they are somehow alive, that they part for me as I walk toward them. I command them and they reveal the next place. Sometimes it's a room, other times I'm outdoors."

She looked down at her plate. She hadn't touched her breakfast. It would get cold.

"Where are you going? Where will this end?" she asked, not sure if she wanted to know the answer.

"I don't know, Judy. I can't be sure, but I feel like I have been on this journey all of my life and that everything else is just a…a roadside convenience. Something to guide me to the main road." He only called her Judy at times of intimacy, when he was telling her something very personal or important.

"Am I a 'roadside convenience,' Steven?" she asked without looking up. She could feel the moisture building in the corner of her eyes and a dull ache forming in her throat.

"No, no, not at all. Never. Please, Judy, please understand me. This…this experience, it's not something I could even share with anyone but you. I know it must seem very strange to you and I know…I know I haven't been communicating with you like I should." He took her hand and looked into her face, searching for the flick of an eye or the upturned corner of her mouth, something to indicate she understood and accepted.

She knew he saw the wetness and felt the tension. She couldn't hide it and she made no attempt to do so.

"I wouldn't do anything to hurt you, not deliberately," he said. He hesitated, as if not knowing what to tell her, how to prepare her.

She studied him, trying to get a sense of his internal turmoil, but aware that her frustration was turning to smoldering anger.

"Judy, I need to try an experiment with my dreams," he said, his tone matter-of-fact, as if discussing an accounting problem. He was still clasping her hands between his.

"What are you going to do?"

"I'm going to put myself into a very deep sleep, kind of like self hypnosis. I want to finish the journey, to see where it goes. I need to find out what that other world is like." His voice was pleading, like a boy asking his mother for permission to stay out late.

"I'm afraid, Steven, afraid of what you are doing. How do you know that you'll wake up, that you can come back from this *world* of yours? How can you be sure? Have you ever hypnotized yourself before?"

Now she was crying, her anguish revealed for him to see and for her to admit. Previous unspoken fears were released in a torrent and she begged him to reconsider. He reminded her of their happy life together, twenty years of contentment, a satisfying union of relaxed understanding between themselves. They had always tolerated, even welcomed, each other's differences. Usually they were minor and their life together had not been marred by serious storms. This was their first real crisis.

She and he talked through the day, strolling briefly in the garden, sitting on the floor in the living room before a fire late into the night with a bottle of wine. He told her more about his dreams, his ability to interact with and direct their outcome. She listened intently, trying to find something she could cling to or use to advantage. He was confident and she slowly yielded to his enthusiasm and persistence. He would enter a deep sleep, what he called his cloud world, in two days. He would spend one day in meditation, not eating, drinking only water, to prepare himself mentally and physically. He would remain awake that night and close his eyes to sleep the next morning. He would not talk to her once he began meditation. She was not to waken him, even if it took several days. He had also prepared written instructions for her to follow if for some reason he didn't emerge from his trance in seven days. He assured her he wasn't using drugs or anything else beyond his own mind to enter the dreamscape. The instructions were in a desk drawer and she wasn't to open the envelope before the designated time. He made her give her solemn word she wouldn't interrupt the experiment prematurely.

Reluctantly, so very reluctantly, she agreed. She loved him and she wanted this obsession to end. That night they parted, as if he was leaving on a business trip. He assured her again, kissed her, and walked into the guest bedroom to prepare for the journey. She stood in the hallway and whispered his name one more time before entering their bedroom and closing the door.

A FLASH OF RED, THEN YELLOW AGAINST AN ORANGE background. A curtain goes up and there is a meadow of lush grass and bright flowers, an idyllic pastoral scene complete with large spreading oak trees in the background and a small brook noisily lapping over smooth stones in the foreground. Songbirds flutter and chirp nearby and dragonflies dart and hover over the water. The aromas of early summer, the humid smell of luxuriant plant growth, a rich soil teeming with countless creatures, of land, water, and air filled with life at its reproductive peak. Cool grass caresses the bare soles, blades sliding between toes, a soft carpet on which to bounce with gigantic leaps across a living trampoline as lungs fill with perfumed air.

Is this not the essence of life itself? I can leap ten feet or more, as if I was in a garden on the moon, and touch, actually feel the touch of…ah, no dream this. One doesn't feel things in a dream. I never did. The world—this world—is mine! It is ours!

I turn to her and see her straight golden hair almost covering her brilliant eyes, eyes shining like stars in a summer sky. She smiles, that cool seductive smile of promises to be filled, promises of answers to questions I have not yet asked, but I will. Her hands reach out and our fingers touch just as the clouds roll in from stage left and right, covering the meadow and obliterating our world. Her mouth opens and I see the fright in her eyes and she is about to scream and before there is a sound she fades, dissolving into the gray mist. The curtain falls, but this time it is a sickly yellow and smoky gray.

"Mr. Watson has a stronger pulse, his eyes have opened and he seems to recognize his wife, although he still hasn't spoken to her," reported Chief Nurse Windham.

"Has he said anything to anyone?" asked Dr. Schumacher, chief of neurology, shuffling through the clinical notes and other records before him.

"He sometimes mumbles to himself, rather incoherently, but for the most part he just lies there, staring about the room without focusing. On occasions he seems to watch us as we work in his room, making his bed, taking his vital signs. We talk to him, but there is no direct response."

"What about his wife? How does he react to her?" asked Schumacher.

Dr. Rao shifted in his chair, started to speak, looked toward Nurse Windham, and lowered his head.

"Mrs. Watson asks him how he feels and he sometimes nods his head or his lips tremble, almost as if he is trying to answer, but little else," the chief nurse replied. "Once or twice he responded to his name, especially when she held his hand and whispered close to his ear. But then he seems to lose interest, almost as if he was suffering from a severe attention deficit. His mood is always calm, almost trance-like." She looked over at Dr. Rao, but he remained silent, as if reluctant to voice an opinion.

"So, we can assume he doesn't know where he is or what has happened to him?" asked Schumacher, his attention now fully directed at the attending physician, Dr. Rao.

Rao looked up at him, glanced at Mrs. Windham, and cleared his throat. Ranga Rao was the chief neurology resident, a slim dark fellow from southern India who spoke with a noticeably precise British accent.

"Well, this a very strange case, Doctor Schumacher. We

have been advised by Mrs. Watson to say nothing in front of our patient about his surroundings. But it should be obvious to him he is in a hospital, if he is aware of anything at all."

Nurse Windham added, "my staff and I were explicitly instructed by Mrs. Watson to not discuss his case while we are in his room. It is most unusual, but she seemed very insistent on this."

"Any reason given for this request?"

"Not to my knowledge," replied the chief nurse. "In fact, she became very upset when one of my night nurses asked her if her husband needed additional medication to sleep. I have no way of knowing if Mr. Watson heard the question, but his wife immediately ushered the nurse out of the room, closed the door behind them, and chastised my nurse in the hallway."

Schumacher looked again at the chart in front of him. "I see he was admitted by his wife eight days ago. He was in a deep coma and an initial medical examination yielded nothing other than dehydration. Doctor Rao, were you on duty when Mr. Watson was admitted?"

"Yes. I ruled out the usual concerns. He has no history of diabetes. His blood sugar was depressed, but he had been in an unconscious state for several days prior to admission."

"Did his wife say why she didn't seek medical help earlier?"

"Another strange aspect to this case, Doctor Schumacher. Mrs. Watson didn't offer us much information. At first we thought he might be a possible drug overdose, but we couldn't find anything in his blood or urine. If we had, it might have explained why she brought him to us instead of the County E.R. I was still suspicious and it was only after I threatened to call the police that she told me he had hypnotized himself."

"Is he a practitioner of hypnosis or a member of a cult of some kind?" asked Schumacher, pushing the records away and leaning back in his chair.

"Mrs. Watson denies any social aberrations or connections with the occult," explained the resident. "She told me he had been experimenting with meditation and dreams."

"And something went wrong?"

"It is difficult to say," replied Rao. "He apparently left instructions for her to seek help, but only after several days had passed. She seemed depressed but resigned to his condition. She gave us written consent to run diagnostic tests, including blood work, but we were not to use any drastic means to extract him from his coma. No drugs, electroshock, or other procedures that interfered with what she called his 'trance.' And, of course, the instructions about not revealing to him that he was in a medical facility."

"You've done an EEG?"

"Yes, it isn't in the chart yet, but it appears to conform to what we have seen in lucid dreamers on other occasions—strong prefrontal, parietal, and occipital-temporal activity, but, interestingly, we saw no external R.E.M."

"No eye movement?"

"None. I have never seen a sleep record like it." Rao handed him the report.

Schumacher pushed his chair back and stood. "I'd like to talk with Mrs. Watson and get to the bottom of this. Is she in his room now?"

"No, but she usually returns at about four in the afternoon. She goes home every morning after breakfast, changes clothes, and returns to spend the evening and night with him."

"Have either of you detected anything negative between

them, something I should know that might help us to understand what's going on?"

The chief nurse answered without hesitation, "No. And nothing has been reported by the staff. She seems upset, but she appears to care and is dedicated to stay with him."

Once again, Rao shifted uneasily in his chair and seemed reluctant to speak.

"Yes?" prompted Schumacher. "Have you something to add to this, Doctor Rao?"

Rao hesitated. "It may be nothing, nothing at all. Patients emerging from comas are often disoriented and confused. Not that it is clear he has been in a coma. I am not sure what his status has been or is at the present."

"Of course, understood. What do you have?" asked Schumacher.

"Well, umm…he did repeat a question several times during the first few hours after his initial responses. He asked, in a strangely clear voice, 'who are you?'"

Schumacher looked at the nurse, then back to Rao. "What's so unusual about that? If he didn't know he was in a hospital or the people around him, why wouldn't…"

"Excuse me, Doctor Schumacher," interrupted Rao, "but he didn't seem to be talking to people in the room. He appeared to be talking to someone else. Actually, with himself. He seemed to be listening to something, then responding."

Nurse Windham nodded agreement with Dr. Rao's account. "It is the only thing we have heard him say in a clear voice. The rest is mostly soft mumbling,"

Schumacher looked at his resident. "Do you recommend a full psychiatric consult, doctor?"

Rao smiled for the first time. He recognized the potential economic ramifications of retaining the patient for extended observations. "No, I do not believe so. Mr. Watson appears to be medically stable and we cannot detect any organic pathology. Other than the strange EEG, neurology exams are normal and the patient is passively cooperative. In fact, we could probably discharge him tomorrow except that Mrs. Watson has asked us to keep him for a few more days, just to be sure."

"Sure of what? I thought she wanted to avoid all references to medical care in his presence."

"She does," said Mrs. Windham. "But when we broached the subject of his release, she became irritated, almost afraid. She told me she'll pay for any extra hospital days and care beyond what their insurance covers. Since we are at low capacity right now, I didn't see any reason to insist we discharge him."

"I see," replied Schumacher, stroking his chin and glancing again at Watson's medical records. "I'll talk to her this afternoon. I'll recommend we transition him to long-term nursing care."

The meeting concluded at 10:30 in the morning. Dr. Schumacher did not meet with Mrs. Watson that day nor did Mrs. Watson see her husband that afternoon.

A THICK FOG COVERS THE GROUND, LIKE DRY ICE VAPORS on a stage. It blows here and there, parting for a moment, then gathering anew, as if obeying instructions from a capricious offstage director. I can see her under the distant juniper tree, waiting patiently as I approach. A trace of false dawn lights the distant hills behind her.

"Hello," I say as she steps away from the tree. We look into each other's eyes. She doesn't smile but her eyes fix and hold mine. She doesn't speak or move. Her arms hang at her side and her shoulders slump. She seems tired, but her eyes never waver.

"I'm ready now," I say.

She says nothing. She waits.

"When the morning comes, I will go. Without you. Do you understand?"

Silence.

"Don't come back. I won't be here," I say with as much finality as I can.

"I won't. I can't," she replies, tears appearing across her freckled cheeks.

"I love you," I tell her, not knowing what else to say, not expecting an answer.

She looks down at her feet then back at me, her eyes glowing like burning embers. "I know you do."

I kiss her, lightly at first, then with increasing passion, savoring the slight taste of cherries on her lips. It has been a favorite of hers for…a long time.

The light in the east grows steadily and the landscape slowly emerges from the darkness. I turn away from her, trying to remember her features, her soft face, her inquisitive eyes. I turn back to see them one last time but she is a shadow and the shadow grows dimmer as the fog swirls between us. I swallow and a sharp feeling of despair fills me as I turn away.

I can't turn back can I?

YOU KNOW THE ANSWER, STEVEN.

Judith Ann Watson left the cashier's window of Nolan

Memorial Psychiatric Hospital at 10:45 a.m. and quickly walked down the front steps to the main parking lot, opened her car door and entered. She started her car and immediately pulled out of the lot, looking back only once at the receding tower in the rear view mirror. The tears came again, as she knew they would, but she drove on, putting miles between her and the hospital, her husband, and twenty years of memories.

"Good morning, Mr. Watson. Isn't this a beautiful day? Let me open the shades a bit further and let the sunshine in."

Sweet voice is back. Where has she been? There have been other voices, some female and others male. Some were familiar, many were not. All of them wanted something. I don't care. They should go away. I don't need them.

YOU DO NOT NEED THEM.

The big voice again. Not so imperious as before, but a commanding presence still. I always pay attention to this voice. It surrounds me. Is it me? Many times I ask that, only to reject the idea. If it is me, then I could choose to obey it or not. I don't believe I have that option anymore.

"Mr. Watson? Are you asleep again?"

Sugar, sugar. The hummingbirds must love you. Can I love you? No time for that now. I am almost gone. Maybe I can try, just one more time…

Like before, the dream appears abruptly. This time it emerges from a tropical sea of blue and green, aquamarine tints swirling about a symphony, slowly rising in volume and tempo.

Which piece is this? I can almost identify it. It is familiar, in fact a favorite of mine. When? Where? It doesn't matter. I listen intently, humming along, moving my feet and hands in time to a clearly pronounced bass, thumping boldly like a stampeding herd as the chorus rises in volume. The swirls of color also keep time and they become waves of marching mountains, sharp spikes forming a parade across a uniform pink landscape. Beautiful are the colors and the music—I am consumed by and drawn into the tornado of color and music. *Carmina Burana! Of course, how could I forget?* The Wheel of Fortune spins and the mountains pass and I am swept forward to the horizon of a breaking dawn. I pass briefly over a city of empty streets and darkened street lamps. Upward over the mountains, like the soaring flights of my boyhood dreams. Surrounded by a maelstrom of color and synchronous chanting, I rush on. I have no fear.

YOU ARE IN CONTROL.

I am?

I AM.

I fly higher and higher, into a deep black sky filled with countless lights, into an infinite expanse of space and time. I will fly forever. There will be no gray clouds. I am in control.

"He must have left after I straightened his bed. He was sitting upright in the chair, dressed in the clothes his wife brought him yesterday. I thought he was asleep." Anna was trembling, on the verge of tears. "Mrs. Watson didn't say anything about him leaving and he didn't give any indication he would or could walk out on his own."

Nurse Windham looked at Rao. "Doctor Schumacher is not going to like this."

"Have you contacted Mrs. Watson?" he asked.

"No, I haven't been able to reach her. I left a message on her phone to call us. The medical bills have been paid to date, so there is no financial obligation involved, but I need to get closure for his medical records."

"I'll tell Doctor Schumacher we have a walkaway and ask him if he wants to alert authorities," said Rao as he turned and walked down the hallway.

Nurse Windham looked at her young staff nurse and put a hand lightly on her shoulder.

"Did he say anything to you this morning?" she asked gently.

Anna looked at her chief nurse.

"Only one thing," she said slowly. "As I was leaving the room, the last time I saw him, he smiled and said in a remarkably clear voice, 'Sweet dreams.' That's all, just… 'sweet dreams.'"

ONLY A PILE OF LEAVES

What are important events in a lifetime of sharing and interacting and
where do the obligations of love stop and end? What problems arise from
the seemingly routine and trivial challenges in our lives? What seems
insignificant at one moment can become overwhelming the next.
Where there's smoke…

knew I had neglected the simple task too long. Not a big
deal, I told myself—I'll get to it and even if I don't, so
what? No one is harmed, no one will remember, no one
cares. Well, that's not completely correct. She cares. How
much, I'm not sure, but enough to remind me they're still
there, covering the back lawn, an irritation visible from
the kitchen door. She sees them while preparing meals or
whenever she walks into the kitchen, which is often. I see
them too, but they are just there, not calling out or waving
imaginary arms, not in distress, hardy noticeable unless
you care about those things. I don't.

That must be the problem, the itch that intrudes on
many relationships—the differences in caring about the
trivial events in a life occupied by insignificant people,
places, and things. So many things, so many opportuni-
ties to find a wedge, a lever that can separate and divide.
Leaves. Dried brittle leaves on top of the pile and wet, moldy
leaves on the bottom, sticking together and clinging to the
ground. I had created a mini-compost pile without effort

or forethought. How clever of me. How disturbing it was for her. Not that she was hostile to compost piles, in their proper place and serving their valid function, but the thing on the lawn was neither proper nor valid, not in her eyes.

It was late winter and the promise of an early spring forced me to begin the annual task of raking the lawn of the previous autumn's leaf fall. I usually let the leaves over-winter to provide an organic medium for the native grass that tried to survive on an otherwise semi sterile ground of hardscrabble basalt and gravel. I could have spent a small fortune on trying to cultivate a proper lawn like my suburban neighbors, but I had neither the money nor the inclination. I preferred the natural cycle of death and rebirth to do my work for me, to let nature provide its own fertilizer.

The problem was the late and unexpected snowstorm that arrived before I could bag the leaf pile. I got the first part of it, the brittle upper level, and left the rest for the next day. That day came, about a week later, and covered the neighborhood with three inches of white. The pile was out of sight, out of mind. I like that. But the sun did its job, the snow melted, and the pile was once again an eyesore to my delightful spouse. I promised her I would have it gone before the next rainstorm rendered it too heavy to bag and haul.

Once again I removed the top layer to be confronted with a blackened sticky glob of organic material. I ener-getically dug into the heap but quickly realized if I left the litter to fulfill it's proper destination I would create a whole yard of glorious decomposing nature. Not just under the pile, but the entire surface of the yard was now blanketed by a slick dark mat of alder and wild plum leaves, mixed with a few juniper sprigs. A metal rake barely penetrated the coating—it was going to take some sustained back and shoulder work to remove a half acre of the goop. Each succeeding rainstorm only congealed the residue further. It gave me a great reason to prolong the task, to hope for a long dry spell to loosen the muck. She logically commented that procrastination had only made it worse. What could I say? I guess it had.

I tried to analyze why this year had been different. The amount of leaf accumulation had been greater last year. Or had I not raked as often, removed as much as in other years? I couldn't remember. The winter had been wetter, not colder than usual, but wetter. With less snow, it seemed an earlier spring was on its way, but no, late snows and more rain continued to delay the job of leaf disposal. I bent down to look at the black material in more detail. It had almost a greasy feel to it, slick and moist. The leaves stuck together in sheets that had been compressed by the winter snow load. There was a rich, not unpleasant smell to them, a fermentation that promised new life, new growth and green stuff. That was good. Things besides dandelions might grow in this substrate. To hell with hundreds of dollars of turf supplements and fertilizers—here was the real deal. I knew I was right and that always makes me feel good.

My backyard neighbor disagreed. She looked over the fence from time to time, obviously distressed that my 'natural' approach produced a questionable presence in the subdivision. Her thick, bright green, and intensely manicured lawn was the icon of suburban presentation and management. She didn't say anything, but I had few delusions about her darker thoughts and desires for a different neighbor. I walked back to the kitchen, past the pyramid of soggy leaves that had now attained the status of a memorial, both to my environmental naturism and to my determination to prolong the inevitable.

Oh yes, there would have to be an end to the standoff. My adorable spouse would see to it. Her first volley in the war of the leaf pile was delivered like a threat. There are people, professionals, she emphasized, who will come out and remove the pile and clean up the rest of the yard. She smiled at the thought of a real yard, one with real grass suitable for lawn parties and badminton and, heaven forbid, croquet! Who in the hell plays croquet anymore? I don't even know where to buy a set. I know the answer, of course. Online—I guess you can buy anything, even a new lawn, online. Who would we invite over to play? Although, the more I thought about it, mix in a few drinks beforehand and croquet might actually become an amusing alternative to just having more than a few drinks.

I wasn't opposed to someone else doing the work—that always seemed like a decent solution to the world's problems—but there was the small matter of money, the same kind of resource I had designated for other pleasures and even a few necessities. Curious, I asked one of my better-informed neighbors who had a similar sized lot, how much he had spent on rehabilitating his grounds. After the blood drained from my face and he had reached for his phone to dial 911, I whispered "thanks" and stumbled back to my house. I looked at the pile again, sipping on a double bourbon, trying to calculate how many more drying days it would take before I would once again attempt its removal.

A week later, the phone rang. It was for my wonderful wife but she was shopping. A strong baritone voice announced he was from the Greater Vistas Yard Team, following up on a call from the lady of the house. Would it be convenient for him to tour our property and provide an estimate for their services in helping us establish the yard of our dreams? Hmmm. I informed him, in my best masculine bass imitation, that we were already in possession of the yard of our dreams and the time would be terribly inconvenient. However, I promised him we would call him back if the dream didn't go as anticipated. It was two days before my special lady of the house asked me if we had heard from the yard specialist she had contacted. By then, I had spent considerable time in staring at and envisioning practical solutions to our environmental problem. I informed her, proudly and decisively, I was ready to spring into action. The day had arrived and the nuisance pile would disappear forever. She stared disbelievingly out the kitchen door at the yard, still undisturbed since my last partial efforts. What about the rest of it, she asked. Will you finish the job and get rid of all of it? Every last leaf?

I reassured her every bit of brown and black organic residue would be removed. Sunday would be the day and I would begin making preparations on Saturday. Monday the yard would be clean and no longer the scourge of our neighborhood. Order the croquet set, I said. We'll be able to play a round or two the following weekend.

Saturday she was once again on the road, shopping for groceries, some clothes, and, she told me with a wink and a whisper, a croquet set. I laid out the garden hoses, put two shovels within easy reach, and tested the leaf layers. Yep, dry as a bone and as loose as the neighborhood gossip's lips. It wouldn't have been an overwhelming task to rake them, but I had a much better plan.

The wind was minimal, barely a breeze. I lightly sprayed lighter fluid along the west edge of our property, the same igniter I used for our infrequent barbeques. I turned on the faucet and a steady trickle ran out of the hose behind the ready fire line. I lit the fluid with a long-stemmed match and watched in satisfaction as the fire spread in a steady line across the lot, licking at the leaves. I watched as they disappeared, curling into a line of smoke rising lazily into the cloudless sky. Patrolling from end to end with a shovel, ready to pounce on any wayward flames, I followed the incendiary progress toward the house. A two-foot firebreak separated the scattered leaves from the house foundation, more than enough to provide a safety barrier. In retrospect, I probably should have soaked that safety zone before lighting up. Yeah, that would have been the thing to do.

Unfortunately, I underestimated two aspects of the clearance project. The first was the accumulation of leaf litter. It was deeper and denser than I had calculated, especially where the previous autumn winds had driven it near the house. The safety zone was not quite as wide as I had perceived. The second factor, which I had no control over (it's not my fault), was the sudden appearance of a stiff morning breeze blowing from, you guessed it, the west.

When my precious partner drove up in our car filled with groceries, she had to park two houses away. Fire trucks filled the street and their hoses covered our front yard. The final cleanup had started and the day's entertainment was done but not forgotten. I had just finished my report to the fire chief and patrolman and accepted from the latter a summons for endangering the neighborhood. Our insurance agent was on the way and our gracious backyard neighbor was behind me, hands on hips and muttering to some of our other neighbors about living next door to a fool. You could still make out some of our house, that is, the outline and about three feet of the walls above the foundation. The remains were very black, still smoking, and producing a distinct odor, like a barbeque gone bad. My wife, my beautiful bride, stood at my side, staring at the charcoal. A big pile of black charcoal.

SAFETY PIN

Love isn't easy—we all know that, or should. The open arms, the confident miles-wide smile, the sparkling eyes—cue the orchestra and let the background music swell to a crescendo as the lovers walk arm-in-arm into the sunset. Or, maybe it doesn't go quite according to script.

Lisa makes one last check in the floor-length mirror by the front door, her fingers spreading to smooth the dress across her slim belly and out to her sides, catching the flair of hips and dropping halfway down her thighs. She is forty-two, physically attractive, softly buxom but appearing fit. Brunette and five-foot-six, she has a friendly face and pleasant complexion with a few light freckles that hint at time spent outdoors. Tilting her head slightly, she poses as if in front of a camera. She flashes a brief smile at her image, revealing a set of braces.

It will do. Here I go.

She hurries through the apartment door, closing it with a turn of her wrist while listening for the lock to click as she walks down the hallway to the elevator. Her high heels tap a staccato percussion on the Spanish tile floor, reinforced by a faint echo from sterile walls that lack softening adornments. She pushes the down button, glancing at the floor indicator above the elevator door.

Damn! The seventh floor again. What do those people do up there, sleep in it? Should I walk?

She looks at the stairwell door a few steps to her left, but the passageway down four floors to street level is cold and dimly lit. The light flickers and the elevator moves—upward.

Damn! Not today. I don't need this.

Whirling on one heel, she moves toward the door with sudden fury, her purse flung to the side, brushing the wall. The door handle is slippery, as if some kid with buttery hands had massaged it, preparing it just for her. Jerking the door open, she wipes her hand hastily across the door-frame and hurries to the concrete steps leading to the lobby. Footsteps echo as she descends, the rhythm changing as she reaches and turns at each landing. Approaching the second floor, she stumbles and almost falls. Her ankle twisting sideways, she grabs the heavy black handrail. Regaining her balance, she pauses, momentarily grateful for avoiding another disaster.

I could be lying in a broken heap while he waits in the lobby. Might not be discovered for weeks.

With an involuntary shudder, she cautiously continues the descent while rummaging through her purse for a tissue. She finds none and closes it with a snap.

Great, I must have used the last one yesterday. Why don't I ever replace anything?

She pushes the stairway door open and enters the lobby, moving toward a full-length mirror on the far wall. Staring at her approaching image, she is visibly panting. She stops in front of the mirror for another critical appraisal.

Four flights downstairs and I feel like I'm running a marathon. I'm out of shape. What the hell am I doing—is he really worth this?

As she had feared, her hair is already disheveled, flopping across her forehead, negating the time, the effort of preparation. She had hoped to achieve a professional look, not business formal, but one exuding competence and control.

I look like some over-dressed schoolgirl who has missed her bus. No, that's not right. I won't be mistaken for a girl, will I?

Reflexively, she presses the front of her dress with one hand and reaches for her hair with the other, hoping to brush the wayward strands into place. She recoils in horror. A dark, grimy smear stretches across her dress, contrasting dramatically with the bright teal green fabric. She looks down at her outstretched hands, at the greasy, soiled palms in the bright light of the lobby.

Shit! That filthy handrail, have to get back upstairs and…

"Hello Lisa."

She hadn't seen him. Startled, she turns toward the voice, placing her purse in front of her.

"I guess the elevator wasn't available," he says. His voice is calm, level, reassuring. He stands about two paces in front of her, relaxed and smiling. He wears a tailored, lightweight two-piece suit. His tie is simple but elegant, the kind chosen by someone who knows the difference between fad and fashion. He wears Italian shoes, black with short laces, shined to a pleasant but not mirrored gloss. Not a hair is out of place. He has a trim figure, not athletic but one attesting to carefully managed fitness. He might be easily mistaken for a leading man on a daytime soap opera or a male model in a clothing ad. There is no one else in the lobby.

"You look…perfect," she manages.

"Perfect? Ha…I don't know about that, but I feel good." His laugh is easy, as if he has handled comments like this most of his life. "How about you? How are things going, Lisa?"

She stares at him without focusing, as if mentally denying him an entrance onto the stage she is ready to exit. Another strand of hair falls across her forehead, coming to rest over her left eye.

"Uh, I…I had to use the stairwell."

"I know. I saw you come through the door."

"Oh….I'm sorry." She looks down at her dress, at the dark stain behind her purse. His eyes don't leave her face but she can't look up, can't make eye contact.

"Lisa? Lisa, look at me. Sorry about what? You look great. I've been looking forward to this all week and I hope you have as well. If you're ready, we'll go. I don't have anything until four o'clock so that should give us a couple of hours to eat, talk, and relax." He holds his right hand toward her, palm up.

Lisa looks at him and again at the elevator, as if it could offer her refuge from the disaster that seems to be unfolding. The elevator is still on the sixth floor. Dropping the purse to her right side, she hesitates, then places her left hand in his. Still smiling, he moves effortlessly to her side, taking her full arm in his. They walk out of the lobby and onto the sidewalk, confronting the downtown bustle of a humid New Orleans summer afternoon.

Did Rob see the stain? What if he did? Relax, dammit! Take a breath and relax.

She breathes in slowly and deeply, her elbow tightening on his arm as she looks at the faces of women rushing by, silently challenging them to lower their eyes and notice her dress, her misfortune. She doesn't worry about men's eyes—they almost always focus on her breasts, jiggling in a loose bra under a thin dress.

The hot air and the rhythm of their walking calms her

and she smiles for the first time when she notices an older man sneaking a not-too-subtle glance at her in passing. It lifts her spirits, taking her mind off of the oppressive heat, the wetness that will soon envelop her.

Does anyone ever get used to this? How does he wear a suit and tie in this climate and stay so cool?

The tension in her arm lessens and the sway of her body takes over, hips moving in the soft feminine swing that some women produce naturally, without exaggeration or intent. Her footsteps lengthen to match his and they stride together in time, moving purposely but leisurely along the busy street. She has always been a hiker and preferred low shoes to heels.

***

During their last meeting she told him that her teeth had been her ongoing shame, the residue of an impoverished rural childhood that had followed her through high school and college. As a result, her smile in the presence of most people was close-mouthed. She had withdrawn, staying in the shadows, never one of those at the front in a group photo. Her yearbook picture was one most people couldn't name. She was the neighbor and coworker that formed the anonymous gray backdrop to other people's lives. After her recent move to the Big Easy and the acquisition of a steady job, she had decided to have her teeth straightened. The orthodontist had warned her it might be as long as two years before the procedure would be completed, but she could feel the transformation begin as soon as he installed the shiny hardware. Almost overnight, her lifelong shyness evaporated. As if compensating for lost time, she became assertive, at times aggressive. She was also aware that not everyone appreciated her dramatic change in personality. Instead of being rewarded with long overdue popularity, she became increasingly isolated from coworkers and neighbors.

She has known Rob for seven months and he had treated her differently from the beginning. He encouraged her to see the orthodontist. Recently he remarked about her braces providing an interesting and seductive contrast between her mature femininity and a measure of little girl innocence. She began to lose her long-standing embarrassment in his presence, smiling openly like a teenager, the silver metal flashing in the sunlight.

"Where shall we eat? In the mood for anything special or different?" Rob asks. His voice has a silky quality, a baritone resonance that most women find soothingly attractive, making them feel like they are with their lover and father at the same time.

"Nothing fancy. I didn't find anything to wear so I just put on this old dress." She bites her lip.

Lie. Liar. I bought this yesterday, just for this occasion. Damned elevator.

He senses the slight change in tension, subtle shifts in posture as they walk. He pats her hand and reads her like a textbook, as if each emotional swing is highlighted in Day-Glo. He is careful to preserve her dignity, to counteract her insecurity and preserve his observational and analytical advantage.

"I know just the spot. They have great Creole cuisine and we can share a pitcher of beer. Maybe some étouffée? It's also a great place to talk, tall wooden booths, almost private."

She nods agreement and gives him a flirtatious sideways glance, sincerely appreciative of his decisiveness.

Maybe it's dark and cool in there. No one will see my dress. And, a beer or two sounds great. Anything to beat this heat.

She looks at him again, marching confidently forward, always forward. "Never look back," he had told her. Don't waste a lot of time regretting and trying to undo the past— you can't do it. Spend your time on the future, Lisa. Look forward." It has been her mantra for the past several months, words she has taken to heart since meeting him. *Look forward.*

———

ROBERT JOSEPHSON HAD BEEN RECOMMENDED BY A friend as a counselor, someone to help her adjust to accumulating recent failures in her social and financial life: a part-time lover gone full-time absent, a family inheritance withdrawn, friends passing from her life, and finally, the death of her mother. She was supposed to call his office for an appointment, but before she did, they were introduced at a small party and he invited her to dinner the next weekend. She accepted, never telling him she had been about to seek his professional help. Rob was charming, smiling at her awkward, inane platitudes that served as introductions. It was Robbie—never "Bobby" when he was young, he told her in a hushed, conspiratorial tone. He was clever, always quick with an appropriate compliment, able to discern her uncertainty, to anticipate her unvoiced needs even though they were mere acquaintances. And yet…

Yet, I can sometimes feel a certain detachment, as if he is experimenting with me, more curious than concerned. My imagination? Maybe. Why am I so self-conscious? Those days are past, when I waited patiently for someone else to make all the moves. That probably cost me—poor Alex couldn't handle the change. "You're a different woman," he told me on the way out the door, "but not a better one." It hurts still, but I don't want it like it was, always wondering, always dependent on someone else. With Rob I eased off on the accelerator, not pushing the relationship forward, always forward. I could have probably had him in bed by now instead of playing an adolescent dating game. I let him set the pace. This is our sixth meeting, including four meals, a walk in the park, and a cruise on the river. All so innocent, but I won't complain. He's been a gentleman, the perfect companion, well behaved, well dressed, turning other women's heads...yes, there are a few benefits, aren't there?

THEY STOP AT A CORNER, WAITING FOR THE LIGHT TO change. A swirl of wind provides an all-too-brief respite from the summer swelter. She feels the perspiration overcoming the deodorant and she knows it too will leave its mark. The breeze pushes her hair across her forehead and occasionally into her eyes.

Wetness, mildew, the dank smell of growth everywhere. A bobby pin or a scarf, why don't I ever have what I need? For the want of a nail a shoe was lost...

The green walk signal flashes but it doesn't stop a few cars from cheating toward the next Canal Street intersection. A block later, he guides her down a nearby side street.

He knows the city so well. After two years I still haven't been to half the restaurants within a few blocks of my building.

The restaurant is unpretentious but the aroma is not. The interior is refreshingly air conditioned and cozy, imbued with that down home feeling for which so many New Orleans eateries are justly recognized. A compelling gastronomic invitation is created by the smell of fresh bread, spices, the ambiance of soups and stews, the hint of delicacies familiar and not. Lisa trades her anxieties for anticipation as they slide into a tall wooden booth along the wall to the right of the door. She watches cars and pedestrians moving past the window, but they seem distant now, as if projected onto a movie screen. She is in a crowd but not part of it, surrounded by solid barriers, protected from the outside world. He smiles at her from across the table.

"How is this? Better? I think you will like this place. I've never had a bad meal here. The bread is home made and the desserts are something to die for."

Better? Better than what? He must have seen my clumsy attempts to recover in the lobby. Damn!

Frowning, she nods, and then looks up as a thin middle-aged man in a white shirt, black bow tie, and black shiny pants, partly hidden by a red apron, appears with menus and two glasses of water.

"Welcome to The Hole," he says, placing the glasses and menus before them. Taking a note pad from his hip pocket, he smiles at the man and turns his body toward him with one hip cocked to the side. He barely gives her a glance as he inquires of Rob, "Do you know what you want today or do you need some time?"

"Anything special today?" asks Rob, returning the waiter's gaze with a neutral but not unfriendly expression.

"Just me, like always, you should know that." The waiter replies without hesitation, in an affected nasal singsong.

"Johnny, you need some new lines. Who knows? Maybe you'll get lucky and score sometime."

"Oh, I do, I do, but just not often enough and not with the right men. Like they say, the good ones are already spoken for." A quick glance toward Lisa emphasizes his lament.

Lisa looks at the waiter and then at Rob. "I'm fine with whatever you recommend," she murmurs and pushes her menu to the end of the table. She takes a long sip of water.

Damn. I hope Rob's not gay. I didn't even consider that, a perfect gay gentleman.

"Two orders of étouffée and a pitcher of the Czech beer I like so well," Rob says, handing the menus to the waiter.

"Two mugs or one?" asks the waiter with a wicked grin and a wink.

"Two, Johnny. One for my friend Lisa…"

"Hi, Lisa," says Johnny, never taking his eyes off Rob.

"…and the other for me." Rob turns to smile at Lisa as the waiter walks away with a smirk and an exaggerated swish of hips.

"You must come here fairly often. The waiter is very friendly." Lisa speaks quietly and slowly, not looking up from the table.

"Johnny? He's a crazy kid, a middle-aged kid, been working here for years, probably knows everyone in the city. He's as gay as a carnival and flirts with everyone. Everyone male, I mean."

"I noticed. He barely acknowledged my presence. If anything, he seemed impudent." She frowns, looking into her glass.

"Lisa, relax. Johnny wouldn't flirt with you if you were Cleopatra. And, in many ways, he is a kid. He's immersed in his own dramatization of what a waiter in a N'Orleans café should act like. I'm not even sure he's really gay, that is, in the sexual sense."

Cleopatra? Long dead, bitten by a snake. I bet her dress wasn't covered with grease.

"Perhaps. I mean…Rob, if you'll excuse me, I'll just visit the facilities."

She slides from the booth and walks toward the back of the restaurant. Entering the women's room she pauses in front of the mirror, examining the stain. It isn't as obvious in the dim restroom light as it had been in the lobby of her apartment building. She steps up to the sink, removes a paper towel from the dispenser, dips it under the warm water faucet, and squeezes the excess water out. Wiping the damp towel carefully across the stain, she sees the fabric darken. Frozen in front of the mirror, she stares at her dress, at herself helplessly clutching a wet towel. A dark wet spot diffuses from under each arm. Her hair hangs in limp, uneven strands, as if she had walked through a steam bath.

This is all a mistake. I should have told him I was sick… or busy…or something. I'm not ready for him today. Dating a therapist no less—what the hell am I thinking?

The door opens behind her and a slim young blonde enters, glances at her and enters a stall. Lisa opens her hand and lets the paper towel drop to the floor. She makes a desperate attempt to push the hair out of her eyes and realizes she left her purse and comb in the booth. Her ankle hurts. She becomes aware of it suddenly, as if she had just banged it on something.

What the hell, I must have twisted it harder than I thought.

She can feel it throb as she exits the rest room and walks back to the booth while controlling an urge to favor it.

He won't see me limping like some cripple. I should have stayed in bed.

Rob nods at her as she sits down. A pitcher of beer has arrived during her absence and two full glasses sit in front of them. Each has an inch of foam, enough to whiten upper lips when sipped. She recalls his litany from a previous dinner. "That's the way it should be, Lisa. Just enough foam to know you are drinking fresh beer, not something left over from last night's party."

He is so damn precise, so perfect in everything he does. He probably spends hours practicing, pouring beer, laying down a foam layer that's exactly one inch…

"Lisa? Lisa? Come back." He says it gently, but persuasively, leaning forward to look up into her downcast face.

"Uh…sorry, I don't seem to be myself today…do I?" She half asks, half suggests, inviting him to agree but not sure she wants him to. Her hands are tightly folded under the table.

"How about a toast?" He grabs his glass and holds it up, waiting for her to do the same. The overhead light reflects from the dark rich lager, as if it was a large piece of amber, a bubbling jewel. She gives him a quick nervous smile, a twitch of her mouth and lifts her glass to lightly touch his.

"Cheers," she mumbles and matches him as he takes a moderate sip of the brew.

Rob sighs, placing the glass on the coaster in front of him. "That's the ticket. A good beer will wash away almost any problem." He says it as if to himself, but she wonders if the message is intended for her, telling her to forget the past week.

This past week, office rumors about a layoff or at least a reduction in pay, snide remarks from colleagues, her building supervisor not responding to her calls about a leaky sink, the damn elevator, the dirty stairwell. Going forward?

As she holds the glass in front of her, she studies his face, trying to read it. He looks at his watch, unaware of her scrutiny. Each movement is precise, orchestrated for maximum efficiency.

Is he patronizing me? Does he really understand how I feel or is all of this just subtle mockery?

Lost in thought, she lowers the glass to the table but misjudges how close it is to the edge. It is out of her grasp even as she realizes her mistake. The cold liquid fills her lap and runs down her legs as she stares at the empty glass bouncing across the wooden floor. Rob is on his feet in an instant, handing her extra napkins. He quickly looks around the restaurant as several people stare at them. For several agonizingly long moments, there is silence around them.

"Lisa, are you all right? It's okay. Wait. I'll get a towel." He waves at Johnny and the waiter approaches nonchalantly, retrieving the rolling glass with one hand and handing Rob a large dishtowel with the other.

"Hmm. Tipsy already, are we?" He smiles at Lisa but she is staring at the very large, very dark stain in her lap. Beer drips from the hem of her dress onto the floor. "Not to worry, honey, I'll get a mop." As Johnny leaves, Rob bends over the table, extending the towel to Lisa.

She looks at him. For once, he is not the smooth, confident man in charge. He looks worried, as if she has exceeded the limits of silliness in a bad slapstick movie. Again, he glances at his watch and looks up quickly.

Will he walk out, demanding his money back, disappointed in my performance?

She sits, dripping beer, smiling at him with mouth open,

braces flashing. But this smile signals fear, the same grin a cowering monkey displays under duress, calling for help or begging for mercy.

"Now you see the real me, the klutz. Maybe we should leave before I do something even more outrageous for an encore."

"Lisa, take this and dry yourself." He speaks matter-of-factly, his voice blunt and neutral. He looks around the room briefly, but most of the diners have resumed eating. The towel hovers before her but he stands back, as if afraid that getting closer might contaminate him with her clumsiness.

She takes the towel and begins soaking up the wetness in her lap and dabbing at the puddle on the seat next to her. Johnny returns with a clean glass and a small mop with which he sponges up the beer near her feet. He works quickly, without looking up. Lisa watches him, as if each movement, each drop removed is a significant victory, promising to redeem her, to make her whole again. Each swipe is also an indictment, a testimony to her fall from grace.

It won't, will it? It will never be the same. I have disgraced myself and embarrassed Mister Perfect beyond any hope of forgiveness. If I could just vanish, without a word, without a trace.

Rob takes his seat and carefully pours her another beer, placing it in front of her but almost in the middle of the table.

She hands the waiter the wet towel. Her little girl voice is feeble. "Thank you."

"All in a day's work, my dear. That's how I stay healthy, you know, running to booths to…"

"Okay, Johnny, thank you. I'll take it from here." Rob looks at him with a steady this-is-not-funny-so-get-lost look that even the irrepressible waiter can't ignore.

She stares into the glass, watching the bubbles drift slowly upward. There is very little foam this time. She can feel the dampness around her waist and over her thighs. Her ankle is pulsating, keeping time with a mounting pressure pounding behind her eyes.

The first signs—a migraine coming. Do I have something with me? Yes, I put them in my purse this morning. Should I take them now, here, with him watching me?

Rob picks up her glass and moves it closer to her, setting it down gently, as if afraid he too might dump it in her lap. His smile is reserved, tinted with concern, the steady face of a professional counselor.

"Do your patients…I mean, clients, ever tell you about things like this?"

"Like what, Lisa? Spilling beer in a restaurant? This can happen to anyone, at any time. I am sure Johnny could tell you countless stories about spilled drinks, dumped food, and worse occurrences. In restaurants you see everything and everybody. Please, have some beer, it'll help you relax. And Lisa, you're *not* my client." He sits back, one arm hanging casually along a ledge at the side of the booth, trying to follow his own advice. His tie is crooked and a dark strand of hair is hanging in front of one ear. He doesn't seem to notice it.

"If I didn't know better, I might think you were trying to get me drunk." She says it half-heartedly, seeking further encouragement. He sits immobile, looking at her without offering a response.

I should return to the women's room, try to dry out, take a Tylenol. But that means walking on this ankle and seeing myself again in that damned mirror, looking worse than before.

He looks at his watch, the third time. "It will still be a few minutes before the food comes. Are you okay? Do you need to go back to your place and change clothes?"

No surprise—he's ashamed of me, a woman who drenches herself in beer in a place where people know him. And...I need those painkillers.

Resigned, she slides across the bench and stands, picking up her purse and covertly testing her leg, determined not to betray her latest injury. "I'll see what I can do here," she says, without looking at him. It hurts but she manages a steady gait to the restroom. A few people look up as she passes and one young woman giggles and leans close to her companion to whisper something.

Forward, ever forward.

Lisa enters the rest room. It is empty and she is once again in front of the mirror. Although the front of her dress is much wetter than before, that isn't what catches her eye. Instead, she is amazed to find her dress very visibly ripped underneath the right arm. With her attention focused on the oily stain, she hadn't noticed the damage.

What a worthless piece of shit, a rag. What damned difference does it make? I can't go back out there, not like this!

Aware of the increasing pain in her foot and throbbing forehead, she finds the Tylenol in her purse and takes two, followed by a small cup of water. Staring at her dress, she resolves to try something to salvage the afternoon. *A safety pin! I always have one for emergencies.* Hoping for a bit of luck, she makes a hasty search, but...still no luck.

Nothing! I have to face Rob in a torn wet dress. Small wonder that woman laughed at me. Shit! No, I won't. I quit.

Rob will have to understand. That's his profession, isn't it, understanding? Let him understand that I can't sit there, watching him smile at me.

She slams her purse shut, whirls and limps through the door and across the floor to their booth. The loud, uneven footsteps turn more heads and Rob looks at her questionably as she stands over him. Two plates of food are on the table.

"I'm going back. Back to my place," she says, defiantly. "Not even a damned pin!" Without further elaboration, she turns and hobbles toward the door.

"Lisa…Lisa, you will return?" She doesn't pause. "Should I come with you?" He remains seated, shoulders slumped forward. He looks at the food, at his watch, at Lisa disappearing through the door. He reaches for his glass of beer.

⁕

Lisa walks onto the sidewalk, holding her head high, eyes forward, trying to ignore the occasional stares of others. The streets are busier as the afternoon rush hour begins. The heat and humidity wash over her anew, but she barely notices. Cars and people rush by, noises rise in a tumultuous frenzy from which she is disconnected. She walks as if in a trance, replaying the day, the week, her life.

It's all a bad dream. The elevator, the stairwell, the ankle, the beer, and not even one damned safety pin! And Rob, damn him! Mr. Cool back in the booth, trying to be casual. "You will return?" Yes, I'll return, when Hell freezes over.

She moves from the curb before the light turns green, her eyes staring ahead, purse swinging at her side. Her steps are now measured and deliberate, anger overwhelming the pain. She moves…forward.

Forward into the path of a taxi. The driver makes a desperate attempt to hit the brakes and swerve, avoiding all but a brush against the woman. It pushes her back to the curb and she sits abruptly. He jumps from the cab and rushes to her as several people gather around. She is dazed but otherwise unhurt. One of the bystanders remarks that she smells like a brewery and others reassure the cabbie that it isn't his fault. Another, an elderly black lady bending over Lisa, is more charitable. "Poor lady. I guess this isn't your day."

Lisa picks herself up, mumbling that she is okay and walks away as fast as her swollen ankle will allow. She notices the dull ache in her left side from where the cab made contact.

So close, so quick, what else today?

She enters the front door of the apartment building and limps across the lobby to the elevator. The black lady's words keep returning, "…isn't your day…isn't your day." Lisa pushes the up button and the doors open immediately to admit her. She turns and briefly spies her image in the lobby mirror as she presses button four. The door closes and the elevator climbs.

The only damned thing that has gone right today.

As the car moves smoothly upward toward security and salvation, Lisa opens her purse for the apartment keys and there it is: a packet of tissues. The tissue wrapper is decorated with small yellow smiley faces. A safety pin lies on top of the packet.

————— • —————

WITH THIS RING

Love is symbolized by what? Hearts? Flowers? Sweet endearments? What about the iconic artifact of western culture that accompanies engagements and marriage? How easy is it to put it on, wear it, or take it off? With this ring, I do thee wed...

He had been studying the newspaper intently for twenty minutes, reading slowly as if his life depended on every word. She observed him quietly, the calm before the storm, picking her moment to initiate the confrontation. She was ready.

"Where were you last night?"

"Last night?"

"Yeah, you know, between sunset and sunrise," she replied. Her voice could slice cucumbers.

"The usual places." He didn't look up from his newspaper.

She didn't need to see his eyes. His hands gripped the paper loosely, fingers moving slightly on the margins. He never could keep his hands still when he lied. She stared at the front page, as if she could burn a hole through it and him. She said nothing, playing the game, waiting and watching his anxiety mount. Already a tremor in his right hand was increasing and soon it would be shaking and he would have to lower the paper and make eye contact. He would give her that in exchange for her forgiveness. Humble eyes, trembling hand, the nervous and repentant husband appealing to her dependable sense of mercy.

The silence in the small living room was relieved only by the soft, steady tick of the clock behind her. She shifted her weight on the couch and counted each click, each passing moment as if it had a special significance but, of course, it didn't. It was just another wasted moment, a passing interval of time that begged for a resolution that wasn't coming. He shifted in his chair and his fingers twitched. The paper began to quiver and she could tell he was attempting to control his left hand without her noticing it. He uncrossed his legs—he was losing the battle. Just a few more ticks, a few more twitches, then it could begin.

As casually as possible, he put the paper aside and reached for a coffee cup on the table to his right. The old clock began its countdown to eleven o'clock, filling the room with a reverberating chime that seemed incompatible with the calculated pause that hung between them like a cheap curtain. His hand brushed clumsily against the cup, and it crashed to the wooden floor, shattering in fine porcelain flakes. Light brown liquid spread and beaded on the waxed surface as he stared at it. She ignored it, her eyes never leaving his. She would not let him divert her attention.

"It'll be different next time," he said, his eyes still fixed on the coffee, as if he could will it back into an intact cup.

"No it won't. There won't be a next time."

His hands twisted in front of him, the fingers sliding over each other, as if he was washing them, removing sticky cobwebs without much success. She once again noted the absence of his ring. Even in the dull yellow light she could discern the whitened indentation on his third left finger. She rubbed her right thumb across her own ring, the mate to the pair they had exchanged so many years before.

Careless or does he just not give a damn? What difference does it make?

He cleared his throat and glanced up at her, but for only a moment. He resumed his appraisal of the spilled coffee. She studied his posture, sitting on the edge of his chair, hands still moving.

He must be wishing he could have the moment back, to grab the cup more decisively, to remain in control.

"I'm sorry."

"Are you saying that to me or to the coffee?"

"What can I do to make it up to you? Just name it, Becky." This time he looked up at her, staring into her face, searching for a sign she would soften, once again relent, forgive him, take him to bed, sleep on it, and awake in the morning to a routine of breakfast, newspapers, phone calls, maybe a weekend night out.

Rebecca's stare collided with his halfway, like two wizards dueling, hurling balls of light across a deep chasm.

Oh yes, a night's sleep will wipe out last night and all of the other days and nights. This is you, isn't it Jack, your usual feeble attempt at an apology?

She could anticipate every word and move. She frowned but said nothing.

He reached into his pocket for a handkerchief, touched the ring, and hesitated. He slowly withdrew his hand without the ring, looking down at his long, neatly manicured fingers. They weren't shaking as much as before. He looked again into her eyes, his confidence visibly returning.

She noticed as well. She folded her hands across her chest and sat back in the couch. *Regaining control, Jack? That didn't take long. You won't say anything—you'll try to out-wait me, to counter my anger and frustration by a show of contrition and an appeal to reason, just like last time and the time before that. Always the confident salesman, the meticulous manipulator, aren't you?*

It was a reassuring movement for Jack—it meant she was ready to talk. She would accuse, perhaps even yell at him, but she would talk and that usually gave him the edge. He wasn't a salesman if he couldn't sell her. He had seen her pissed-off wife routine a thousand times, from stony silence to sarcasm to screaming. He reluctantly admitted she had a right to complain. He had been careless lately, especially with regard to the ring, the missing band that often became the focus of her rage during these confrontations. But he could deal with it, just like he handled the displeasures of business clients. It was all part of the game—appease, please, and ease on down the road.

"Jack, you are a bastard, you know that?"

"Yeah, you're right, I admit it. I'm sorry, I really am. It won't…"

"Jack, SHUT UP!"

He sat back and let her run with it. She needed to get it out and done. He glanced up at the clock, marking the time. It was late but not a workday tomorrow. She always repeated his name during her initial anger phase. At this pace, he calculated she'd be spent in less than fifteen minutes.

"I could understand it better if you had waited a few more years, waited until my breasts sagged, wrinkles showed. Hell, I wasn't even twenty-four when I caught you the first time, less than a year after our wedding. Was that really the first time, Jack? LOOK AT ME, DAMMIT! Do those whores of yours have so much more sex appeal? Can they do it better?

What do they give you that I don't? Do they have perky boobs? You always liked tight perky boobs."

"It isn't you Becca, you're still…you know, a great looking woman. I just lose it. It's me."

"Lose it? Yeah, you're gonna lose it. At least you are not denying it anymore. Why is that, Jack? Is your lechery so commonplace that even you've grown tired of the repeated lies and feeble excuses, or are you just too damn lazy or stupid to invent anything?" She leaned forward, her hands dropping to her side, fists clenched. "Where is the ring, Jack? Do you still have it or did you lose it in some bar or in some whore's bedroom?"

"C'mon Becca, it's not like that, I've got it, right here, it's just that…"

"Fuck you, Jack! I've heard all I want of your stupid excuses.…We've been through this…how many times? I know damn well what you expect. I rant and rave for an hour, cry for several minutes, then you hug me and tell me you're sorry, then we go to bed and…of course! Sex makes everything okay. Then it's just a matter of how you want your eggs cooked tomorrow. Right?"

He said nothing, head down, his hands gripping each other, fingers interlocked. This wasn't her usual script and he began to suspect he might need to take a different approach to reconciliation.

"RIGHT?" She glared at him defiantly, simultaneously demanding his silence while daring him to say something clever, something she hadn't heard before.

"I guess…I…you're right. You know you are. I'm a bum and you have every right to be angry. What can I do to make it up? Anything. Just say what you want." His fingers disengaged and he held his hands out, palms up, as if to receive her blessing. "Take my hands, Becky. Tell me you'll forgive me. Tomorrow night is New Year's Eve. We'll be with friends and have a great time. We can start all over, a new year for us."

She stared at his left hand, at the extended bare third finger. She spoke softly and slowly, with monotonic emphasis on each word, delivered with the hardened, mechanical precision of the ticking clock. "I won't take your hand, Jack. Not this time. Maybe it's time to sever this relationship, this joke of a marriage. Tonight, Jack, you're sleeping by yourself. I don't really give a damn where, on the couch, on the floor, with your whore, I don't give a damn. By morning I'll know what I'm going to do. Right now I can't think straight. I've had it." She rose from the couch and started walking toward the bedroom.

"Becky, I'm really sorry. I know you're upset. I don't blame you. I'll make it up to you. I promise. I'll never take your ring off again. I swear."

She didn't turn. As he stared at her retreating rear, his left hand reflexively formed a well-practiced gesture, middle finger extended. The bedroom door slammed and he was alone.

He walked slowly into the kitchen, grabbed a broom, dustpan, and sponge. After cleaning up the coffee and pieces of cup, he put sheets and a pillow on the couch and undressed. One of the three bedrooms was being repainted and the other was filled with furniture and stuff from almost twenty years of marriage. The clock struck midnight and the chimes again filled the living room. He sat on the edge of the couch, thinking about the evening and whether he could have exerted better control.

It's been a long day, work, the workout, the brief fling

afterwards, then I forgot about our dinner company, and then…all of this. Who needs it? Screw it all and screw her.

Only once before had she excluded him from their bed and that was because he had been caught with a neighbor, a friend of hers. That time it had gone very badly. They had only been married about a year and it occurred soon after her discovery of an affair with an agent in his office. She had threatened divorce but a vacation in Hawaii, complete with a Honolulu shopping spree and some romantic beach walks, had smoothed it over.

If I hadn't forgotten about that stupid ring and if I had been on time for our dinner date with the Wilsons, this time might not have been any worse than the others. If…if she wasn't such an uptight bitch. I need a drink, something to calm my nerves and help me sleep.

He returned to the kitchen and retrieved a glass from the cupboard, looked at it for a moment, and put it back on the shelf. Taking a bottle of whiskey from the liquor cabinet, he broke the seal, walked slowly into the living room and sprawled on the couch. *Real men don't need a glass.* He took a healthy slug, relishing the burn sliding down his throat. *The first gulp is always the best, whether it's beer or bourbon.*

Jack slumped against the wall in a t-shirt and briefs, his legs spread at a ninety-degree angle. He surveyed his body, starting with his chest and waist, flexing the muscles in his arms and legs. *I've kept in pretty decent shape for a guy in my late forties, unlike some of the jerks at my office.*

Selling real estate involved a lot of sitting, computer time, driving around, but he made a point of working out whenever he could. The spa, in fact, provided the perfect excuse for arriving home late. "Working out with some of the guys, honey." "Got a big bet on a racquetball match, tonight, Becca, don't hold dinner for me." "I'd love to hon, but keeping these abs and pecs requires discipline. You, know, healthy body, healthy mind." He took another drink, relaxing further. His hands gripped the bottle firmly, decisively. Another drink.

I should put the ring back on. It'll look good when she wakes me up in the morning. Good thing I'm off tomorrow… today.

He looked at the clock—half past twelve and ticking. He was feeling light headed and laughed aloud as he rose from the couch and stumbled toward the stuffed chair, clutching the bottle carefully, lovingly. He wouldn't drop this stuff on the floor. He folded his pants carefully over the back of the chair.

No, no, don't wake my precious Becca. She probably won't be in the mood to press them tomorrow so no sense in making work for myself. Fishing in the pants pocket, he pulled the thin gold band out and held it up to the light.

"Damn piece of shit. You've cost me a bunch, haven't you?"

The ring didn't say anything to him. He stared at it for a moment, rolling it around in his palm, sliding it over the smaller fingers. It fell to the floor and rolled toward the kitchen, as if trying to escape. His left foot stopped it, the heel covering the gold circle for several seconds before he slowly reached down to retrieve it. He slid the ring on and took another drink. The warmth of the amber liquid brought increasing numbness.

Nothing like it—warmer than a woman's body and much more reliable. It doesn't care where you've been or who with. I could love being an alcoholic if there was any money in it. But no one wants to buy a house from a sloshed agent, do they?

Bloody hell. I've got to do something about all this. I wonder what she's going to do. Something dramatic? Probably not. Where in the hell would she go? Who'd want her? Maybe I'd be better off. Let her go. No problem, I can find someone else. Lots of good stuff around, especially if you're in shape. About a third of the fifth left. What did that come to? A twelfth? No, that isn't right. But not much. Might as well finish it.

She ain't bad looking, my Becca. Actually, there might be any number of guys who'd take her to bed. Like some of the jerks in the office. That's all they talk about. Sex. Sex with the office clerks, sex with their clients. Some of them manage to get the client's wives in the digital shots they take of the properties. The women don't suspect that the electronic zooms nail them up close while the jerk is taking shots of the kitchen or bedroom. The bedrooms are their favorites. They like to add these to their office computers as if they were conquests. "Check this out Jack! Cant'cha just imagine this babe in here, without the clothes?" *Yeah, in your dreams, buddy. Not in your lifetime. I'm doing the bedding while you're doing the boasting. You won't see any bedroom shots on my computer.*

The last chug came at two-thirty. The empty bottle rolled across the floor as he swung his legs onto the couch and made a half-hearted attempt to pull the sheets up.

Becky's damned lucky to have me. I make good money, provide a decent house in a decent neighborhood, two cars, whatever she needs. Needs. The kids. She hasn't brought that up lately. Couldn't have kids. Not my fault. I can have kids. I can have any woman I want. She won't do nothing. Not a thing. Damned lucky.

He was asleep within seconds. The lamp glowed, the clock ticked, and Jack snored. His left hand hung limply, dangling over the side of the couch, the gold ring gleaming, reflecting the kitchen light in the doorway.

"He must have been totally wasted. I don't believe he even knows she left," said Ustin. He put his notebook into his jacket and looked at his partner as they walked slowly from the living room.

"You think?" replied Lima, the older officer. "You don't get a call like this every day."

Mrs. Wilson, the next-door neighbor, took the house key from the living room table and followed them to the front door. "I'll stay here and finish cleaning up, if that's all right?" She looked at them and they nodded.

She paused in the doorway, cleared her throat and said, softly, almost shyly, "I only called you because she asked me to as she was leaving." She looked down at her feet, then looked up at them and continued. "He had it coming, you know. He was always running around on her. Everyone in the neighborhood knew and we all wondered why she took it as long as she did. I don't know where she went, but I'm sure she will be better off without him." The last word she spit, as if it was an obscenity.

"Thank you, ma'am," answered Lima. "If Mrs. Russell does return or she calls you, would you have her contact us?"

"I don't think she'll be back, but if she does, I'll tell her. Will you keep the note?"

The two officers looked at each other. The neatly printed note had been taped to an empty bourbon bottle and placed on the coffee table:

Jack, it's over. You can have the house and everything, except the ring. It's mine. Don't look for me.

—B

Ustin couldn't completely suppress a grin. "Yeah," he said, "we'll need it for evidence, especially if he wants his ring back."

The ambulance left the driveway as the two police-men closed the front door behind them and stepped off the porch. Lima looked back at the trim white house and nodded toward the blue sedan sitting in the driveway. "She could have rolled off with the new Lincoln, instead of taking the compact. According to her neighbor, she didn't take much, just a few clothes."

"Well, he's going to be really pissed when he comes off the sedatives and realizes what she did take," said Ustin.

"Yeah, I guess we'd better get out a bulletin for Rebecca Russell."

"Too bad that's necessary." Ustin looked at him as they got into their car. Lima slid behind the wheel and turned the key in the ignition. Ustin sighed. "It wouldn't have been our problem if it hadn't been for that sorry bastard's finger."

"Yeah, I guess so," Lima agreed. "Not sure what she used but it was clean and fast. She was probably out the door before he was fully awake.

Ustin gave him a sideways glance. "Considering how much bourbon he probably consumed, I doubt if he even woke up."

"Yep, helluva way to start out a new year."

———◆———

INTERLUDE I:
PANDORA'S SECRET

Love can be generous and it can be greedy. This story began
as an often-used exercise during a writing conference workshop hosted
by John M. Daniel in 2002. The goal was to compose a short-short story in
exactly ninety-nine words. This evolved into a related short with additional
words. The current term is flash fiction, an appropriate term for this
particular piece. Both versions are presented here.

THE ORIGINAL NINETY-NINE-WORD
SHORT SHORT STORY

"Is it magic?" he said.

"I don't think so," she said.

He reached for the bright blue ring, but she withdrew.
His eyes narrowed.

"Where did you get it?"

"Found it."

"Where?"

"It's a secret."

"Let me see it again."

"No. You want to touch it. I can't let you do that."

This changes everything, he thought.

Suddenly, he grabbed her arm and twisted. He removed
the brilliant green ring and slipped it on his little finger.

Odd. Green?

Emerald brilliance flashed from his finger. It was his. It was magic. It was the last thing he saw. Forever.

THE MODIFIED SHORT STORY

"Is it magic?" he asked.

"No, I don't think so," she said, keeping her hand closed.

He reached for the bright blue ring, but she drew her hand back.

"Let me see it," he insisted.

"That's close enough," she said, stepping back, wary for any sudden moves.

His eyes narrowed and he stepped toward her.

"I'll trade you something for it."

"Not interested. This is the only one and I'm keeping it."

"Where did you get it?"

"I found it."

"Where?"

"It's a secret. I promised not to tell."

He hesitated. *Tell? Someone else must know about the ring. He couldn't just take it from her, even though he was older and stronger.*

She put her hands behind her as she stepped back again. He stepped forward, keeping the distance between them constant.

"Please let me see it."

"No. You want to touch it. I can't let you do that."

He froze. "I can't touch it? Why not?"

"You just can't. It's part of the secret."

This changes everything, he thought. Suddenly, he grabbed her arm, twisting it as his hand closed over the ring. She cried softly as he removed it and slipped it onto his little finger. He stared at the green brilliance flashing from his finger.

Odd. Green?

He held it in front of him and the sun reflected from its emerald surface. It is magic. He held his breath. *The ring is magic and it's mine!* The bright green light was blinding—it was the last thing he ever saw.

Pandora crouched over the boy lying on the forest floor. Smiling, she gently took the ring and slipped it on her finger. Sapphires are beautiful but they seemed pale in comparison to the color in her eyes.

DEATH IS A MAN
I KNOW

Love can seem unreal. Maybe it really is, but who should judge and what criteria should be used? Another story about lucid dreaming and manipulation—but who or what is the manipulator?

Sometimes when I lie down for a rest in the afternoon, I mentally prepare myself for not waking up. I don't mean waking up later than I should or oversleeping because of fatigue and the need for those extra minutes or hours of undisturbed quiet. Instead, there is a premonition that the next time will be the last time I close my eyes. Whatever awaits me on the other side of life will be finally and irreversibly revealed. Or not. It hasn't happened yet—perhaps it's only a vague foreshadowing. It also occurs before I go to sleep at night. Not every night, but when my mind isn't preoccupied with the daily routines of survival, when I am drifting on the sea of random memories before the curtain of unconsciousness descends, the thought appears unbidden: this is it, the end of existence as I know it.

Strangest of all, this isn't scary, not something I dread. In itself it has never kept me awake or made me afraid to let go and enter the dark realm and confront whatever is lurking there, if anything. Most often it is a curiosity, a window of speculation about the unknown and about what I would leave behind, the emotions, the thoughts, and the aftermath among those I know, I knew, those I love, I loved, those that I don't and didn't. Sometimes it manifests itself as regret and sadness, the part involving the loved ones left. I regret that I can't do anything for them when I die. I don't mean insurance or other assets for them to divide. I regret that I will no longer be a person, a factor in their lives. No one will look upon my grave and realistically ask me for help or comfort. If I don't provide it now, it won't matter when I depart.

Depart? For where? Anywhere? You understand I'm not afraid, that death is more about the question itself, one asked by billions of people since human consciousness evolved. The answer, according to many, implies a mind-body separation, a spirit that leaves the physical body with a separate existence and fate. Maybe the spirit never was part of the body—it was only a case of mistaken identity, a convention to give the body meaning and the spirit a home. I know I am not the only one that has asked those questions and thought about the answers. The older one gets, the more one suffers, the larger the question of death looms. Even those who claim a religious dispensation for a life afterwards can't help wonder about the experience of dying. Everyone thinks about death, except those who are young and have never seen an animal or a person die. Once they do, a new reality imposes itself, even if only a momentary and superficial one.

At the age of fifty, life is good. Divorced and with no encumbrances, I still have some romantic prospects. I am in good health and I take care to stay that way. My friends like to use the word moderate to describe my habits: "she eats and drinks moderately" or "she dresses moderately," always with the insinuation that I am not expected to exhibit some shocking extreme in behavior or appearance. And I haven't, not since high school. I was a bit of a rebel then, an idealistic semi-hippie that rejected most of the traditional church, family, and social values in my white, suburban, and very Southern community. Unlike many of my peers, I married late and managed to avoid pregnancy.

I work full time for an environmental group, a non-governmental organization, or NGO, that advocates for wetland preservation. Most of my job involves correspondence with individuals that are either for or against our activities, but I also track various media for news and items related to our cause. It isn't all glory and excitement but it is sometimes interesting and my colleagues are an eclectic mix of old hippies, young politicos, and others who believe they are doing something to save the world. I have no such visions of grandeur or importance—it is a job, I am good at it, and it pays the bills.

The first night he appeared, I had arrived at sleep's door promptly, exhausted by a day of frantic telephone and email communication about an upcoming legislative action that threatened our environmental objectives. I had grabbed a quick bite on the way to my two-bedroom apartment, read a couple of files to prepare me for continuing the advocacy battle the next day, and fell asleep on the bed, still dressed with the lamp on. The next morning, I had an unusually clear memory of the dream.

Dream recall was not new for me. I had experienced many such occurrences from the time of adolescence to the present. Not only could I recall many of these nocturnal fantasies, I could often manipulate them. I was aware of dreamscapes and lucid dream control well before films and novels brought it to the attention of the general public.

Therefore, the vision of a man dressed in black, holding out his hand to me and mumbling something indistinct, was not an image of special concern or cause for alarm.

I thought about the fading image as I ate breakfast and dressed for work, wondering as I often did, where did *that* come from? Another long and intense day at work ensued as the legislature debated and we stood by providing our lobbyist with relevant information and opinion polls. Overtime was followed by another fast food encounter on the way home and an early crash, but only after a shower and donning warm pajamas. Sleep came almost instantly.

I rarely have sequential reoccurring dreams, that is, the same dream in subsequent nights. Reoccurring themes, such as flying off a cliff, watching a train approach from a distance, or trying to run away from danger in slow motion, had been part of my dreamscape repertoire for years. But these repeats, never quite the same in detail, were usually spaced months to years apart. When they did reappear, I welcomed them as familiar old friends.

This night was different. The man in black was waiting, holding out his hand. He wore a black cowboy hat and a black long-sleeved shirt, open at the neck. The hat cast a shadow over his forehead and eyes, leaving his lower face bright, as if lit by a spotlight. The lips seemed redder than normal, not as if embellished by makeup but more like the natural lips of a young child who has been running on a cold day. His left hand reached toward me, palm out, fingers and thumb extended. The image was close to what I had seen the night before, but the voice was new.

"Caroline," said the man, in a drawled but clear baritone reminiscent of the voiceover from manly pickup truck commercials. The background seemed foggy, a vague backdrop to the scene. I knew I was dreaming—it had all the signs. Although I tried to back up, I was having trouble moving, as if my feet were slogging through thick mud. I couldn't see my own hands, even though I tried hard to put them in front of me. But, the surprise, the exception, was the word, "Caroline." It was my name and I had never heard it in any dream before. He repeated it, the hand coming closer. I woke up.

It was three-twenty on the night clock. I lay quiet, thinking about the dream and my name. I had learned many years before to wake myself from nightmares, not always successfully, but often enough to bring relief if it was a particularly bad one. This wasn't. The man appeared to be more mysterious than sinister. I didn't feel endangered, but hearing my name for the first time had startled me. My pulse was fast and I had been sweating. I wondered if I had moved or said anything aloud. Sleeping alone had its rewards and disadvantages. My ex-husband had remarked on numerous occasions about my sleep walking and kicking as well as occasional vocal outbursts.

I drifted back to sleep and the rest of the night was peaceful. I awoke feeling refreshed, ready to start a new day. But unlike other mornings following a night of nocturnal imagery, the dream didn't fade, as if the replay had embedded the scene into my long-term memory. It was Friday and I was supposed to meet a woman friend for dinner and a few drinks that evening. The change in my usual routine would probably prevent me from dreaming or, at least, having the same dream again. I pushed the man in black into the background as I entered the office and joined the bustle.

Marjorie was my age and my major confidant. She knew about my speculations on death and we shared an interest in lucid dreaming. While sipping on rum collins and picking at a plate of cheese sticks, we discussed the man in black.

"Maybe he's your guide to the underworld," she said, an evil grin inviting an equally evil response.

"If so, I hope he's good looking. I don't want to go out with an ugly guy. Bad for the reputation, you know."

She considered the scenario for a moment, staring at the lime wedge in her glass. "Well, there's going out and then there's going out. Of course, if he turns out to be a nasty one, maybe you can just tell him no."

That wasn't unrealistic. Marjorie and I had both experimented with dream control, the practice of not only ending unpleasant dreams, but also manipulating the event, changing the actions or outcomes to a more favorable result. "I suppose I could say no. But before I do, I'm curious about who or what he is and what he wants. I probably won't have a chance. It's unlikely the same dream will appear again anytime soon."

"Speaking of second chances with a man, are you still seeing Jonathan?" She was looking at me with that I-hate-to-ask-you-but-I-will-anyway countenance.

Jonathan had been an on-again, off-again man of interest for the past few months. He was a lawyer, working for a paper company that was trying to relocate one of their plants. Their move would use water resources that directly compromised the wetlands we were hoping to preserve. He had represented his corporate clients at a morning meeting with our environmental group. I had participated and later he asked me to lunch. He was affable and took some pains to inform me he only represented his client but didn't necessarily agree with their objectives or stance. This led to several traditional dates of dinner, films, and a couple of intimate nights, one at his place and one at mine. He was in no hurry to hook up in a long-term relationship and I was willing to let things slide. Marjorie, however, was an inherent matchmaker. Divorced, she was always on the scan for a companion, long or short term. If she couldn't find one for herself, she was ready to help her friends, whether they needed it or not. It was the one point of minor contention between us. Usually, a couple of cocktails put the world right and we pursued other topics.

"Saw him last week. We went canoeing on the lake," I answered, sucking the last of the rum collins from the ice cubes. "I think I need another." She gave me the hard stare. "Another drink," I clarified.

"Canoeing? How did that come about?" She signaled to our waitress for two more.

"I told him we needed to do something outdoors for a change, and that didn't mean a blanket under a tree. He suggested we get 'environmental' and take a boat on the lake. So we rented one and we paddled around for a couple of hours, followed by hamburgers at the Do-Drop."

"Romantic, no doubt," she said. "Will you tell him about your mysterious man in black?"

"No, he's not ready for that. Or, I'm not ready for that, I'm not sure which. You're the only one I've mentioned this to and I want to keep it that way."

She looked at me and laughed. "Not to worry, honey, I don't say nuttin' to no one."

The waitress brought our drinks and we continued to banter about work, Marjorie's love life—usually a short conversation, and how my job was going. We left the club at eleven and I was home in bed just before midnight, feeling completely at ease. With thoughts of a leisurely and unplanned Saturday before me, dreaming was not on my mind when I turned out the lights.

"Caroline."

The same baritone, the same outfit. The only difference was the shadow from his hat just barely covered his eyes and forehead, leaving his nose and cheeks exposed. He held out his left hand as before, palms up. I must have answered him, although I couldn't hear myself. It was more like an intention, the desire to answer, asking him "what do you want?"

His mouth formed a slight smile, neither friendly nor hostile, almost whimsical, as if my unvoiced question was either frivolous or meaningless.

"Caroline, it is nearly time." He said it matter-of-factly, as if I should recognize the truth of it, as if I had always known this would be said at this time and place. I must have asked something else, "time for what" or something similar.

"Caroline, come with me. Take my hand."

His continued and persistent use of my name was unnerving. I tried to see past him, to see where he might want me to go. The background was amorphous and gray, swirling like the carbon dioxide clouds in gothic films. His hand dropped and for the first time, he turned. His back was to me and he slowly stepped away. Somehow I was following because the distance between us didn't increase. Again, movement was slow in the familiar foot-dragging pace of dreamland. He turned back and looked over his shoulder. I still couldn't see his eyes. I needed to see them because they would tell me if he was someone I could trust, a friend or foe. Without a change in distance, he became less distinct, as if the fog was forming a blanket between us. He faded from view and I woke.

It was five twenty-five. The sun would be up in less than an hour. I reviewed the dream as I touched two fingers to my wrist and felt my pulse pounding. Ninety-six, I was breathing faster than normal and wet under the armpits. My forehead also felt damp. I arose and walked into the bathroom, glanced in the mirror, and observed a disheveled woman who looked every bit her age. After relieving myself, I wiped down with a cold damp washcloth, got dressed, and went to the kitchen. Normally, I would grind coffee from beans and enjoy the luxury of two or three cups along with a nice omelet. I had the makings, but I didn't have the patience. I boiled water and used the instant coffee. A bowl of cold cereal and a piece of toast would have to do. I waited until nine before calling Marjorie. She wasn't home. I was still trying to sort it out when Jonathan called just before noon.

"Caroline, how have you been?" asked the cheerful voice at the other end. Unlike my mysterious man, Jonathan was no baritone. He had a soft high tenor, almost feminine in quality.

I could never picture him wearing black—it was gray or blue flannel by business day and casual knit pullovers in the evening and on weekends. When we were on the lake, he wore a pair of shorts, conservative white, as if on a yacht or at a country club.

"I'm fine, how about you?"

"I've got tickets for a ball game this evening. Wanna go?" I knew he meant the Jackson Mets, a double-A minor league baseball team affiliated with the New York Mets. I had been to their games a few times and had mentioned it once to Jonathan. *He probably doesn't forget anything, like a gray flannel elephant.*

"Sure, why not? Meet you there?" I lived close to the ballpark and Jonathan lived on the other side of town, so meeting him seemed a reasonable accommodation. Marjorie would have been outraged. She, like many of her Southern friends, considered dating to be a formal ritual and the man was expected to pick up his date. The woman was also supposed to be a bit more circumspect in accepting the offer, especially on short notice for a Saturday night. My quick response was prima facie evidence that I had nothing, translatable to no man, in my life at the moment. I didn't care.

"Sure, meet you in front of the box office at six-thirty. And, don't eat beforehand. Ball games are as much about beers and brats as they are about balls and bases."

I smiled and hung up. Jonathan liked to indulge in alliteration whenever he could, as if compensating for a law degree from a third-tier university.

Jonathan was nothing if not punctual. I walked the four blocks from my apartment to the park and arrived at six twenty-five—he drove up two minutes later. We walked into the stadium hand-in-hand and found our seats along the third base line. Hot dogs and beer took us to the national anthem at seven and the first pitch shortly thereafter. Like at most minor league parks, the atmosphere was casual and friendly. Hits and errors came often and beer went down easily on a warm humid Mississippi evening. By the bottom of the fourth, I excused myself to visit the restroom. As usual, there was a line and I stood in the covered corridor waiting my turn. A roar from the crowd made me turn to the right and I saw him, my man in black, hat and all, unmistakably watching me.

The space beneath the bleachers was only partly lit and a shadow fell across his eyes and forehead. He smiled at me and held his hand out in the all-too familiar gesture. The noise from the crowd around me made it difficult to hear, but his lips formed my name—I knew he was calling me. I wanted to turn around, to go into the bathroom and have time to think, but I couldn't. I was frozen in place, facing him. He didn't come closer and there was no further conversation.

I awoke next to Jonathan. We were sitting in our hard wooden seats, it was the bottom of the fifth, and bases were loaded. The score was tied and the crowd was going wild. Jonathan looked at me and smiled.

"C'mon the game isn't that dull. We're putting on a pretty decent rally."

I looked at the crowd and at the brightly lit field. The sun had set and a breeze was blowing from left field, bringing relief from the stifling humidity. I had to go to the bathroom. Hadn't I just gone in the fourth inning? What happened? Had I really fallen asleep? I didn't remember finishing my break or returning to the seat.

"Excuse me, gotta go," I said, getting up and edging past his knees.

"Yeah, you said that about twenty minutes ago. Women and their small bladders."

I stopped in front of him and looked down at the top of

his head. He moved it back and forth, trying to see around me in what was a crucial moment of the ball game.

"Jonathan, I have to ask you something."

"Right now? I mean, can't it wait just a minute and could you stand to either side?"

I shifted back toward my seat and crouched so I didn't block the people behind me.

"Last inning, did I leave my seat and go, you know, to the restroom?"

He looked at me and then at the half cup of beer next to my chair. "Are you serious? Don't you know whether you went up there last inning?"

"I'm not sure. Maybe it's the beer, but I thought I had. I remember standing in a line to get into the lady's room. I saw something strange and then I woke up here...." I looked at my watch, "...about twenty minutes later. I don't remember anything in between."

The crack of a bat brought a roar from the crowd, now standing and yelling. A quick glance at the field showed everyone in motion as the ball sailed into right center field. Their outfielder misplayed it and the ball bounded to the wall. The bases were cleared and the batter was standing on third. Jonathan was yelling and smiling, looking around him, relishing the moment. He saw me looking at him and I must have had a strange look on my face. I felt strange and he quickly sat down and took my hand.

"Sorry, I didn't mean to..."

"It's all right," I assured him, "but now I really do have to go. I'll be back in a minute." We were still batting so I figured the crowd wanting to use the bathrooms might be distracted for the moment. I was right and walked in, but not before looking around for the man in black. Not there.

While I squatted, I tried to recall what happened earlier and I thought about what to tell Jonathan, if anything. I could depend on him to remember my remark about seeing something strange, so I needed to either tell him about my dreams or provide him a plausible but harmless story. We still didn't know each other that well, so maybe he would buy a confession about sun, beer, and fatigue. It had been a long and trying week at work and I had shared some of my frustrations with him. We usually didn't talk about my job because he represented the corporate "bad guys," as I had occasionally reminded him.

Leaving the bathroom, I again looked carefully down the corridor for signs of my, what? Phantasm? Specter? What do you call a dreamscape figure that enters real life? Or did he? Was I sleeping or in some kind of diurnal trance while next to Jonathan? Did I actually see someone in the corridor or was my imagination beginning to override my common sense, my moderate common sense for which I was so frequently credited? I walked into the open and down the steps to my seat. The inning was over and Jonathan smiled at me as the Mets took the field for the top of the sixth.

"Everything okay? Feel better?"

I nodded and picked up my beer, slouching in my chair and sipping slowly. I wasn't a big beer drinker, usually stopping after two. This was my second but I resolved to finish it. Jonathan watched me as I drained the last of it.

"Need another one?" he asked. His look told me he was merely being solicitous rather than recommending additional brew. "About what you saw…"

"It was nothing, just my mind wandering around without proper supervision. I guess I was more tired than I thought."

"Do you want to leave now? I can have you home in a couple of minutes."

"No, I'm fine. I want to see the rest of the game. We don't win that often so let's watch it." The score was seven to three in our favor, but last minute rallies and turnarounds were common.

We settled down to see the Mets win it nine to eight. He dropped me off at the front of my apartment complex. I think he wanted to come in but I was emotionally and physically drained. I told him so and he nodded. A quick peck on the cheek and he drove off as I entered my apartment, not knowing what to expect. Did I want to fall asleep and observe more of the unfolding drama or did I want to avoid another encounter? Did I have a choice? If I didn't like the story, could I stop it or change it? The ballpark reverie had changed the rules. I hadn't been in my bed and I wasn't in control. What would the next chapter reveal? I made a cup of hot chocolate, got dressed for bed, and turned off the light at eleven fifteen.

SUNDAY MORNING BROUGHT A BRIEF RAINSTORM FOL-lowed by bright sunshine and blue sky. There had been no dreams and I took my time rolling out of bed. Still wearing pajamas and a robe, I indulged in the full weekend breakfast I missed the day before. The sound and smell of grinding coffee obliterated thoughts of men in black and swirling clouds. I didn't have any plans for the day and decided to pick up a novel I had been reading sporadically for the past two months. That didn't necessitate getting dressed, so I curled up on the couch, nibbling at the remains of cinnamon toast. *A cat would be nice, purring and snuggling against my fleece pajamas.* My cat had remained with Roland, my ex. I couldn't have one in the apartment so he had agreed to keep her when I moved out. *Wonder if she is still alive?* It had been three years and he and I didn't communicate after the papers were signed. It was a clean sweep, no-fault, no lawyers, all very civilized. No kids, but he kept the cat.

I started to read, but the ballpark incident kept me from concentrating. I still wasn't sure about what had happened, where reality and fantasy met. Jonathan had treated it as a joke and wouldn't confirm whether or not I had made two trips to the bathroom. At least he wasn't annoyed that I had fallen asleep during the most exciting part of the game. His remark about my "small bladder" implied I had mentioned needing to go. But had I? And, if I had gone during the fourth inning, had the man in black been there?

I stared at the wall across the room. It needed a picture or something to relieve the stark emptiness. I kept meaning to find something inexpensive to give the place some warmth or character and just hadn't gotten around to it. Life was good, as I kept telling myself, but it didn't seem to be progressing toward anything. Even the advocacy work seemed to be directionless. There were no decisive victories or defeats, just an endless parade of legal complications, suits and countersuits, hearings, opinions, and unfulfilled promises. My personal life seemed to be in a similar state. *Jonathan is nice enough but there isn't any oomph, any zest in our relationship. Sex is adequate but not exciting. Marjorie is a friend but all too predictable. Once she finds a man, I'll probably see little of her. Maybe I should get a cat and say the hell with the landlord.*

The day passed quietly and by bedtime I had calmed

considerably. I finally made progress on the book, had a light dinner, did a few aerobic exercises, and ironed some clothes for the coming week. As I pressed the blouse and pants for the next day, I speculated on the dreamscape. I felt confident I could turn it off, wake myself when I wanted and dismiss the fantasy completely. One of the ways to do that was to think about the dream and the action I would take. It was a type of self-conditioning, being able to recognize the onset of a dream and to either terminate it or manipulate it. The latter took more practice, but I had done it a number of times in the past. Except for the ballpark incident, nothing in the dream had been frightening. I was tempted to go further into the fantasy and see where it would lead. *What the hell, it's only a dream. How bad can it get?*

By the time I climbed into bed, turned off the light, and looked at the clock, it was ten forty-five. I resolved to give myself up to the man in black. I needed to know who or what he was and where he wanted me to go. I also realized there might be no answers—it was just as likely a silly dream, a visual montage of nonsense with no definitive plot or outcome. Dreams are more often not an organized story, at least not in my experience. I fell asleep thinking about the man, trying to force his reappearance.

"Caroline, come to me."

By now it was all too familiar, the clothes, the face, the extended hand. But there were also some differences. I could see his eyes. The shadow fell across the top half of his forehead and the eyes looked directly at me. They weren't remarkable—not blazing red or black pits or anything invoking demons or other icons of horror. And the background was no longer a vague blur of gray. We were on a road slanted slightly uphill. On either side there was a white picket fence and to the left was a large tree, probably an oak, overhanging the road. It was dark and the light seemed to come from behind me, as if I was standing between the man and car headlights. However, I couldn't see my shadow nor could I make out one behind the man.

"Are you ready, Caroline?"

Again I noted his constant reference to my name, as if it was a requirement beyond a personal greeting. It spoke of a familiarity at odds with the other elements of the dream. And a dream it was, without doubt. By now I could analyze it while the scene unfolded. I also decided to exert some control, to alter the outcome if I could. I forced myself forward, closer to the man. It was painfully slow but the distance closed. I could see his hand in front of me, close enough to touch if I could reach out. But I couldn't. I could not make my own hand come into view. It was as if I didn't have a hand or an arm. I was a disembodied observer, able to approach but not permitted to contact the stranger. I tried to tell him I was ready but no words came. He looked steadily into my eyes.

"Not yet. Soon, but not yet, Caroline. We will wait." He faded from view, again obscured by a layer of fog that suddenly appeared. I woke and looked at the clock: three-forty. Between three and four seemed to be my prime time for nightscapes. It had always been, conforming to what most dream scientists believed was the period of sleep featuring the longest and most intense bouts of rapid eye movements.

Perhaps I should contact a sleep clinic and have them test me during these encounters. Would there be a correlation or was this some other kind of mental event? I thought about it for several minutes, the advancing revelation of facial features, the new appearance of surroundings, and his message about waiting for me to be ready. I was frustrated by my inability to interact, to ask questions. He seemed to be leading me further each time, but at an agonizingly slow pace. And to where? It was then I began to think about the man in black in relation to my previous thoughts on not waking up. What would happen if I did follow the man, if I took his hand and we walked down the road together? Would I be able to return, to wake up?

* * *

Monday morning, I called in sick. I wasn't really, but I didn't feel like poring over reports, answering the inevitable inane questions about our wetland policy proposals, or dealing with people in general. Solitude was the only thing I could face. I took the time to make an omelet and grind the coffee. I sat in my robe and ate slowly, listening to Dvorák's Slavonic Dances. They inspired melancholy, matching my introspective mood, but provided enough uplift to slowly transition me into active preparations. I called Marjorie and she answered. She had Mondays off and I told her we needed to talk, that the man in black was back and more intense than ever. She listened quietly and said she would be over for lunch in thirty minutes. She made it in fifteen and we sat on my small veranda sipping the last of the coffee.

"This is depressingly sober of us," she remarked, holding the cup in front of her like a precious family artifact. "This topic begs for a martini or some other serious libation."

"I though most of you Southern belles refrained from hard liquor until after four," I answered.

"Only before eleven, dearest—after that it is righteous to drink whatever."

She called me dearest when she was concerned for my health or welfare. After giving her the details of my latest fantasy, she admitted she was concerned.

"Don't go with the man, Caroline. I have a bad feeling about this. Do you want to see someone? I have a friend, a really nice young woman with a doctorate in counseling. I have confided in her a few times and she is down to earth, really a great one to share this with."

"I don't know, Marge, I feel so stupid, even telling you about it. I'm like some naïve little girl afraid of the boogeyman and the dark. But, even stranger, I'm not actually afraid of the man. There was nothing in his eyes to make me want to turn back. He said I wasn't ready yet. I can't decide what that means."

"You still haven't said anything to Jonathan about this?"

"No, I can't. He is already a bit spooked about what I did and said at the ballpark. If I start ranting about a man in black and a foggy road, he'll write me off as a certified loony. He might be right." I looked at my friend, hoping for words of refutation. Marjory regarded me like I was a hopelessly lost puppy, with affection but resignation.

"Sure you don't want to break out some serious sipping stuff?" she offered again.

I shook my head and thanked her, but by two she was on her way and I was alone to confront my options for the evening. One was to spend the next several hours exercising in an effort to disrupt my usual sleep pattern. A deeper sleep resulting from exhaustion could preclude REM activity and associated dreaming. Another option was to take a sleeping potion. I rarely needed one, but it might also interfere with the course of events. The third option was to go to bed as usual and to welcome a return of the mysterious man. One thing bothered me about the last option, however. I had a strong premonition that a replay of the scene would be decisive, that a resolution of one sort or another would occur. Was the man's wait over? What did he want? More important, what did I want?

I answered a few letters, paid a utility bill, and heated a dinner of leftovers. As the evening wore on, I began preparing for a journey. No clothes were packed or transportation arranged, but I focused on the small things I could control. I left no dirty dishes in the sink or clothes scattered about the bedroom. Everything was in its designated place and accounted for. I spent the rest of the evening watching a light-hearted musical, something to enjoy without a lot of concentration. The next day was another workday, but I was prepared to blow it off. I'll call in again. *No one is irreplacable—maybe that's part of the problem.*

There was still one task I hadn't faced. Should I leave a note for Marjorie? It seemed silly. I was going to sleep, I might have a dream, or not, and I might decide to take another day off work, hardly the stuff of big decisions or confessions. What about Jonathan? Should I try to explain my behavior to him? By the time I stepped out of the shower and dried myself, I had rejected the idea of a note to anyone. *Let it be. It is a mystery to me and it will be to them if something should happen.* I smiled and turned in at ten thirty, not sure what would be waiting for me on the dark road.

As expected, he was there, dressed as before, his entire face exposed by the light from behind me. He didn't say anything but his extended hand beckoned me forth. The smile was subdued but welcoming and his eyes told me all I needed to know. They were open and bright, the reassuring eyes of an old friend. I raised my hand as I approached. The oak leaves rustled in a slight breeze, the gentle sound distinct and soothing. Our fingers touched and it was warm as I stood beside him. I heard myself say clearly, without hesitation, "I'm ready." The snow-white fog closed in around us, swirling, obliterating everything as we walked up the hill together.

AUTUMN CATS

Do animals love or do they just respond to us in anticipation of receiving food and other gratifications? What about us? Is it a form of mutualism—I'll satisfy you if you will satisfy me—or are we really altruistic, giving without required reciprocation? Perhaps we share more than we realize.

She is dreaming again, her butt quivering in slight arrhythmic spasms, pressed against me. Outside, autumn aspen leaves fall in their own asynchronous fashion, disturbed by a light breeze and soft rain. Together, they produce a sensual orchestra, tactile and auditory, accompanied by sighs of our predawn breathing. The glowing red numbers of the bedside clock indicate three forty-four, the hour of the dead and dying. Yes we are, but that's nothing new. As I have reminded her and myself so many times, we started dying at conception—nothing to be concerned about. Lie back and enjoy the show.

The dull pressure of a full bladder pushes me out of bed to the adjoining bathroom. The cold air brings the first reminders of winter. We don't turn the heat on until necessary, meaning, when I require pajamas in a shared bed. She wears them anyway, even in summer. It makes her feel secure, she says, warm and protected. I relieve myself, wash my hands, drying them so I don't touch her with cold wet fingers. She hates that. I leave the toilet unflushed. Her dreamtime is important, assuring her a good night's rest.

She is a cat, through and through and nine hours of sleep is her norm. She doesn't get that on a working day, so I disturb her as little as possible.

She has been a cat all of her life. I guess most cats have been. We have known each other for eight years and lived together for six. We find comfort in each other's company, laughing and loving together, occasionally fighting, then making up with little time lost to regrets. She wanders away from time to time. To see what is out there, she explains. Cats go where they want and when, unless confined by the clueless and heartless. Sometimes she tells me where she goes and what she does—sometimes it is a mystery, another prerogative of the feline spirit.

We have a real cat, the four-legged kind that has her own secrets. She is a runt, a six-year-old kitten with a squeaky voice and pumpkin-colored short hair. She's a one-trick kitty—rolling over onto her back with feet waving help- lessly in the air, an inducement to scratch her belly and butt. When we do, it sends her into throes of ecstasy, the closest thing she will ever know to sex. Unlike my woman, kitty doesn't go outside. I am not clueless, but I am heartless. I am also tired of paying veterinary bills to repair outdoor cats whose adventurousness overcomes prudence. Kitty is a birdwatcher and she utters twittering noises accompanied by a tail imitating a metronome. The jays tease her, coming up to the glass door, separated, but only a few inches from paws and teeth that would gladly greet and eat them.

Kitty is fascinated by other cats, those that prowl around the house and walk across our porch with impunity. Like the jays, they know the glass barrier will hold. Some are met with soft growls and cries of despair, accompanied by a bristling tail and puffed hair. As the visitor walks around the house, our cat dashes madly between windows and doors to keep the intruder in sight. Others are greeted calmly, with much sniffing and quiet pacing.

The woman laughs at kitty's antics and says she understands. Understand what? I ask. Her reaction to other cats, she explains, holding a warm cup of chocolate with both hands.

It is Saturday morning and we have nothing planned. We can talk and eat a leisurely breakfast. We are watching kitty watching birds through the dining room glass door.

They are probably female cats, she says. Kitty and I don't like other females. She smiles and lowers her head to sip. I know this to be true. She doesn't have many female friends. She has always preferred men and I am grateful for that, being of the male persuasion myself. Strangely, there is no jealousy or concern. She doesn't stray. She wanders but always returns. I never smell the scent of another on her. I can tell.

The yellow and brown leaves clutter our deck. I'll have to sweep and bag some of them before the heavy rains and snows arrive. I leave some of them on the grass to provide compost for the spring revival. She and I agree on our compact with nature. It is one of the few un-catlike things about her—she won't kill anything unless necessary. Mosquitos and cockroaches are fair game, but spiders, beetles, and even scorpions are ushered outside with gentle hands and wishes for their continued existence. I look at the dry leaves and she looks at me. We both understand the portent of the season and we accept it, although not graciously. It is also part of our destiny.

Kitty spots a wren sitting on a branch near the porch. The bird's tail flicks back and forth, providing an additional element of attraction. The cat's tail responds in kind. I look at the woman and she smiles, knowing what I am thinking.

"Do I still attract you like that?" she asks. It is a rhetorical question because she knows the answer. I mention her dreams and warm butt and ask her if she remembers what it was about. Maybe it was a bird, she says, and stretches her arms out in an expansive yawn. Her bathrobe falls open. She is still beautiful and slim in her fifties. Cats don't seem to age like other animals. They are young, they mature, but they vanish when they get too old to hunt or respond to other cats. Kitty, like my woman, is middle-aged but young at heart. I'm not so sure about myself. I am twenty years older than her and I'm not a cat.

We got drunk one night and I asked her about us, what would it be like when we became really old. She doesn't like talking about it because she knows I will leave her some day. It's just the way it is, I tell her. We knew that when we hooked up. She smiles. Hooking up is what younger generations do—we cohabitate, she says. I tell her we are shacking up, a term from my generation. "Should I put you down when the time comes?" she asks.

I can tell she is saying this deliberately, trying to shock, her way of telling me she doesn't want to discuss winter endings. I remind her she actually likes winter, the icy landscapes and the quiet solitude. It prepares the way for the rebirth of spring. Not for us, she says, we have only one cycle. She starts to cry and I put my arms around her.

The wren has flown and kitty comes to us, flopping on her back. She rubs herself on the carpet, legs flailing in the air and we reach down to satisfy her craving. My woman's hand lies on top of mine as I scratch kitty's belly. The three of us ignore the burst of wind that brings a fresh scattering of leaves to the porch.

A NIGHT ON BIG RAT ISLAND

Remember the boys from the diner in the first story?
Seems they are back, a few months older and wiser. Well, maybe older.
This is not so much about love as about misadventure. Also, ignore all those
insincere assurances of "any resemblance to actual persons or events being
strictly coincidental." The strictly part is somewhat questionable.

We had never heard of Big Rat Island. We weren't alone. People we talked to later hadn't heard of it either. Rats weren't on our minds when we rented a boat one Sunday morning in the spring of 1962 to cruise the sloughs near Suisun, California. Charlie, Melvin, and I were enlisted airmen, newly arrived trainees at a nearby air force base hospital. We had known each other for almost a year, buddies in earlier training courses at other places. Our status came with a blue ribbon guarantee: we were short on money, privileges, and girlfriends. On this particular Sunday a boat excursion promised something different to relieve the boredom. It also had the virtue of being cheap entertainment.

Melvin was the oldest at twenty-six, a bright, introverted guy from the Midwest—an artist with an artist's sensibilities. He was usually reserved when sober but could light up a room after a few drinks, emphasis on few. Charlie was almost twenty-one, a Tennessee prankster who was serious only under the most serious conditions, like when he was asked for identification in a bar. Of course he had it, but he hadn't paid much for the phony driver's license and that often led to serious explanations. I was nineteen, didn't have a drivers license, but I used a phony school ID that raised even more questions than Charlie's. Melvin owned our wheels, a beat-up old Ford that was good enough for local use but not to be trusted for any distance. Although we spent a lot of time together we didn't have that much in common. We were as different in background, interests, and ambitions as any three men could be. All of that was about to change.

The idea to rent a boat for the day had occurred to us the week before. The base had a small wharf and rental facility at the head of the slough. None of us had any experience with small boats or outboards, and we had never been in the maze of waterways that comprised the extensive estuary above Grizzly Bay. But, we figured, what the hell, what could possibly go wrong? We knew there were some pretty stupid, drunk fishermen out there on the water, so it should be no problem for three smart guys like us.

It was an early spring day, presenting a few puffy clouds, a gentle breeze, and a bit of morning chill. We arrived at the rental shack and the man checked our identification, our real military ones. Melvin signed an agreement stating we had been issued a boat, a motor, a tank of fuel, two oars, and three life jackets. We were told to stay in the estuary and to have the boat back by sixteen hundred that evening, in time for closing. We tried to be as non-military as possible when off base and agreed to have it back by four.

"And one last thing," he warned us as we climbed into the rowboat and lowered the outboard, "don't leave the slough—

don't even think about crossing the bay. Understand?" He was a retired master sergeant, known to everyone as "Sarge" (what an unusual nickname) and his authority on this or anything else wasn't a matter of debate.

"Yes, sir," answered Charlie, always the quickest to defer but the least military minded of us. He took control of the motor as we donned our vests and took seats, Melvin in the middle and myself at the bow.

Without further comment, we were under way, rounding a bend and out of sight, intending to spend the day prowling the meandering waterways of the brackish marshes. We had packed sandwiches, chips, and some water. We thought there would be a place to get drinks at the boat rental, but because it was Sunday the adjacent bait and beer store was closed until noon. We also had a small map of the slough that included some landmarks, such as numbered buoys, and a few piers and shacks here and there. Each of us took a turn at the motor while the other two relaxed, spotted birds, waved at a few fishermen, or checked the map. We planned to be back before three, giving us almost five hours of cruising with no destination, no plan, not even a fishing pole.

It was by sheer chance that one of the many channels we navigated happened to open on the bay around noon. The sun had been relentless and our water was almost gone. Although all of us could legally drink on base, Melvin was the only one who could buy beer off base. We looked at the bay and it seemed relatively calm. Winds were mild to moderate and we had time. A large boating facility across the bay would have the precious suds, so the decision came down to whether we wanted to spend the next three thirsty hours wandering the marshes or make a dash for the beer.

Charlie was again at the helm as we shot into open water at full throttle. We picked up the first small waves and the exhilarating spray, in sharp contrast to the quiet backwaters we had just left. Several minutes later, we were far from shore, any shore. Surrounded by open water, we suddenly realized we were the smallest boat in sight. Undaunted, we continued toward the pier and fuel sign ahead. The waves became whitecaps and the wind delivered a sting as the salt spray whipped across us. Fortunately, we had windbreakers and the water evaporated readily in the hot sun. As we pulled closer to the marina, we commented on the underlying swell that indicated a strong inbound tide through the Carquinez Straits.

We pulled up to the pier, tied our boat, and Melvin went in for the beer. Charlie and I waited in the boat, speculating on how long it would take us to return. It was close to one when we left the marina and started back into the bay at about half throttle. Each of us was sipping on a cold one and eating a sandwich. There is something special about cold beer, sun, and salt water. As we eased into the tidal flow the boat began to rock against the waves striking our port side. The wind had increased and the swells became noticeably larger as we made our way north toward the slough entrance.

At first, the chop was exciting, slapping against the metal hull and evoking images of men struggling against the sea. Occasionally, waves crashed over the sides, forcing Melvin and I to employ a plastic bailer.

"Bail for your lives boys, we're taking on water," laughed Charlie, as if he was in an overflowing bathtub at home.

Melvin and I looked at each other, smiled, and took another sip of beer. We would have a few sea stories to impress our friends with at the base that night. Within a few minutes, the winds increased further and water began to pour over the lower sides of the transom. Charlie, sitting along side the outboard, began to receive his fair share of abuse. We still weren't too concerned but we had slowed down to smooth the bumps and take on less water.

Then it happened. A large wave crashed against the stern and the outboard sputtered and quit. We were drifting eastward with the inbound sea while Charlie tried to restart the motor. We all tried, with the same result. We were still a long way from the marshes and the current was sweeping us toward a low island with a wooden building at one end. Melvin and I deployed the oars to try and cut across the current, but we made little headway. The island loomed nearer and we decided that it was better to beach the boat and seek help rather than stay in the bay. We were also aware the tide would eventually reverse and sweep floating objects out through the straits and westward into San Francisco Bay with the same force by which it was pushing us into the delta.

By this time it was nearing three. Although we still had a few hours of daylight, we would be late in returning the boat. Our most serious problem, however, was being out-of-bounds in the bay. Our bold, cheerful attitudes during our initial crossing yielded to sullen resignation as we beached the boat. A good day had gone bad.

"This might be a court martial, gentlemen, for disobeying orders," proclaimed Melvin. It wasn't unusual for him to seize upon the worst of possible outcomes.

I looked at the outboard motor. "Suppose we don't get it started, what then?"

"Then I guess we're castaways on a deserted island," laughed Charlie, opening another beer. Reality came hard for Charlie.

The narrow strip of sandy mud quickly yielded to dry reeds and grasses. We pulled the boat several yards onto shore, not sure how high the tide would come, but it didn't look like anyplace on the island was more than a few feet above sea level. It was cool enough to keep our coats on, but we left everything else in the boat as we started the two hundred yard walk to the building. A few larger bushes and an occasional tree were the only other features of the isle. Charlie was the first to see the dead seagull lying in the grass. It wouldn't have been remarkable if it weren't for the condition of the body. Part of it was decomposed but the rest of it had been clearly eaten by something.

"Probably dogs," I offered.

"Too bad Walt, that might have been supper," said Charlie.

Melvin and I looked at each other, knowing we had already eaten most of our lunch. Approaching the house, our hopes of finding immediate help began to sink. Although it was a large one-story building on piers with a porch on one side, it had not been painted in years and the wood planks were beginning to rot. Loose shingles were evident but the window glass was intact. A water tower and shed stood near the northern end of the building. We walked around to the front entrance and onto the porch. The house, like the island, was still. Charlie's comment about a deserted island had been prophetic.

Melvin tried the front door. It opened easily and we entered. The main room had a linoleum floor but little furniture except for a junky looking dresser and two chairs with torn cushions. To the right was a kitchen. There were several cans and boxes of food on the shelves, but nothing of recent vintage. Many of the boxes had holes at the corners and sides.

"The mice have been busy," remarked Melvin as we surveyed the room.

"Shit, this is just shit," said Charlie slowly in his southern drawl.

An old range and oven and an icebox were lined up against one wall. The icebox door was open, revealing a bare interior. Newspapers were scattered here and there on the floor, on a small wooden table, and on the shelves that formed a pantry area.

Our footsteps sounded louder than usual as we re-entered the living room and turned into a straight hallway that ran the length of the house. Three bedrooms and a bathroom led off the hall. We stepped out onto the front porch and relieved ourselves. There was no running water in either the toilet or the sinks, which were liberally stained by years of rust. I found a 1947 advertising calendar for a repair shop in one of the bedrooms. Penciled comments on some of the dates included names of people. The dressers and closets contained some clothing, but it was ragged and soiled. Old mattresses, stained and smelling of mildew, lay either on the floor or on bed frames in each room.

"I don't think anyone has lived here for at least ten or fifteen years," announced Melvin as he sorted through loose papers and notebooks lying on a dresser.

I looked out a window facing the channel toward the marina where we had bought the beer. Shadows were growing longer as the sun lowered toward the Carquinez Bridge.

"There's obviously no phone here," I said.

"No electricity, either," added Charlie.

It was almost five and we were an hour overdue.

"Someone might be searching for us by now," said Charlie, still hopeful, still cavalier.

"If they spot the boat on the beach, that should lead them to the house," I stated.

Melvin was skeptical. "Unless they spot us before dark, it's very unlikely we'll be rescued before dawn. Even then, it might be a while before someone thinks to look around the bay islands. We're supposed to be in the slough and that's where they will focus first."

It was about that time I found three candles in a drawer. I suggested we light the candles after it got dark, placing them in a window facing the marina. If the house had been abandoned for many years, the appearance of lights in the house might invite an investigation. Furthermore, one of the dressers had a mirror. Remembering a scene from an old movie about Thomas Edison, I told them we could intensify the light by putting the mirror behind the burning candles. Melvin suggested we use the window shades.

"If we pull them up and down in front of the candles, we can try and signal the marina."

S.O.S. was about the only Morse code any us knew. As desperate as it sounded, we seemed to have few other options. Charlie smoked so he had a lighter and some matches. We found a few in the kitchen but they had long since lost any capacity to ignite. While Charlie moved the dresser and set up the candles, Melvin and I walked back to the boat to retrieve our belongings, including the remnants of our lunch, three cans of beer, and the life jackets. It was Melvin's idea to spread them out on the roof to dry while at the same time indicating our presence on the island. As we trudged back to the house, Melvin again commented on the remains of the sea gull and questioned the fate of the original residents. Being of morbid mind and not inclined to reassure my sensitive friend, I replied that we would probably find their half-eaten remains under the house.

It was dark by the time the life vests were spread on the roof and the candles set by the window, ready to light. We ate the last of our food and finished the beer while we moved the shades up and down in front of the burning candles. Taking turns, we signaled and watched for a response from the marina or anywhere else across the darkened waters, but there was nothing.

"I guess this is home for the night," said Melvin. "Lets drag some mattresses into the living room and sleep there."

We put the least damaged mattresses in a circle at the center of the living room where the damp smells weren't as noticeable as in the bedrooms. The candles were slim and burned rapidly, leaving us in the dark. A half moon had risen and provided enough light to discern our bodies as we settled onto the floor. It was still early and we talked for a while, but it was probably no later than ten when we fell asleep.

* * *

I'M NOT SURE WHO HEARD THE NOISE FIRST. PERHAPS we all woke at the same time. Melvin was the closest to me. He whispered, "Walt, did you hear that?"

"Yeah," I said. "Charlie?"

"Me too," he answered. "It sounds like something scratching."

There was silence, except for the three of us breathing. No one moved and we waited, not sure of what we were hearing or where it was coming from.

A light, swift scratching noise from the direction of the kitchen brought us upright. We could still see each other in the dim moonlight, but we couldn't see anything beyond the living room. Charlie struck his lighter, holding it over his head. There was a dark blur in the kitchen doorway, accompanied by soft, rapid skittering across the linoleum.

"A mouse!" exclaimed Melvin, sounding noticeably relieved. The lighter went out and we laughed at our fears in the dark. The long day and the island's desolation had taken their toll on our nerves.

"Maybe our rodent friends won't be satisfied with dry oatmeal. Maybe they need fresh meat," joked Charlie.

"Yeah, maybe the occasional sea gull isn't enough," I added. Melvin said nothing.

Charlie started to tell a campsite ghost story, but Melvin interrupted him.

"Do you think one of us should stay awake and keep the mice away?" he asked.

I thought a minute and told them I didn't think mice would bother us. Melvin wasn't a bit reassured by this happy news and he volunteered to keep the first watch. Charlie said it was all right with him and gave his lighter to Melvin. I rolled over and prepared to get some sleep.

My efforts were short-lived. The skittering noises started a few minutes later and we all sat up. The sounds came from the kitchen and the hallway. Melvin clicked the lighter and a brief flash illuminated several sets of eyes staring at us from the two doorways. The lighter went out as Melvin and Charlie uttered, in unison, "Shit!"

We stood up immediately. Scratching could be heard throughout the house.

"Damn, how many of these damn things are there in this damn house?" shouted Melvin. He wasn't much for swearing, so this represented a high state of agitation for him. Charlie took the lighter back from Melvin. We still hadn't gotten a good look at them, so we weren't sure whether we were in the midst of mice or rats. We stood in a close circle, facing outward.

"Let's be quiet and let them get closer before I use the lighter again," said Charlie. I could tell Melvin was shaking his head and this was very difficult for him.

"Okay," I replied, "but not too close."

We waited, but only for a few seconds. The noises began again, but this time there were a lot more of them, seemingly from every direction. We held our breath and waited, trying to judge how close they were. We could barely make out dark forms here and there against the walls.

"Now!" said Charlie as the lighter flicked and the small flame lit up the living room. We gasped.

About a dozen or more of the large dark rodents were in the room with us, about six or seven feet away. Many more could be seen in the kitchen and hallways, their eyes reflecting the light. They scurried back and forth, but they didn't flee for the cover of darkness as they had earlier. As we looked on in horror, they returned our stares and a few ventured closer. I brought my foot down sharply on the floor and Charlie yelled something unintelligible. Melvin didn't say anything. The rats, for rats they were, scattered, but not far and not for long. As we watched, the bolder ones crept back into the hallway doorframe. Melvin was breathing rapidly and shaking. He seemed to be on the verge of hysteria.

"Let's get the hell out of here," whispered Charlie, as if he wanted to keep our intentions secret from our rodent companions.

"Where?" asked Melvin. His voice was close to tears.

"The roof. Let's get on the roof. At least we'll be out in the open," I said.

There was no further discussion. We were already wearing our jackets and there was nothing else to take. Moving toward and out the front door, we stomped our feet and waved the lighter. A ladder beside the tower led onto the roof and we climbed up and sat down beside the life vests. We didn't say anything for several minutes. The three of us stared out at the bay, noting that the wind had died, the water was relatively calm, and the tide was now outbound. Our boat was on the beach well out of harm's way.

"Maybe the motor will dry out and we can start it tomorrow," said Charlie.

"Maybe the rats climb walls and we won't have to worry about it."

Charlie and I looked at Melvin. Normally, this would have brought a few laughs and further comments, but we realized Melvin was not in the mood for levity. Come to think of it, we weren't either.

"I don't think they can climb up here," I answered, softly and less sure than I wanted to be.

We didn't talk further. Charlie and I laid down first. It was cold and damp and we remained close together. I remember Melvin was still sitting there, hugging himself and staring out at the water when my eyes closed.

I WAS THE FIRST ONE TO HEAR THE PLANE OVERHEAD. It was about six thirty in the morning and a coast guard PBY search and rescue was circling the bay. I woke the others and grabbed an orange life vest. The plane was coming back, flying relatively low at an angle to the island. Melvin and Charlie also grabbed vests and we spread out on the roof waving them over our heads. The plane passed us about a half mile away and we lowered the vests, discouraged that we still hadn't been spotted. The PBY made a tight turn and came back toward the island, closer this time. Once again, we waved the vests, shouting at the plane to see us, as if they could hear us.

This time, however, the plane bobbed its wings once to each side, then turned and came straight toward us. We waved with our hands as it passed overhead and turned west toward Vallejo.

"It's just a matter of time, now. We'll be off this damned island in no time at all." Melvin was once again among the living, animated and laughing. He was the first one to spot the coast guard cutter heading toward us from the direction of the slough.

With daylight came courage and we clambered down from the roof with our vests, walking toward the beach, relieved to leave the house. By the time we arrived, a dinghy had been lowered from the cutter and two men in blue uniforms were motoring toward shore. They pulled up next to our boat and one of them, a petty officer second class, stepped up to Melvin.

"Are you guys the missing airmen from the base?" he asked without preliminaries.

Melvin hung his head and replied almost inaudibly, "Yes sir, that would be us, sir."

"They've been searching for you all night," he said.

We looked at each other, knowing we were in big trouble. In addition to disobeying orders and not returning the boat on time, we were now officially absent without leave as of seven that Monday morning. We were still in training and failure to report to the hospital was not going to go down well. We stood silent and glum, watching as one of the seamen sprayed something on our motor, waited a minute, and started it. He cut the engine and fastened a rope to our boat. We took seats in the coast guard dinghy, motored back to the cutter, and climbed aboard. We were given warm blankets and seated in the galley, where we were provided with bacon, eggs, and coffee. The skipper of the cutter came down after we were underway and asked us if we were all right. We told him we were, thanked him for his hospitality, and related our tale of the rats.

"It used to be a popular fishing resort," he said, "but it's been abandoned for quite a few years. Every once in a while someone lands and uses some of the wood to make a fire on the beach."

He agreed that wharf rats could be big, but had never heard of anyone being attacked by them. He told us the island had sported a number of names over the years but that it was currently named Roe Island. We suggested that "Big Rat Island" might be a more appropriate name. The cutter couldn't enter the slough, so they put us in our boat, made sure the outboard started, and wished us good luck as we cast off to enter the waterway.

"There will be someone to meet you at the dock," shouted the skipper.

We didn't doubt that for one minute. Our trip back to the boat rental was uneventful. We discussed possible alibis but knew we didn't have one. We had been caught in the wrong place doing the wrong thing. There was little to say except apologize for our disobedience. We tried to imagine all of the possible things that might happen to us and who would be waiting for us at the pier. As usual, we were wrong on all counts.

Instead of the air police from the base, a single deputy sheriff from Suisun was waiting along with the retired master sergeant and a third person. Sarge was truly pissed at us but he devoted most of his attention to the boat and motor. Satisfied we hadn't damaged either, he let us know we were permanently barred from ever using the boat facilities.

"Don't even show up to look at my boats or to buy bait," he said. We promised him the thought would never cross our minds.

The third person was a reporter for the Suisun newspaper. He snapped a picture of us when we tied the boat to the dock and climbed onto the pier. He asked a few questions and took our names. The deputy was more amused than irritated. He knew our troubles would start when we returned to the base, so he wasn't inclined to give us any grief. He listened to our story as he drove us back to the base.

We reported to our duty stations at ten thirty that morning, still wearing our civilian clothes from the day before. Our supervisor told us to get cleaned up and report back to work by noon. We returned to our barracks, showered, put on fresh hospital whites and went to lunch. Nothing else was said officially to us during the afternoon, but we related our island adventure to our barracks buddies a number of times that evening.

The final surprise came the next morning. The three of us, vowing to stick together for whatever was to come, entered the laboratory expecting to be disciplined by the commanding officer of the unit. Instead, applause and a chorus of congratulations by several of our enlisted colleagues greeted us. Only the officers seemed reserved and silent. The reason for the celebration was pinned to the central bulletin board, a newspaper clipping from the front page of the *Suisun Times* with large bold headlines that read:

AIRMEN DOWN AT SEA
Coast Guard Rescues Three Airmen from Travis

Under the headlines was a picture of Charlie, Melvin, and me climbing out of the boat, accompanied by a story describing our ordeal. Backslaps and further questions followed, but there are always dues to pay.

"Gentlemen, if you will come with me…" said Sgt. Pruitt, the noncommissioned officer in charge of the laboratory trainees. He turned on his heels and we followed him to Colonel Sullivan's office. Pruitt knocked and we entered. The colonel, an older black man we respected for his intelligence and sense of fairness, sat behind his desk. To his right was another of the lab officers, a young lieutenant that most of us tried to avoid whenever possible. Sgt. Pruitt took a seat to the left and the three of us stood before the desk at attention.

"At ease, airmen," said the colonel.

Before him was the report from the coast guard, the deputy sheriff, and a copy of the newspaper. He made a point of looking through each document carefully, although we suspected he had read them earlier. We stood and waited, eyes straight ahead but aware the lieutenant was staring at us with no love lost.

The colonel leaned back in his chair and looked at each of us.

"Had a busy weekend, I see."

"Yes sir," we answered, not sure if we should add anything. We didn't.

"I shouldn't have to remind you that you disobeyed orders and you were absent from duty without permission," the colonel said in his slow, precise, deep baritone.

"This could constitute dereliction of duty," added the lieutenant, the lab's executive officer, trying without success to keep the malice out of his voice.

"Yes, I suppose it could," replied Colonel Sullivan, "but that would be a serious charge and might require a summary court martial hearing. I don't believe we want to involve these boys in that, do we?"

The lieutenant didn't have an answer for what was a rhetorical question. He remained silent and Sgt. Pruitt said nothing. There was also no love lost between our NCO and the lieutenant.

"I understand you boys have been barred from base boat rentals for life. Is that right?"

"Yes sir," we answered.

"That should take care of the business about crossing the bay and returning the boat late. As for not being on duty yesterday morning, the three of you will report for a squadron cleaning detail and spend four hours scrubbing floors. Understood?"

"Yes sir."

The executive officer shifted in his seat, started to say something, but a silent glare from the colonel silenced him.

Sgt. Pruitt rose and turned to us. "Attention. Dismissed."

We left the office, not believing we had escaped both the rats and the dark shadow of military justice. Later, we learned the colonel was mostly amused by the incident and found the newspaper headline hilarious. It was he who posted it in the laboratory for everyone to read. For a few days the three of us were celebrities in the hospital. Almost everyone, including the airman in charge of our work detail, greeted us with smiles. Everyone, except our executive officer. He would find some other way to provide us with an appropriate punishment. But, as the well-worn saying goes, that is another story.

FOR MARVIN AND JON

INTERLUDE II: SIX-WORD STORIES

The passion for writing, expressed in prose or poetry, entails a love for words. One of the interesting challenges offered by a writing workshop is to construct a story in six words, no more, no less. One other requirement: the story has to have at least two sentences. Here are some examples. What can you say in six words? Try it yourself.

Graveyard summons. Two days left. Waiting.

I love you. Forever. Maybe not.

Rich man sends love. How much?

Chili cooking champion chokes. Bad beans.

I win. You lose. Still friends?

Road to nowhere. Nowhere to go.

You want me. To do what?

Eternal rain. Boat not ready. Gulp!

Write me! No one else will.

LAWNMOWER TED

You find love—and misadventure—in strange and unexpected places. This story is a modified excerpt from a forthcoming novel, *The Party House*, set in 1970s Texas. Well, not actually Texas, but on a barrier island purportedly part of the Lone Star State. I assure you, it was a different country then, pardner.

Lawnmower Ted was old and scraggly, a man of few words and few beers. The latter because he couldn't afford more, the former because he was able to express his entire philosophy of life, which he did often, in a loud cracking voice directed to the bar more than to the people in it:

"Fuck 'em all."

That was it. Very little else came from LT, except an occasional grunt or "shit" or something completely unintelligible. LT's daily schedule was also simple: borrow a lawnmower from a local resident named Johnnie, push it down the street, and find someone who needed a lawn mowed. Most lawns in town weren't worth mowing. A few sparse weeds growing out of the sand and shell comprising the barrier island "soil" was the best most homeowners could hope for. Renters could have cared less and most of the summer beach town was renting. Still, Ted was able to find an occasional patron willing to give him a dollar or two to cut some of the weeds. They knew what he needed it for, and no one wanted to begrudge a seventy-year something his suds.

He worked for an hour or two, depending on the sun and how long he had looked for a lawn, and returned the mower. Johnnie left his garage unlocked and the mower was always there by early afternoon. By two or three, Ted was in the Party House, sitting next to the jukebox, sipping on a draft. Drafts were twenty-five cents, a good deal even during the seventies. The mugs were chilled and LT could make a beer last almost an hour before ordering another one. The first two or three were usually consumed in total silence. Ted would focus on the mug he held firmly with both hands, watching the bubbles rise slowly to the surface. When they stopped, he was ready for another. Sometimes he stared at the Corona sign over the bar, lost in his own universe of weedy lots and a past he never revealed to anyone.

We sometimes speculated, usually on a slow afternoon, just what it was Ted contemplated. Maybe a new lawn mower of his own or about a place where they had real lawns? Probably not. My friend Mitch speculated about how many more beers he could do a day if they were twenty cents instead of a quarter. Sometimes, we bought him one or the bartender poured him an extra. Ted added color to the bar and kept some of the more easily offended tourists away.

I don't remember how he got the name "Lawnmower Ted." I think it was one of our more colorful drunk patrons that first called him that, but within a week everyone knew him without knowing him. He showed up in late April, before the students hit the beaches and the fishermen manned their deep-sea charters. Johnny must have known him first because he started mowing yards soon after arrival. His first "fuck 'em all" graced the Party House on his first night at the bar and the expression became his handle as much as his nickname. One day, Sherry, the irrepressible

Party House bartender, kept a tally of how many times he expressed himself before he stumbled out of the bar: twenty-seven utterances between one in the afternoon and eight that evening. He didn't stumble because he was drunk—Ted always stumbled, coming into the bar, pushing the mower, or walking about town.

Ted had at a room in the old Flounder Inn, a large hotel that had once been the pride of the fishing town, but had seen better days. In the 1940s, Franklin Delano Roosevelt had stayed there during a tarpon fishing trip. Ted paid for it and an occasional meal with his social security check and a bit of broom pushing for the hotel. But mowing lawns was for beer, Ted's hard-earned justification for living the life of luxury.

Mostly Ted drank his beer and left everyone alone. There was an occasional exception. One afternoon, about five, a group of students dropped in. This in itself wasn't unusual. The Party House was near the docks and in proximity to two restaurants and several other watering holes. Two guys and three girls, all of them with early college freshness and few other clues to life stepped in and up to the bar. Ted, as was his habit, pointedly ignored them, secure in his corner by the juke. One of the girls, a perky brunette with short hair and a revealing tank top, stood behind Ted and next to the jukebox. She pulled out a couple of quarters and turned to select some songs. She punched two or three but couldn't decide on the next. She turned back to Ted and said, in an overly cheerful voice that only the perky can muster at that time of day, "What'cha wanna hear, sweetie?"

Ted didn't respond, despite the fact that she was almost breathing down the back of his sunburned neck.

"Maybe something old-timey?" she says, winking at one of her male companions.

Several of us farther along the bar, sitting at tables or playing pool, watched in anticipation. Entire hours could pass inside the bar without some excitement or drama. Surely this brazen intrusion into the lawnmower man's personal space would do it. Sherry, putting mugs in the chiller, decided intervention might be the best course, but whether it was to rescue Ted or the girl wasn't clear.

"I think you might best just leave him alone," she drawled. "What can I get y'all?"

One of the guys indicated they would all have longnecks and Sherry was just about to start checking ID when Ted stood up. He wasn't tall but the perky one was still several inches shorter. She backed up a step, not sure what Ted was going to do. He looked at her, looked at the jukebox, then out at the bar without focusing.

"Fuck 'em all," he bellowed, and walked out.

After a moment of stunned silence, the brunette turned to us, eyes close to watering, a slight but noticeable tremor in her voice.

"Did he mean us?" she asked, first to no one specific, but then to Sherry.

Sherry could have said no, that this was Ted's only way of communicating his deep and carefully considered thoughts to the world. Instead, she said slowly and carefully, like a female John Wayne, "Sure did, honey. That's exactly what he meant. I have never heard him so upset." The brunette went running for the door and the rest of her group followed. We never saw them again.

Sherry could be that way. She didn't own any part of the business and she got paid the same and drank the same, whether customers were there or not. She was the old lady of a Gulf shrimper and also didn't care much for college kids, especially perky brunettes.

The second notable time Ted was demonstrative was when we loaded a new record on the box that he particularly liked. It was "Why Don't We Get Drunk and Screw" by Jimmy Buffett. Buffett was a favorite on our music lists—his songs about laid-back island life and drinking resonated with most of us. This particular song wouldn't play at some of the family restaurants or tourist-oriented taverns, but it was just right for the Party House. The first time it played while Ted was occupying his stool, the effect was immediate and transformational. Ted looked up, turned around, stared at the jukebox, and said, "Well, I'll be damned."

Henry, one of our regulars, was still selecting songs and Ted stood behind him as he punched the buttons. Henry looked up and asked him if he liked the song. Ted nodded, so Henry punched it again. From that time on, whenever Ted was in the house, someone would play Buffett's raucous piece. Ted would usually sing along or bang his mug in time. Once, after several hours of sipping, he actually stumbled through his interpretation of a solo two-step.

Unlike most business establishment jukeboxes, the Party House owned this one and the records on it. The community of Party House regulars was solely responsible for the contents and we contributed to the collection, changing the repertoire according to our whims. The screw song was never taken off, even after Ted disappeared.

The only other things that seemed to trigger a predictable reaction from Ted were the dogs that frequented the bar. There were several regulars and a few occasional short-time strays that could be found either on the porch or inside, usually under a table. We kept several water dishes in various corners and they also helped keep the floor clear of dropped pizza, chips, and whatever. Ted liked them and often stooped to run his gnarly fingers through their coats or give them a pat on the butt or head, whichever was closest. He once poured part of his beer into an empty water dish on an especially hot day. This had to be a big sacrifice for a man who nursed his suds as carefully as Ted did.

"How old do you think Ted is?" asked Willie, one of the three Party House owners, one night. We were sitting around with a bottle of bourbon and some setups. The question also paraphrased the introduction to another song on the box, one that Ted occasionally requested.

"Gotta be at least seventy-five, maybe more," offered KC, another of the bar owners. "Hard to tell. He's spent a lot of time in the sun. Probably did manual most of his life."

"Scrawny people live long. His arms don't have muscles, they're made of wires," offered Sherry. She was off-duty, drinking heavy, and sitting between Mitch and Willie. We thought about that a while. None of us had reached forty, and we talked about how someone comes to a town from nowhere, settles in at Ted's age, and becomes a fixture with minimal needs and wants. Most of us had arrived in our twenties; a few had been born and grown up on the island. But elderly newcomers like Ted were a rarity in "our crowd." Typical retirees on the island stuck to condos and a whole different lifestyle.

"What's his story?" Mitch asked, not expecting an answer. "Why, 'fuck 'em all?' What do you think triggered his bitterness?"

"What? You're some kind of psychiatrist? What the fuck do you care?" snorted Willie, downing another shot of Old

Crow. He was almost as shit-faced as Sherry. With her old man shrimping in the Gulf for three weeks, we could guess how this night would end.

Sherry put her arm on Willie's shoulder, gave him her best closing time horny grin and said, "Let's go play Ted's favorite song." It seemed an appropriate and timely invitation, so Willie did.

A year later, almost to the day he arrived, Lawnmower Ted stopped showing up at the Party House. He had rarely missed more than two days in a row and it had been a week since anyone had seen him. Johnnie came in and sat down. Asked about the man, he just shook his head. "Hasn't borrowed the lawnmower in a week. Don't know nothing."

Sherry called the Flounder Inn and asked her friend at the desk if she had seen Ted. About five days ago, she was told. He wasn't looking too good, but I've been off for several days. I'll ask around.

That was all we knew for another week. On a slow Thursday evening, Mac, our favorite town cop, stopped in. "Need a cold one?" asked Sara. She was making pizza for Mitch, Willie, and me, the only customers in the place except for the town's rag-tag Airedale. The dog was asleep and wasn't inclined to share his opinions anyway.

"I'm on duty so I need to pass on it, but I've got some news about Ted. Thought you oughta know." We could tell from Mac's face the news wasn't good. Mac was usually happy-go-lucky and as close to being a Party House regular as the law would allow.

"The coroner in Aransas Pass called us this morning and asked if we could identify a body they pulled out of the Intracoastal. He was an old guy and didn't have ID, but they thought he might have fallen off the ferry. It looks like he had been in the water for a couple of days. An autopsy is pending. I went over and identified him as Ted. We checked at the bank and found his social security account. The checks come in for Charles Littlestone. A search for relatives is underway, but there might not be any. Can you guys or anyone else you know add to that?"

We sat in silence. There was nothing to add. We told Mac to check with Johnny and he left. Sara served the pizza and poured us all a beer. We ate and drank slowly, still silent, thinking about what we had just heard.

Lawnmower Ted was a stranger we had accepted as one of our own. But he wasn't really. We never knew him and he didn't know us. What impact did his presence make and what ripple resulted from his passing? It was hard to understand the emptiness that it left. The Party House was sometimes quiet and lonely, often crowded and noisy, but it was never empty. Emptiness is more than just too much open space. It is more a feeling of hopelessness, of the dreaded inevitability of mortality. It is a somber reflection on us, the survivors. We will age, we will die, and our party will end. Did Lawnmower Ted choose to leave the party or was the choice made for him? We would never know.

A quarter hit the slot and Sara pushed a button. Ted's favorite song filled the bar. Willie and Mitch looked at each other for only a moment and then shouted simultaneously, "Fuck 'em all."

SPARKLE

How far would you go for love?
To the ends of the earth for the one who is like no other?
Maybe that's not far enough.

The sun is creeping over the horizon but the morning chill won't dissipate for another hour. The high desert landscape looks monotonously simple to someone who is ignorant about its geological complexity and variety of life forms. Sagebrush and occasional cacti are the dominant features, scattered across the coarse sands and gravels of the arid plains. It is a quiet landscape, seemingly abandoned and peaceful. An occasional breeze disturbs dry branches of rabbit brush, and a lizard scurries for cover to avoid daytime predators. Later, hawks will circle overhead, but not until additional warming provides the updrafts to make soaring almost effortless. Most of the desert's predators are nocturnal, and they have already retired to their sanctuaries. A few, however, remain cryptic and ready to ambush the unwary.

A few million years ago, the region had been a sea bottom. The land rose and the waters disappeared. More recently, lava flows deposited black layers of basalt across the surface, some forming horizontal tubes and closed caverns. Other tubes and caves collapsed, adding a dramatic dimension of rugged crevices and chasms to the desert floor. These dark places, seldom visited by people of the region, provide concealment for living things and for precious artifacts.

The sun climbs into the sky and the substrate bakes. Like a mirage, two upright figures appear in the distance, their shadowy outlines distorted by a shimmering heat wave rising from the sparkling sand. They walk next to each other, close but not touching. One is larger than the other, but, from this distance, their features cannot be discerned. If a camera had been present, it might have recorded the unhurried but decisive progress of the two. There is no camera—they are unwatched and unrecorded.

Suddenly, the larger figure collapses to the ground. The smaller one appears to bend over the other for several minutes, the shadows forming one poorly defined lump, like a distant boulder. Many more minutes pass before a single figure, the smaller one, rises, remains still for a moment, and then continues in the same direction as before, toward a small state highway in southeastern Oregon and the rural community of High Plains.

A rattlesnake crawls slowly under a ledge. Disturbed during its mid-morning sunbath, it reluctantly struck and transmitted some precious venom, but the intruders are gone. Only a slight depression in the sand provides evidence of their passing and the temporary presence of the fallen one.

TUESDAY, WEEK ONE

SHE WATCHES THE ROAD FROM A SMALL HILL, PARTLY out of sight of the occasional passing truck or car, but not well hidden. Anyone who takes the trouble might spot her and wonder about a young woman standing by a gnarled juniper, but no one does. There is a town about two miles west, and she starts walking, a bit back from and parallel to the highway. She doesn't trust the speeding vehicles—they make her uneasy and she isn't sure what she would do if one of them stops. She needs a place to stay, a way to get food, some additional clothes, and time to make preparations. If all goes well, she can recover in a month or less. If not, it could be a lot longer and infinitely more difficult. Being alone is not something she had planned on.

Based on the change in sun angle, she calculates it has taken her about two hours of steady walking to reach the highway. She is not too dehydrated but can feel the unfamiliar discomfort of thirst. They could have made the trek during the dark, but the dangers of the desert were greater at night and the land was unfamiliar. *That worked well, didn't it?* She also makes a note to carry water in this terrain.

Following her shadow, she reflects on what she knows and might expect in the near future. Her orientation to the region is not detailed but she has a general familiarity with the immediate area, including some knowledge of the town ahead. *I will be a stranger, but when am I not?* She smiles and forces herself to relax. The trick is not to be too much of a stranger. This is one of her essential advantages, the aura of casual confidence she creates, establishing a nearly instantaneous familiarity with those she meets. She has practiced it often and it hasn't failed to ease her way into a new place. She requires a few close contacts in order to be successful in recovering from the accident. She doesn't know who her helpers will be or exactly where she will find them, but it will happen. She smiles again as the sun warms her back.

Approaching the outskirts of the small community, she notes the serenity. There is little noise aside from passing cars and trucks on the road. The horizon reveals only two buildings that rise more than one story and no people are visible as she approaches the first one-story buildings on the other side of the highway. She waits until a large semi passes before crossing the road and walking slowly over the gravel parking lot. To her left is a small motel with an office and a row of attached cabins. The sign states "High Plains Motel, locally owned and managed." Under the sign, a smaller neon sign proclaims "Vacancy." Directly ahead of her, the sun glares from the windows of a highway diner. A car and two pickup trucks are parked in front and she sees people moving behind the glass door as she approaches. She enters and is greeted by the aroma of fresh coffee and bacon and a low hum of conversation. The hum stops briefly as she steps to the counter and faces a thirty-ish woman in a black uniform near the cash register.

"What can I do for you, honey?" asks the woman as the background hum resumes.

"I'm looking for work. Do you have a job?" She stands straight, her shoulders back, hands held in front of her, and flashes a smile. Her clothes are a bit damp from perspiration and more than a bit dusty from the desert walk.

"That'd be Mamie, around the counter and through the opening." The waitress points to an area behind the counter.

"Thank you," she says and moves to and through the opening. At her right is an office and a desk. Behind it sits an older woman, cigarette in mouth, looking up at her.

"I'm Rozelle," she states, "and I need a job."

The older woman takes a long drag on her cigarette but doesn't move from her chair. She looks at the young woman carefully, appraising her with the experience of many years as the owner of a highway diner. She considers herself a good judge of character and has been proven wrong only a few times and not recently. Mamie notes the sweat and dirt, but otherwise the stranger appears to be eager and friendly.

"I might need someone. Had any experience waiting tables?"

"No ma'am, I haven't been a waitress, but I learn very quickly, and I am available to start immediately."

"Rozelle, huh? Do you have a last name?"

"No, I just go by Rozelle. That's all." She holds her hands behind her and gives Mamie a generous smile. Her eyes seem to flash, lighting up her face.

"Where are you from, honey?" Mamie leans forward and puts her cigarette out in an ashtray that hasn't been emptied in some time.

"It's a long ways from here, a small place that you wouldn't know."

Mamie sits back and folds her arms across her belly. "Got any work references?"

"No one you can reach, ma'am, but I work hard and I am dependable." Another flash of her eyes, as if she has an internal spotlight that intensifies the deep blue irises.

Mamie feels uneasy but can't identify the source. Despite her lack of anything that would qualify as background, Mamie is drawn to the stranger. "I don't like to hire a complete unknown, mainly because they usually come and go within a few days. If I'm going to train you to wait tables, I'd like to know you'll be here for awhile. I also have to know if I can trust you around the cash register."

"Yes ma'am, I can promise you a few weeks at least,

perhaps longer. You do not need to worry about me taking anything that doesn't belong to me." Every word is pronounced distinct and precise.

Mamie nods her acceptance while still wondering why. The girl—if she is a girl, her age is difficult to judge—is a complete stranger. No last name, no place of origin, and no identification cards or papers. Her way of talking is also a bit odd, no accent, speaking like she was reading from an English primer. Mamie has never taken a chance like this before. She agrees to hire her on a probationary basis, paying cash and no social security until she is officially put on the payroll.

"Where are you staying, Rozelle?"

The girl looks a bit confused and admits she has just arrived in town and hasn't found a place yet.

"The motel next door might be able to help. See the manager, Phil, and tell him I sent you. I think he's looking for someone to do some light housecleaning and you might be able to work something out for a room. I expect you ain't got much money, right?"

"No ma'am, I don't"

"And not much in the way of luggage either?"

"No ma'am."

"Okay, I'll stop asking questions. Go see Phil, get yourself settled, and be here at quarter to six in the morning. We open at six sharp and the morning is our busiest time. Hope you don't mind serving a bunch of grumpy old men and truck drivers, 'cuz that's most of what we have." Mamie finally gives her a smile.

"Thank you, ma'am, I appreciate…"

"Call me Mamie. That's good enough. And ask Faith at the cashier to loan you twenty dollars from the till. You can pay it back at the end of the week."

"Thank you, ma…Mamie, thank you." With a smile and a flash, Rozelle leaves the office. *The first step accomplished. On to number two.*

PHIL SALVIA IS BEHIND THE LOBBY COUNTER WHEN Rozelle enters the motel office. It has been a quiet day, not unusual for a High Plains weekday. A strange good-looking female always commands Phil's attention and he turns on the charm immediately.

"Good morning, I mean…afternoon," he laughs. He immediately notes the absence of a car in front of the office.

Rozelle walks to the counter, stands two feet in front of Phil, and looks into his eyes. "Are you Phil?"

"At your service." He stands about an inch taller and sucks in his gut, pleased that she knows his name. "Looking for a room?"

"Yes, I am. Mamie told me you might require some help with cleaning. I will be working for her and I need a place to stay." Her eyes flash as she smiles at him. It is not a seductive smile, but it captures his attention, all of it.

Phil beams. "I'm sure we can work something out, miss…uh, miss…"

"Rozelle, just Rozelle. I don't have identification, and I am new in town, and I need to remain private about who I am and where I am from. Will that be a problem?"

Phil is still smiling, completely mesmerized. "No problem, Rozelle. If Mamie vouches for you, that's good enough for me. We don't have a lot of customers this time of year, so we have several empty rooms. You can have your choice of any of the ones in the back line. If you'll clean up the occupied rooms, usually four to six per day, I'll provide you with your room at no cost. You can take it now, if you'd like. Do you need any help with luggage?"

"No, Phil, I travel light." Her eyes flash as Phil reaches for a key and hands it to her.

After she leaves to inspect the room, Phil shakes his head, trying to clear it, wondering how he agreed so readily to terms he would never propose, even to someone as attractive as his newest employee. He'd need to inform Ray about her and ask his night manager to keep an eye out, despite Mamie's recommendation. Young good-looking women just didn't show up from out of nowhere, unattached and without some story. That was another thing. Phil could keep someone talking until he knew him or her better than they knew themselves, yet he had only exchanged a few words with her. He sighs and vows to learn more about Rozelle during their next encounter.

Rozelle enters her room, locks the door behind her, and walks into the bathroom. She looks at her image in the mirror. *Time to clean up and rest up.* She removes her clothes, turns on the shower and washes herself thoroughly. Looking at her clothes, a short-sleeved blouse, a pair of jeans, socks, and underwear, she decides they need washing as well. She scrubs them with hand soap in the bathtub and hangs them to dry over the shower rod. Exhausted, she climbs into bed naked and pulls the covers up around her. A few minutes later, she is in a deep sleep.

It is late evening when she awakes. A small clock on the bedside table reads 7:37 and she quickly gets out of bed. She returns to the bathroom and dresses. Her clothes are still slightly damp, but the desert dryness has helped and she feels refreshed but hungry. *I could have eaten at the diner earlier, but sleep was a bigger priority. The twenty dollars will need to do until I collect some salary and tips. Fortunately, I don't need much.* She leaves her room without locking the door—nothing of hers is present—and walks to and along the highway.

⁂

SOME SAID SHE WASN'T ALL THAT MUCH TO LOOK AT, while others just couldn't get their fill. The men talked about her, watched her, and flirted when they could, always hoping for a smile or a flash of eyes in their direction. No doubt about it, Rozelle was a sensation, from the morning she started serving coffee and breakfast to the customers of the High Plains Cafe.

Rozelle pronounced her name with a hard z, a zing released through pretty white teeth. Her eyes were deep green, sometimes a shade of blue-green, depending on the light and, perhaps, in keeping with her mood. The boys weren't sure, because she seemed to be changing all the time. She had short strawberry blonde hair, not like a man's but in a pixie bob, short in the back with a few strands falling loose over her forehead. Her smile was quick, as if it came easily from a lot of practice. In retrospect, she just didn't seem like the kind of woman who would come off the road. That kind was usually hardened by less than pleasant experiences, more cautious about themselves and leery of others.

There was another thing to add to the mystery: her age. Everyone had an opinion on how old Rozelle might be. Some thought she wasn't much over nineteen, maybe early twenties at best. Others talked about her maturity, her grace in serving the usual assortment of diner patrons. No matter what happened or what someone said to her, she responded in a disarmingly casual manner. The broad smile and flashing eyes made everything good. Whether the customer was angry, sullen, horny, aggressive, shy, depressed—it didn't matter. Somehow, after Rozelle's attention, the person seemed to be in a better mood.

Most of the women liked her as well. Not all of them—that would be impossible, wouldn't it? Other waitresses and the few women customers regarded her as a pleasant addition to the cafe. Most of them knew about her from hearing their men talk about the new sparkle at the High Plains. That's what some of them started calling her, "Sparkle." "Got some more coffee, Sparkle?" "How are ya today, Sparkle, anything good for breakfast?"

Most guys would notice a woman's figure first. They would be more inclined to comment on a woman's curves than on her white teeth or a few freckles or eye color. Rozelle's figure was trim with the usual standard equipment, but nothing spectacular. It was the way she seemed to look into your soul, as if putting you in a hypnotic spell. When she smiled, you didn't even notice the rest of her.

Almost everyone seemed to be fascinated with Sparkle. Except Ed. Ed didn't even seem to know she was there at first. He was a regular customer, stopping off at the High Plains every morning for the same order. Coffee, black, two scrambled eggs, two strips of bacon, well done, one piece of sourdough toast, and a glass of juice. Sometimes it was tomato, sometimes orange. He usually arrived within ten minutes of eight o'clock and sometimes sat at the counter by himself. More often, he joined one or two of the others at a table to discuss happenings around town.

Ed Ferguson was a bachelor of forty years. Tall, thin, and balding, he wouldn't have qualified as any woman's dream catch. But he had an asset—his own business, a

U-Haul rental on the edge of town, and he lived in a trailer behind the U-Haul office. Most people knew him from the business and the cafe. He didn't socialize much individually, although he contributed regularly to the chamber of commerce, appeared occasionally at rotary lunches, and bought cookies each year from the Girl Scouts. Most people liked Ed, but few would claim to know him well. He definitely wasn't a womanizer—you'd know that in a small town. It wasn't that he disliked women as much as they just didn't seem to be a part of his life. He stopped dating in his twenties and spent most of his time and energy in building the rental franchise. He read a lot, visiting the county library, prowling the two local bookstores, and buying other books by mail order. He was pleasant but not overtly charming, a competent businessman but not one to either aggressively solicit or to overindulge customers. As others often respectfully remarked, "Ed was straight."

The first morning Rozelle served Ed breakfast, he barely noticed her. That was his way. He usually ordered with a minimum of words and acknowledged the arrival of his breakfast with a brief thanks and that was it. He would talk to the men beside him or read the paper or just sit there, lost in thought. That first morning was no different. He was talking to Ray, the night manager of the Motel 6 next to the diner. Rozelle had been working all of two hours as a waitress when she stood in front of Ed and waited for him to look up. He didn't.

"The usual, with orange juice," he said.

"Usual what?" she replied, with just a hint of amusement in her voice.

Ed raised his head and met her smile, her bright eyes. She had a pad and pencil ready, unlike most of the waitresses who worked there. He paused, as if trying to remember what his usual was. Except for choice of juice, it had been awhile since he had specified breakfast.

"Black coffee, two eggs, scrambled with milk and two strips of bacon hard," said Ray, smiling up at Rozelle.

Ed glanced at Ray then back to Rozelle.

"Yeah, I guess he's got it right. And a piece of sourdough toast."

She smiled and walked away, scribbling quickly on the pad.

"New gal, just started working for Mamie this morning," offered Ray, his eyes following Rozelle's rear to the order window at the kitchen.

"Hmmm."

"Well, don't get so worked up, Ed. I've seen more excitement from you about a shipment of baling wire than the arrival of a new, not-so-bad-looking, woman in town."

"Hmmm."

"She's staying at the motel. Mamie sent her my way because we need someone to clean rooms. I think she's going to do a room for work deal with the owner." Ray paused and looked at Ed for comment. There was none.

Rozelle returned with a cup and a pot of coffee. She set the cup in front of him and poured slowly, making sure she didn't spill any. Ray watched her as if he had never seen anyone pour coffee before. She walked down the counter, giving just the slightest emphasis to her swaying hips. Ray held his breath while Ed sipped the hot coffee slowly, staring straight ahead.

Mamie came out of the kitchen, watching Ray's reaction. She stopped in front of him, but he didn't notice. His eyes followed Rozelle as she made the rounds of the small diner, filling empty cups, and asking if everything was all right.

"Ahem," grunted Mamie in a voice that resembled sandpaper passed over rough wood. "I'd ask if you approve of my new hire, Ray, but I can already see that would be a wasted question."

Ray startled and looked up at her, face reddening, like a small boy caught with his hand in the cookie jar. Ed winked at Mamie and she smiled back.

"Tell me, Ed, why is it always the married men that go gaga over the young women but the eligible ones, like you, never seem to notice they're in the room?"

Ed paused and gave the same response he always delivered in this situation, "Guess that's why I'm still eligible and they're not."

Mamie shrugged, turned, and followed Rozelle with a pitcher of water.

"It don't hurt none to look," said Ray in a low voice. "Does it?"

"I guess not. It's free and no one seems to mind and…" replied Ed with a wicked grin, "I won't tell your wife."

That was Ed's first meeting with Rozelle—nothing more than that. She served him breakfast, he left his usual ten percent tip next to the plate, and Mamie took his money at the register. He walked out the door, nodding to a few of the men on the way, but not looking back at the counter where Rozelle was clearing his dishes. She could have been a push broom for all of the attention he gave her. The next several mornings went the same way. She wasn't always the one who waited on him, but when she did he recited his usual order and said thanks when she brought it. He didn't ask questions and she didn't offer any information.

Some of the men were curious, however. One or two, in fact, were prompted by their wives to see what they could find out about Sparkle. A couple of them were bold enough to try the direct approach, but most opted for discretion and asked Mamie when Rozelle wasn't in the room.

"Where is she from?"

Mamie wasn't sure. Maybe somewhere from the Midwest she thought, but she was as clueless as they were.

"What's her last name?"

Mamie didn't know that either. Rozelle declined to provide it. Since Mamie was paying on a cash and carry basis, no taxes and no social security, and Rozelle didn't fill out any forms. Mamie didn't bother with the formalities until someone decided to stay longer than a week or two. The motel staff couldn't add anything. She was Rozelle. No last name, no date of birth, and no home address.

Direct questioning yielded the same results. She parried the questions with a smile and a response that answered nothing. "I'm nobody from nowhere, but I'm here and I'm Roz-zelle," she said, elongating the "z" as if it belonged to both syllables.

"How long you planning on staying?" Ray asked her one morning. She had been there two weeks, about a week longer than most of them had figured she would be. The town of High Plains wasn't exactly a magnet for younger people. The few that stopped stayed for a night or two. If they needed money, they worked for a few days, a week at the most, then left as suddenly as they came.

"Don't have a clock on me. I'll be gone when I go, but I'm still here. More coffee?"

TUESDAY, WEEK THREE

SO IT WENT. THE MYSTERY SURROUNDING SPARKLE GREW even as the patrons of the High Plains grew accustomed to her presence. She worked six days a week, getting her choice of a weekday off. That quickly became the next point of speculation. No one seemed to know where she went during her day off. As far as anyone knew, she didn't have a car, and no one recalled seeing her around town. She sometimes did a little shopping after work, but she vanished in thin air once each week. Ray became obsessed with finding the answer and told Ed on Tuesday morning about his latest theory on Sparkle's whereabouts.

"I figure she's got a man somewhere here in town, Ed. It has to be. Probably somebody married that needs to keep it quiet. She sneaks to his place early in the morning when no one's up, spends the day inside, and doesn't leave until well after dark." Ray was doing serious damage to a stack of hotcakes, and he offered his thoughts between mouthfuls.

Ed looked at him for a moment and shook his head. "Don't you have anything bigger or better to worry about than her? Even if you're right, so what? She looks like she's of age and can do what she wants. And if you're wrong, well, you're wrong. Either way, there's no sense in starting a bunch of rumors that could hurt her or someone else. It might even chase her away." Ed took another sip of coffee and bent over his plate, as if Ray had vanished.

Ray stopped eating for the first time in ten minutes. He stared at Ed, his mouth slightly open, syrup leaking from one corner of his mouth. He was frozen, his fork in mid-air. He swallowed, put the fork down and wiped his mouth with a napkin.

"Damn me, why didn't I think of this before. It's you, isn't it? It's not some married man or young kid. You're the one that's bagging Sparkle. Why you sly old…" Ray got no further.

Ed stood up, straightening to his full height of six-two. "Ray, that's enough of this crap. I don't want to hear anymore of it. And if you're smart, which I'm beginning to have serious doubts about, you won't share this with anyone else either." He dropped a bill beside his plate that was more than enough to cover the tab and tip and walked decisively to the door and out of the cafe.

Although Ray had teased him in a voice heard only by Ed, everyone in the cafe heard Ed's response. Most of them had never seen him agitated, much less angry. Ed's rapid departure, without a nod or glance to anyone, left no doubt about the man's mood. Ray, having completely misjudged the effect his remarks would have, was stunned into silence. He returned to his pancakes with considerably less gusto. Mamie watched from the kitchen doorway, but said nothing.

The other customers didn't know what had provoked Ed's anger, but Mamie had caught enough of it to know it was about Rozelle. It had been her one concern. Rozelle wasn't the most beautiful woman she'd seen, but she was alluring. She had charm and it attracted attention, for better or worse. Normally, Mamie welcomed having a waitress like her. The truckers would stop more often, the regulars liked her, and she had learned the job quickly, like she said she would. She handled the orders and the patrons as if she had been a waitress for years instead of two weeks. But this, this wasn't good. Ray wasn't the only one speculating, and some of the wives had continued making inquiries. It didn't seem natural for a woman of Rozelle's age and looks to be living in a motel room and to have no last name or anything else to identify her. Some speculated she might be hiding out, either from the law or from an abusive husband or lover. Whatever, Rozelle was starting her third week and

Mamie was obliged to start deducting social security. That also meant getting some information.

Rozelle didn't smoke, didn't patronize any of the three taverns in town, nor did she keep company at the motel. Ray could testify to that. As night manager, he kept watch on the closed circuit television monitoring her corridor. There was nothing to find fault with, yet many people were not satisfied. Mysteries in small towns provoke a disproportionate share of angst and curiosity. In answer to Ed's question, no, there weren't bigger and better things to do.

WEDNESDAY, WEEK THREE

ED DIDN'T SHOW UP FOR BREAKFAST THE NEXT MORNING and neither did Ray. Mamie noticed and was contemplating what, if anything, she should do about it. One of the women in town that used to work at the High Plains was asking about a job again. She wasn't Mamie's favorite, but she was competent. Should she replace Rozelle? And if so, on what basis? Mamie decided it was time for her to have a private conversation with Ed. She valued his judgment on business matters and this was, after all, a business matter.

Mamie went into the back part of the kitchen to a phone where she could talk in private. She dialed Ed's office, but there was no reply. She tried his trailer, but no luck there either. As she walked away from the desk, Rozelle entered the kitchen with a stack of dirty dishes. Mamie waited while Rozelle deposited them next to the sink.

"Honey, there's something I need to ask you. You got a minute?" Despite her gravely voice and hard exterior, Mamie could be motherly at times.

"Yes ma'am. My last order won't be up for a few minutes. What do you need?" Rozelle's face was open, without a trace of guile. At times she seemed like a young child.

Mamie cleared her throat and leaned against the wall, fishing a cigarette out of her apron. She lit it and took a slow drag. "Rozelle, you know I don't want to meddle in your business. What you do when you're not working is nothing to me. You have been a hard worker and I'm pleased with how you conduct yourself."

Rozelle waited, her expression not changing from a look of eager anticipation, as if she was being offered a raise. "Yes ma'am, thank you. I try to do my best."

"I'm sure you do. And listen, this is probably no fault of yours. Hell, you weren't even here yesterday when it happened."

"What happened?'

"Oh, not a lot. It was just a couple of the men talking, gossiping really, like a couple of old hags. But it seemed they had a falling out."

Rozelle's sparkle dissolved. Her mouth slightly open, eyebrows arched, she waited.

"It's Ed and Ray, honey. They got into a dispute and I think it was about you. Whatever, Ed stomped out of here. This is the first morning in months I haven't seen him, and Ray is almost as regular as he is. He hasn't been in either. I tried to call Ed at home and at the U-Haul, but there's no answer." Mamie paused, looking in Rozelle's eyes, encouraging her to provide any information she might have on the men.

Rozelle was unabashed, as if the men's nonappearance was unrelated to the dispute Mamie had just described. "I think my order is probably ready. I should go."

Mamie reached toward her, lightly grabbing her wrist. "Rozelle, do you know where either of them are right now?"

Rozelle hesitated. "I cannot tell you anything at this time. Maybe later."

Mamie wasn't reassured. She stared into Rozelle's eyes, trying to read signs of deception or something vital withheld. Deep, impenetrable pools of dark green stared back and Mamie lowered her eyes.

"Please do not worry. Everything will be okay. You will see them again, I promise."

Mamie let her go and watched as she left the kitchen. Rozelle's answer was unexpected and the way she said it sent shivers up her spine. What did she mean everything would be okay? What were they doing? Mamie had never doubted she would see them again—until now. She stood there a long time, smoking and watching Rozelle as she moved among the customers, flashing smiles and pouring coffee. She had also forgotten to ask the mysterious waitress about some identification so she could formalize her employment. Mamie would need to get some answers to hard questions sooner rather than later.

THURSDAY, WEEK THREE

THE NEXT MORNING CAME AND WENT WITHOUT EITHER Ed or Ray. The U-Haul store was not open, and a few of the High Plains customers were discussing it.

"Ray didn't appear for his night shift at the hotel. And Ed hasn't opened his store in two days. Anybody here know what's happened to either of them?" Seven of the local regulars were gathered around a big round table in the corner. Usually it served as a meeting space for the businessmen to discuss politics or economics, but today the focus was Ed and Ray. The men were unanimous: no one had seen either of them since Ed had walked out and Ray had left a few minutes later.

"Think we should notify the sheriff?" asked one of the farmers who fished now and then with Ray. "Bill's been on the road since Monday but he should be back tonight."

"Not yet, but keep it in mind," said the town barber. He had known Ed for several years and had seen his moods come and go. "Ed's a private guy and he probably just had to get away for a few days. Might've went camping or something like that."

"What about his truck?" asked another farmer. "Anyone seen his green Ford in the last two days?" No one had, but then they couldn't swear they hadn't either.

"Well, they're both grown men and they can take care of themselves," offered Sam, the pharmacist. "Hey guys, it's only been two days." But he said it without conviction and no one was inclined to provide reassurance.

Rozelle stopped at their table, coffee ready. Silence descended over the table as she filled their cups. It was as if a heavy curtain fell over them, extinguishing all conversation. Sparkle's glow seemed lost on the usually jocular morning group. No one wanted to engage her in small talk or exchange the casual flirtations that had become part of the daily morning protocol. In turn, she said nothing, hurrying back to the kitchen to retrieve the next order.

"Think it's got anything to do with her?" asked the barber.

"Don't know, I just don't know," answered Sam, shaking his head.

The men sat there, saying little, picking at the food set before them, waiting for Ed and Ray to walk in the door and return the High Plains to its normal state of small-town mediocrity.

TUESDAY, WEEK THREE

ED LEAVES THE HIGH PLAINS CAFE AFTER HIS CONFRONtation with Ray and climbs into his green truck. He wastes no time leaving the parking lot, pulling onto the highway ahead of an oncoming semi. The truck driver sees him and slows. Ed mumbles a thank you under his breath and realizes he is reacting to Ray's comments as if he had been insulted. Ray can be boorish, even childish at times, but he means no harm. He relaxes his grip on the steering wheel—he is sweating profusely, even though it is still early in the morning. *I could have finished my breakfast.* He turns into the driveway at the U-Haul, but instead of parking alongside of the office, he continues toward the back and stops beside his trailer. He gets out of the truck and walks quickly to the long silver Airstream, unlocks the door, and enters.

The room is dark, the curtains pulled. He sits down on the couch and stares at the cube on the coffee table. Rozelle's cube. She trusts him with it and it's secret, and he is determined to protect it and her from the small prying minds of High Plains. *Doing a lousy job of that,* he thinks. *I couldn't have called more attention to us if I had taken out a billboard ad. Damn it. Ray caught me at the wrong moment. If I had just thought a bit I could have ignored him or made a joke of it. Now he's convinced we're an item. Who else will he talk to and what will he say?*

The cube measures about two inches in each dimension. It glimmers with an opal-like radiance highlighted by pinpoints of shifting color when observed from different angles. It sparkles. Just like me, she had said and laughed. That first night, a night he wouldn't, couldn't forget.

SUNDAY, WEEK ONE

ED IS WATCHING TELEVISION, A BLACK AND WHITE WAR MOVIE starring John Wayne. He doesn't hear the soft, gentle tapping at first. Unannounced nighttime visitors are rare and unexpected, especially on a Sunday night. The knocking persists. During a lull in the artillery fire, Ed realizes someone is at the door. Frowning at the interruption, he rises from the small sofa that dominates his cramped living room. A lifetime of batching produces an eclectic accumulation of junk and there is little room for anything else. He opens the unlocked door.

Rozelle looks up at him from the bottom of three steps, illuminated by a half moon and the light from his living room. Her larger-than-life shadow is cast across the parking lot and onto the back of the office. Her eyes sparkle, as if they are filled with small blazing diamonds.

Ed stands in the doorway, speechless, unable to move. He recognizes the new waitress from the cafe, but he stares at her as if she is a total stranger. She smiles up at him, as if she has known him forever, a trusted friend to whom she comes often.

"May I come in?" she asks, but in a manner suggesting she already knows he will say yes.

He stands aside without a word and feels her brush against him as she enters the living room and sits on the sofa. The television blares dramatic music as a beach is stormed and rockets roar overhead.

"Uh, I can turn that off," he says, starting for the video recorder.

She smiles and the room is silent and the television blank.

"How did you do that that?" Ed is still halfway across the room and Rozelle hasn't moved from the sofa.

"Maybe you have something cold to drink? It was a warm walk from the motel."

Her direct manner disarms him, preempting further questions. He walks to the refrigerator, opens the door, and then looks back at his unexpected guest.

"Iced tea okay?" He grabs a glass from the cupboard over the sink.

She smiles and watches him fill the glass and add a couple of ice cubes. "The waitress is being waited on," she observes.

After handing her the glass he removes several boxes of correspondence from a chair, the only other place to sit in the room. He sits, facing her, and waits. She sips the tea and closes her eyes, as if it is a long awaited pleasure. As he watches, his initial confusion turns slowly to suspicion about her possible reasons for the visit. After drinking half of the tea, she crosses her legs and sits back against the sofa, smiling.

"What can I do for you, Miss…uh, Miss…?"

"Roz-zelle," she says, her smile unwavering and eyes flashing. She puts the glass down next to a stack of books on a small end table and uncrosses her legs, leaning forward, her elbows on her knees and her chin in her hands. "Ed, I need your help with something, something personal."

"Help with what?"

"Travel. I need to go somewhere and I need your help with the preparations."

"Look, Miss…uh, Rozelle, I think you have the wrong guy. I rent stuff, like trucks and handcarts, things used in moving, but I'm not a travel agent. Someone probably made a mistake and referred you to me instead of…"

"No mistake, Ed, you're the one I need. I know we just met a few days ago but I also know I can trust you to help me without others being involved. I need discretion. I need *you*."

Her determination overwhelms his reservations. Instead of showing her the door and dismissing the meeting as a bad joke or misunderstanding, he continues to wait, curious about the strange circumstances that cause her to seek his help and the odd way she is going about it.

"Why didn't you come to my office? I'm open until six. I could have helped you better there."

"It is important no one see me with you. I can explain, but I must ask you to trust me."

"Trust you? I don't *know* you. I only know you from the cafe and I understand you are new in town. I doubt if anyone else around here knows you either."

"Perhaps some will in time. For now, it will be you, just you. Although you don't know me now, I know you and… Ed, you will come to know me better than you have ever known anyone in your life."

Her smile and eyes fill the room and floating crystals flash in bright whites, greens, and blues, swirling around and immersing him in an ocean of kaleidoscopic color. A roaring sound, like the gusts of a tropical storm, muffles all other noises. The contents of the room fade, replaced by spinning patches of light. He doesn't move. He can't. He is transfixed, surrounded by a maelstrom of light and sound. It only takes a few minutes but for Ed it seems to last a lifetime. When the sound and light show fades, he understands and he knows her. As she promised, he knows her better than he has known anyone in his life and he understands clearly what she needs and why.

Rozelle walks away from Ed's trailer, past the U-Haul office, and along a side street paralleling the highway. There are no street lights but her strides are confident, full of purpose. She is satisfied with Ed's response. As she had hoped, he will be the partner she can trust. The final arrangements are about two weeks away.

TUESDAY, WEEK THREE

ED STARES AT THE CUBE, ENCHANTED BY THE TECHNOLOGIcal wonders it represents. Ten days ago she promised him the chance to experience the universe, to be her intimate voyaging partner, and to exist in a different plane without the limitations of a mortal body. He had accepted her offer as if it was a routine business proposal, a simple rental contract. The decision occurred quickly and decisively, such was the power of the cube and the influential magnetism of its owner. For the past week, his detached demeanor has managed to keep their relationship undetected. But now his angry response to Ray in the cafe barely an hour ago might complicate their secret. Fortunately, the preparations are almost complete.

There is a knock on the door. It is nine thirty and he isn't expecting anyone. The business should have been open by now, so maybe it's a customer wanting to rent a truck. He sighs, puts a tablecloth over the cube, and opens the door. It is Ray.

"I had to see you, Ed. I couldn't let you just leave like that. I didn't mean anything, you know, it's your business and I shouldn't…"

"Forget it Ray, it was my fault. I'm sorry I said what I did." Ed stands in the doorway, mostly blocking Ray's view of the living room. A breeze from the open door lifts one end of the tablecloth and it slides off the cube. The bright glimmer catches Ray's eye immediately.

"Holy shit, what's that? You got something unusual in there?" Ray moves his head back and forth trying to see around Ed. Ed looks back at the exposed cube and realizes Ray won't let go of this—he will need an explanation, something, even a lie.

"Come in Ray. Sit down and I'll get you a beer."

Ray has been there before, although not often. Ed's furnishings don't change much and the cube is not only a new item, but completely unlike anything you would associate with Ed.

"What is it? I don't think I've ever seen anything like it."

Ed looks appraisingly at Ray. "It's an artsy thing someone left here. He rented a truck but didn't want to take it with him, so I said I'd keep it for him. He'll return and get it in a few days." *Will that satisfy him? Ray isn't terribly complex but I'm not a good liar.*

Ray walks around the cube, noting its changing colors. He reaches out and touches it.

"It's warm. Does it have a heater inside?" Ray runs his hand along the edges.

"It might. It's one of those modern art objects, according to the owner. I don't understand it."

Ray bends over the cube, reaching to lift it.

"Don't do that!" Ed's voice has a hint of desperate panic. He has forgotten how impulsive and unpredictable Ray can be at times. "It's very delicate. You might damage it, and I don't have any idea how expensive it is."

Ray stands over the coffee table, staring at the cube, rubbing his hand under his chin, as if trying to think of something else to ask.

"Do you want something to drink, Ray? Some coffee or that beer?"

"Kinda early for a beer, but I guess I could use some coffee. Didn't finish the cup I had at the cafe." He grins at Ed, letting him know all is forgiven.

Can't let him tell anyone about the cube. I promised her no one else would see it. Another screw-up on my part.

Ray is still admiring the rainbow-like patterns as Ed drops the sleeping potion into Ray's coffee. He brings both cups into the living room and watches warily as Ray sips. Ed has used the drug a few times to get some rest, but he put about four times the usual amount in Ray's coffee, hoping it wouldn't alter the taste. Ray makes a slight face with the first sip, but doesn't seem to notice after that.

They chat for several minutes but both avoid the subject of Rozelle. Ray yawns, stretches his arms and rises to his feet. "I need to get to bed, it was a busy shift last night and I had to evict…" He hesitates and shakes his head, as if trying to clear it. He takes two steps toward the door and Ed's heart sinks.

What the hell should I do now, knock him over the head?

He doesn't have to. Ray turns to Ed with an astonished look on his face, raises his right arm as high as his belt and says, "Damn. I feel…" He never finishes. He would have hit the floor if Ed doesn't catch him. He walks him to the back bedroom and lays him on the bed, taking his shoes off, and throwing a light blanket over him. *That should keep him for a few hours, then what? Rozelle will be here later—maybe she'll know what to do.*

Rozelle arrives shortly after two in the afternoon. She looks at Ray's prostrate form, sleeping soundly, complete with snores and a few arm and leg twitches.

"You did the right thing, Ed. We don't want any complications."

"But he'll be missed. He may be late for his shift tonight at the motel. And he's married. There will be questions to answer and…"

"And?"

"And he will eventually wake up and wonder what happened. In this part of the universe, it's not considered socially acceptable to slip someone a Mickey Finn."

"What?"

"An old name for a drug to knock someone out. He'll want an explanation and then he'll wonder about the cube and whether there's a connection."

"Yes. That is true, he must not wake up yet. We must remove him."

"What do you mean? Remove him? What are you talking about?"

Rozelle turns to him, her smile soft and graceful, her eyes piercing, sparkling as if shining from a galaxy of stars in a desert sky. She puts her arms around him. Ed feels himself relax, falling toward her, relinquishing his fears and resistance.

"He will be as happy as you are. You need not worry."

FRIDAY, WEEK THREE

EARLY FRIDAY MORNING, THE THIRD DAY OF THEIR absence, Mamie called the sheriff. Rozelle had not reported for work, her first absence. At eight o'clock, Sheriff Bill Swenson arrived at the cafe, greeting the somber men gathered around the big table. In the kitchen, Mamie explained what had happened and what Rozelle had said to her.

"Do you know where I can find her?" asked Bill. He had been a deputy sheriff for eight years and the sheriff for the last four. He knew just about everything and everybody in the county.

"Can't help you there, Bill. Apparently no one seems to know where she high tails it to on her days off. And this ain't her day off." Mamie was smoking two packs a day for the first time in several years. It didn't help her voice.

"What about Ray's wife?"

"Stella's visiting her mother. She hasn't been here for over a week. Sam's wife wanted to call her, but couldn't find the number. It's possible that Ray is with them, although he didn't say anything to anyone about leaving."

Swenson had his hat in one hand and was scratching behind his left ear with the other. He looked down at his boots, then back up at Mamie. He had known her a long time. She was a tough old bird, and she wasn't one to panic over something of no consequence.

"You suspect foul play, Mamie?"

"I don't know what I suspect. Just a feeling, I guess. You know Ed. Solid. Always here for breakfast at the same time every morning. Orders the same thing every time. He may be the most predictable man in town."

"He might be the dullest, too," added Bill. "Maybe he just needed to break the routine. The argument with Ray was just a trigger, telling him he had been doing the same thing too long."

Mamie looked doubtful.

"Okay, I'll see what I can come up with. By the way, his truck is in his garage, I already checked. So if he took off, it was with someone else or by some other means."

"What about his business? I'm not trying to tell you how to investigate, Bill, but shouldn't he have made arrangements to close the store, put up a sign, or something? It's just not like Ed to let things go like that. And Ray didn't say anything to Phil. He'd surely let the owner know."

"Yep, Phil isn't real pleased about Ray's disappearance. He seems madder than worried, though. Probably figures Ray is goofing off. He's done it a few times before. I'll see what I can find out. From what you've told me, Ed and Ray are probably together."

"For better or worse?"

Bill glanced at her without responding, put on his hat, and walked toward the door. He stopped and addressed the men as a group. "Any of you know anything, about either of them?"

A few nodded in the negative and others only lowered their heads, holding their coffee cups. Bill left the cafe at 8:20, climbed into his patrol car, and drove out of the parking lot leaving a swirl of dust blowing past the windows. Mamie took a long drag and let the smoke out slowly.

Bill Swenson walked along the outside of Ed's trailer, looking under it, checking the doors and windows before stepping up to the main entrance. He knocked loudly. Like earlier that day, there was no answer. He called Ed's name several times as he circled the trailer again. The windows were curtained. Three days mail had accumulated in the box by the road and the same number of folded newspapers lay in the parking lot. He decided to force the lock. He retrieved a crow bar and mallet from the trunk of the patrol car. He jammed the bar into the frame, working it behind the lock, and whacked it several times with the mallet. The lock gave and the door swung open.

"Bill Swenson here. You in there Ed?" He stepped up and into the living room. It looked lived in, full of Ed's belongings scattered haphazardly. Nothing unusual, Ed's home had never been a model of neatness. He quickly toured the interior. The bed was made, towels hung in the bathroom, the toilet seat up. The refrigerator had food. He sniffed the milk—it was fresh. He checked some drawers, but nothing seemed out of place. Ed could have been there at any time that day. The clothes closets were full and there were several pairs of shoes near the bed. Two empty suitcases were stored under the bed.

Bill's deputy was checking Ray's house and he reported no one at home, his car missing, but nothing unusual. His neighbors hadn't seen him in three days. Without evidence of foul play and after only three days, Bill didn't feel this warranted a missing persons report. Not yet. He would give it a couple of more days and try to locate Ray's wife. He would also open the rental office and check the inventory to see if any of the vehicles were unaccounted for.

THURSDAY NIGHT, WEEK THREE

THE CLOUDLESS NIGHT SKY CONTAINED A MILLION OR more pinpoints of light. In a desolate stretch of desert at four thousand feet above sea level, the heavens seemed to reach down and touch the earth. The familiar constellations were all but obliterated by the added detail of countless fainter stars. Interstellar dust, thought Ed as he drove Ray's Lincoln Town and Country along the deserted BLM road twenty miles from the paved state highway. *I never thought in terms of interstellar before. Is this what it will be like from now on? My little world has become the universe?*

Rozelle sat beside him in the front seat. Ray was sprawled across the back seat, unconscious. Ed glanced at the rear view mirror every few minutes, but no one had followed. He'd be able to spot them miles away in this flat stretch of nowhere. He began to relax, realizing they had probably made their exit unnoticed. Rozelle looked at him and smiled. Her hand reached out and touched his on the steering wheel.

"We should be there momentarily. I will recognize the fence and it is only a short distance from there." Her voice was calm and manner direct, leaving no doubt she knew exactly where they were and where they were going.

"I'm still not clear on what we are going to do with him," said Ed, nodding toward the back seat.

He had feared she meant Ray some permanent harm, but she reassured him Ray would be able to drive his car back to town when they were finished. It had been two days, going on three, since Ray had taken the sleeping potion. Rozelle had woken him a few times to give him something to drink and a nutrition capsule. He remained in a daze, probably due to something extra in the capsule. She put him under again when they left the trailer for the desert.

Rozelle held the cube, which was now colorless. "More technology, get used to it," she had told him. Her precise English conferred additional credibility. By that time he was willing to believe anything.

"Stop here. This is it." She pointed to a short segment of scrap wood fencing running perpendicular to the road. It was either the remains or the start of a barrier that had been abandoned—only about a dozen posts with connecting bars stood up from the gravely sand. Clumps of sagebrush could be seen in the headlights.

He shut off the motor and lights. She turned to Ed and pointed into the desert. "Now we walk along the fence and turn toward the east." They got out of the car and she joined him on the driver's side.

Ed nodded. "I'm ready." He glanced once more at Ray. "And he won't remember anything about the cube or coming to my trailer?"

"He will have a hangover, wonder how he got here, and believe he is lucky to be intact." Her eyes were dazzling, lighting up the dark.

"Are you certain no one will ask what has happened to me?"

She laughed. "You aren't going anywhere, remember? I explained all that. You, your physical self, will be the same good old Ed as far as anyone knows. You, the real you, is the one who will travel. With me." She smiled reassuringly.

He looked at her and took her hand. "Yeah, I'm just a traveling…what? I'll make Marco Polo seem like a couch potato."

"Would you really care if people knew? Have you left anything behind that matters to you?"

He shook his head, his eyes meeting hers. "No."

I haven't, have I? The business, the trailer, High Plains? What was it all about? Forty years and what to show for it? What will they say at the rotary club or at the cafe? There'll be rumors about Ed and Sparkle, his disappearance for a few days, hers forever. Sly old Ed had himself a cutie, and a young one at that.

"You have a special place out there, to put the cube?"

"Yes, where it was before, a place no one will find. After we unite as one, the other you can return to town."

"It'll be a long walk. Will the old me, the one that stays

here, be the same physically and mentally? Will I know about the traveling me…?"

She put a hand on his lips. "Ed will forget about us, but almost everything else will be the same."

Almost? He took one look around, at the car, Ray in the back seat, the dirt road back toward town. "Let's go. And watch out for snakes."

The warning had a greater meaning than Ed could know. She simply smiled and said, "Yes."

She held the cube under her right arm as they stepped off the road together. The light it cast in front of them was multicolored and dazzling. At the end of the fence line, they walked into the darkness and out of sight from Ray and the Lincoln.

FRIDAY, WEEK THREE

RAY FINALLY WOKE WHEN THE SUN LINE REACHED THROUGH the back window and fell across his eyes. He sat up, very groggy and stretched out his arms. It took him about a minute to recognize he was in the back seat of his car. Looking out the window, he could see nothing but desert, a few fence posts nearby and a landscape of endless sagebrush. He opened the door and climbed out, looking around. The tracks from his car were obvious. He had stopped in the middle of a dirt road but had been coming from somewhere. Since he had no idea where he had intended to go, he decided to turn the car and follow the tracks back. It was almost nine o'clock in the morning when he drove into High Plains and pulled up to the cafe. He was still trying to remember where he had been and what he might have been doing when he opened the door and walked inside.

Most of the morning coffee crew were paying their tabs and getting ready to head out for the day. A dozen voices greeted him at once.

"Ray!"

"Damn, man where have you been?"

"We've had everyone looking for you."

"Are you all right?"

They shook his hand, slapped him on the shoulder, and ushered him to a seat at their table. Mamie came from behind the counter with a cup and a pot of coffee.

"I might of had an exciting night," he said softly, not sure whether he had or not. Maybe one of them could enlighten him. Maybe he didn't really want to know. He was thankful his wife was out of town.

Mamie stood behind him with her hands on her hips. "Maybe it was three exciting nights. Phil ain't any too happy with you, Ray. You might not have a job there anymore. And Bill and his deputy are looking for you."

He turned around to face her. "What do you mean three nights?" He looked around at the others and was met by silence. Some had looks of reproach while others showed concern. One or two were having trouble suppressing a grin. "Three nights? I woke up this morning about thirty miles out of town on an old BLM road. Don't know how I got there. I was asleep in the back seat, keys in the ignition." He looked around at them. There were a few more grins. He wasn't the only one who had ever lost a night here and there.

"Musta been one helluva party somewhere, Ray. Too bad you don't remember it."

Another added, "Where did you lose Sparkle? We haven't seen her since you and Ed disappeared." Several people laughed and looked at Mamie, who scowled and faced Ray.

"What about Ed? Was he with you when…" Mamie stopped and stared as the door of the cafe opened and Ed Ferguson walked in, nonchalant, nodded at the table of men and Mamie, then sat in his customary seat at the counter.

"I don't remember," said Ray, sipping his coffee, grateful that someone else would be the focus of attention for a while.

Mamie stepped behind the counter and faced Ed. He looked up at her, gave her a brief smile and said, "the usual, with orange juice."

She stared at his face and especially at his eyes—eyes that seemed to reflect a thousand points of light, like microscopic diamonds glittering in a dark blue pool.

ODOMETER MOMENTS

How do you measure your existence? Some count benchmarks, those elusive accomplishments by which they might be known and remembered. For others, it is accumulated assets, the estate left to family and others. For a few, it is far more mundane than all of those.

Life is full of sequential milestones, clocks and calendars, distances traveled, miles to go. As the mortal odometer ticks, our lives pass before us in the forms of anniversaries, commemorations, checkpoints, and deadlines. For some, it is more than a clock, greater than a number.

4101 22 OCTOBER

Eating popcorn—lots of popcorn. The butter oozes out of it and buffers the dryness, the hard shells of partially popped kernels. It's salty and I shouldn't eat too much of it. Bad for the blood pressure, according to those who know. I'm not sure about the butter, but the corn should be healthy, even in this exploded state.

The theatre is almost empty and empty seats surround me. Bombarded by light and a thundering bass soundtrack, I temporarily ignore my isolation. Me, my popcorn, and an oversized Coke (more sugar than I need) with too much ice, but that's what you get for eight dollars. I eat automatically, eyes fixed on the screen, quenching the saltiness with a greedy slurp. I avoid straws—they are not manly.

It's my birthday, my thirty-third. Thirty-third for the nerd, hurray. Birthday dinner was at the Wagon Wheel restaurant. I treated myself to scallops and fettuccini, not the usual hamburger at McDonald's. This is a special day, isn't it? A benchmark, three-three on the two-two of the one-one. The movie isn't great but it is better than television at home. I need to get out every once in awhile. That's what Ginny says and I believe her. She couldn't be with me tonight. She apologized twice.

4115 6 NOVEMBER

Ginny brings me a sci-fi video tonight. I hadn't seen it and she thinks I would like it. We sit on the couch together, not too close but near enough for me smell the lavender spray she uses. She is not beautiful, not like the women in the magazines or in the movies, but she is clean and she smiles and I feel comfortable with her. There are not very many women I can relax with. When the movie is over we eat some ice cream, and I put chocolate syrup on mine. She eats her dessert plain, to keep her figure, she tells me, smiling and shifting on the couch. Her shoes are on the floor, and her legs are curled underneath her. I don't know what to say so I smile back and nod, concentrating on getting the right ratio of melted vanilla ice cream and chocolate in my spoon.

The clock reads ten ten. Ginny has never been at my apartment this late before. Another record for my journal. I started my journal when I turned twenty-five, at 0001. It gives me perspective, a sense of where I am and what has happened. I haven't told Ginny. I have only known her for two months (since 4031), and I decide that I will share this with her at 4200. Or maybe 4300. I will see how it goes. She says goodnight and suggests we have dinner and a movie at her apartment next week.

4163 2 DECEMBER

Winter is almost here. In addition to gray skies and a stiff wind, the overnight dew has turned to frost. I can view the thin coat that covers the grounds as I look from my second floor apartment window. There are twelve apartments in our suburban complex. Mine is number one-one, a nice number, matching my birth month. Ginny is away, visiting her mother who lives in another state. She will be gone for six more days. I decided I will definitely tell her about my numbers at 4200. She is a good cook and she likes the same kind of food I do. But not fast food. She says it is greasy and bad for her complexion. She weighs 117 pounds, sixty-two pounds less than I do. I do not know if I can give up french fries.

4187 9 DECEMBER

Two important things happen today. My car odometer reaches 50,000 miles. I watch it on my way to work. It was 49,999 and then slowly, because I was only going twenty-five miles per hour, the last digit turns, the nine disappearing and the zero taking its proper place. I like the older mechanical odometers because you can savor the transition, unlike the newer digital ones that flash a new number. What fun is there in that? I want to stop the car, park it at the curb and look at the dial for several minutes, but I cannot be late for work. The boss expects me to be in the office five minutes before nine, ready to go. She wouldn't understand the significance of the event. No one can, except maybe Ginny. I still have not told her yet (thirteen more entries to go), but I have hopes that she will appreciate the occasion. Maybe we will celebrate.

The second thing: Ginny returned last night. She calls me when I get home today and asks me to go shopping with her on Saturday. That is four days from now. She wants to buy a small Christmas tree and put it in my apartment. For us, she says, and our presents. This is a problem. I have never bought a present for a girl before. Except for mother, and that was a long time ago. Mother was not easy either, but I do not feel competent to pick out something for Ginny. All I can think of is lavender perfume, but she probably has that already. Ginny tells me she knows what she will get for me, but she won't tell me. A surprise, she says.

4197 13 DECEMBER

SATURDAY AND SHOPPING, AND IT IS ALMOST TIME TO reveal my secret journal to Ginny. She is cheerful and we find a tabletop tree, a natural fir. I do not have ornaments or any Christmas decorations. She does and offers to share her two boxes of tinsel and glass globes, and two wreaths. One is for the door, right under the double one apartment number. The other hangs on the wall of the dining nook. We hang the ornaments and wrap the silver strands around the tree. She pulls a small package out of her over-sized purse and puts it under the tree.

I haven't gotten anything for her yet. I confess and lower my eyes. She steps closer and squeezes my hand. Her face is very close to mine and she is breathing deep, her eyes are half-closed.

It's okay, Ronnie, I don't mind, she tells me. Just being around you is my present. I do not mind her calling me Ronnie. Mother used to call me that but everyone else uses my real name, Ronald. It sounds more dignified, more manly.

This is the closest we have ever been (4198). I think I am supposed to kiss her (that would definitely be 4199) but that would bring me to the moment of revelation and I may not be ready. I am not sure anymore. I also do not completely believe her about the present. People say things like that but they really expect you to give them something. I will but I need time. I can see there might be a lot of numbers in the next few days. I am probably not ready for this. I step back and she releases my hand. I smile and suggest we have something to eat, avoiding a dramatic 4199, at least for now.

4204 16 DECEMBER

SEVERAL THINGS HAPPENED AT WORK, AND I HAVE NOT seen Ginny for a few days. We did not talk about my journal, so 4200 occurred at work. She is thinking about going home for Christmas but she does not want to leave me alone. Come home with me, she says. You'll love my sister, and mom and dad. I've told them about you and you'd be welcome to spend the entire holiday with us, including New Year's Eve. That would be a special moment for me, no matter where I am.

I have time coming at work and I know I can get off for the holidays. Two weeks would be enough, but I do not know what will happen. I bought her a pair of mittens, red ones with white kittens on them. She likes cats. I am neutral about cats and dogs, but I think she will like the present. Today, I asked my boss for the time off and she approved it (4205).

4207 17 DECEMBER

GINNY PREPARES DINNER FOR ME AT HER APARTMENT. She has a nice kitchen with lots of utensils and special pans and bowls. She says she wants to be a professional, a chef with her own restaurant. I believe she could be. I tell her about getting time off and that I would like to go home with her. She can tell I am happy but also uneasy and she sits close to me after dinner. She opens a bottle of white wine and pours it into two special glasses, ones with long stems. I do not own glasses like that. We sip the wine as we discuss the trip. I do not usually drink wine or anything alcoholic, but Ginny says it will be okay. She wants to leave on the nineteenth. Her parents' house is 361 miles from her apartment—it will take all day to get there. I sip more of the cold wine, and it makes me feel strange, as if I am not sure of what is going to happen (4208). She tells me she is happy I have decided to come with her and she puts her left hand on my arm. It is very warm and she sits close, our thighs touching. I take another sip and feel a warm glow beginning to spread, starting in my stomach and moving up and down. I believe this is supposed to happen, the feel of the wine I mean.

I look at Ginny and she has leaned back, her eyes closed. She is the perfect picture of ease, breathing slowly. I feel the opposite, not sure what I should do. If I do nothing, will she be insulted? Is she waiting for me? Can I delay this? The clock hits eight even and it is 4209. I reach toward her and kiss her lightly on the cheek. She doesn't move and her eyes are still closed, but she smiles.

Did you do what I think you did, Ronnie? She asks, still smiling. Now she opens her eyes and turns toward me.

I am frozen, unable to answer. She puts both of her arms around my neck. She closes her eyes again and pulls me toward her face. My eyes remain open as our lips meet (4210). They are warm and soft, slightly moist. She presses them tighter and they give, as if melting into mine. I can feel my heart pounding, afraid that she will hear it and think I am afraid, unmanly. I close my eyes and the kiss continues for several seconds. I lose count but it must be ten seconds or longer.

Now her eyes are open and our faces are about a foot apart. She is looking at me, as if expecting me to say or offer something further. I cannot think of anything profound so I say thank you.

She smiles and tells me I'm welcome. She pours the last of the wine into our glasses and holds her glass up. Here's to us, Ronnie, for our safe trip, she whispers, as if we should not let anyone else know about our adventure. She looks at my glass, and I raise it to clink with hers. I saw that in a movie once.

It is my first toast (4211). It is 8:05 on 17 December, a Wednesday, and I have experienced a kiss just like in the movies. They aren't my favorite kind of movies, but the real thing is surprisingly enjoyable.

4214 17 DECEMBER (CONTINUED)

USUALLY MY JOURNAL ENTRIES ARE SHORTER. I TRY TO BE precise, like mother taught me, but this day is an exception.

At 10:36 p.m., still at Ginny's apartment, she asks me if I want to spend the night. For the past hour I have been debating whether to tell her about the odometer, even though it is still a long way to 4300. She and I start another bottle of wine and I am definitely not myself. In fact, I am recalling events only with difficulty, and the numbers are harder to remember. We have the next day off, and she says she can make me the best breakfast I have ever eaten. We never ate breakfast before, and I can imagine it will be remarkable, definitely countable. At first, I think she wants me to come to her place the next morning, after I get up, but no, she wants me to stay the night at her place.

Where would I sleep? I ask, looking at the couch.

I have a big bed. There is plenty of room for both of us, she says, as if describing a real estate feature to a prospective client.

I do not have a toothbrush or any of my other bathroom things, I reply, beginning to feel very uncertain. I do not want to reject her offer of hospitality, but I never go to bed without brushing my teeth. I also do not have pajamas with me. All of this would be a greater worry if I was clear headed, but I am not. The warm glow remains and my apartment seems a long way away. She waits patiently as I continue my internal debate. At 10:39 I nod yes and follow her to the bedroom. It is my first time in the bedroom of a young woman (4215? I think that's correct).

She slips into the bathroom, and I sit on the edge of the bed, trying to remember how this came about. I hear the toilet flush and the water in the sink. At 10:46 she emerges, wrapped in a bathrobe.

Your turn, she says and gives me an encouraging smile as she crosses to the bed. I walk into the bathroom, shut the door, rinse my mouth with tap water, and relieve myself. Another first, using a woman's private bathroom. The number is fuzzy. It's 42-something, but I will have to recall it later, when I revise my journal entries. I remove my socks, shirt, and pants—my shoes are in the living room. Wearing only my underwear, I enter the bedroom. It is dark but I can make out her shape on the bed, under the covers.

I'm right here, Ronnie, nothing to worry about. We'll just sleep tonight and talk about things tomorrow morning, okay? Her voice is soothing, smooth.

Yes, it is okay. I pause. Ginny?

Yes, she answers, low and gentle.

I'm not afraid. I tell her, standing about three feet from the foot of the bed. It is just…it feels different. I have never done anything like this before. I watch her form shift under the covers. My confession does not sound manly, but I do not feel manly. I feel I am out of control.

Never done anything like what, Ronnie? There is a hint of amusement in her voice, not like she is making fun, but as if she is enjoying it, a game. I'm not sure what the rules are or what winning or losing means.

I don't answer as I reach the edge of the bed and she holds the covers open. Her night clock reads 10:52 as I slip under the covers, staying close to the edge on my side (4218? 4219?— Where am I?). Will I remember this tomorrow?

Make yourself comfortable, she murmurs. Her pillow is close to mine and she is on her side, facing me. I can feel her breath on my face. It is a big bed, but she is in the middle of it. I turn toward her, suddenly aware that the warm sensation has returned, threatening to overwhelm everything else. Her hand touches mine, and the numbers start to swirl and I can't count anymore.

18 DECEMBER

SITTING AT THE DESK IN MY APARTMENT, I LOOK OUT AT the lawn and parking area. A small junco is nervously hopping from branch to branch in a leafless tree. I'm calm, but try as much as I can, I don't remember the last numbers from yesterday. I blame it on the wine and on Ginny. Did I get to 4300? I relieved myself at 3:17, aware I had slept only briefly and Ginny was waiting again for me. I told her about the numbers but there were distractions, and I couldn't remember the details and it just didn't seem to matter.

She kept her promise, a great breakfast, served in bed. Yesterday I would've been shocked to see her naked, bringing me food while I sat naked in her bed. We talked about the trip and what to take with us. After three cups of coffee, we dressed and parted.

The journal is open before me. It seems best to start over. 0001 would be breakfast and 0002 would be the best coffee ever and 0003 would be…well it would be the best morning of my life. However, I write nothing, close the book about a quarter after eleven and pick up my travel bag. Ginny and I have 361 miles and two weeks ahead of us and that's only the start of a longer journey. Ginny likes my journal but she says I need a bigger odometer.

ANOTHER CUP OF COFFEE TO GO

Sometimes it doesn't take much to open the door, to invite someone in.
It's even better when the savage beast is soothed at the same time.

Just about everyone in Prairie Pines will be at the twenty-fifth anniversary celebration of Pines Stop and Eat. Everyone except me. "Don't bother," Jonesy had told me. "It's an after-hours affair, closed to the public." Now, according to him, I'm public. Now they don't know me. But, they will.

Another cup of coffee. I pour it slowly, watching the steam rise, catching the aroma. It's only instant, not the real thing with the full rich flavor, but it's expedient, satisfying my now need. I hold the cup with both hands, transferring the warmth inward. It doesn't overcome the chill of the room, but it's still too hot to sip. The fire hasn't had time to disperse the cold penetrating under the door and through the cracks of the cabin. Outside, the morning fog shrouds the nearby bushes—the trees are invisible, but I suspect they haven't left. Coffee calms me down, just the opposite effect for most people. Another reminder that I'm not like them.

Cougar wanders by, expecting a random scratch or, at least, a few words of encouragement. I consider it. He is my only companion. Fierce and independent, *like me*, he approaches his dish in the kitchen corner, sniffing it to see if I've added anything fresh since yesterday. I haven't. Again he is underfoot and this time I reach down and rub him behind the ears, earning a brief high-pitched mew. Too high a note for an outdoor rat chaser, but it is his way. He is straggly, unwashed, *like me.*

"You and me, Cougar. Want some coffee?"

He looks at me. Comprehending? He doesn't refuse but I ignore him and he walks away, tail erect, nose down, sniffing always sniffing. You never know when you will run into something to kill. Today is the day. No, not to kill something, but to let Jonesy know I'm still out here and I haven't forgotten. He probably hopes I've left, moved far away and won't show up like I promised.

Well, Mr. Thaddeus L. Jones, I will show up and remind you of the day you humiliated me, turning me out of your pathetic slop-hole of a diner, running me off in front of Misty and Grace and three or four customers. As if I was some unwanted neighborhood nuisance, not good enough to eat at the counter, an object of your derision, and subject to your dismissal. Grace was no help either, as she stood there with her arms folded, nodding her head as her husband pointed to the door and bid me adieu. She mumbled something to him but I didn't catch it. Not a compliment or a protest to defer his holier-than-thou behavior, I can be sure of that.

The coffee is reaching that perfect sipping temperature, too hot to gulp but just right to take in dainty slurps. "Imagine that, Cougar? Me, dainty?" I laugh but the cat has no sense of humor, mostly ignoring me as he licks his butt. The coffee reminds me once again of Misty, the only gem that glistens in Prairie Pines. Not that there is any competition—most young girls and boys leave town as soon as they graduate from high school, some before then. No jobs, no future, *nada*.

Misty is an exception because she is the only one in her family left to care for her infirm mother. She is eighteen and works part time at the diner and part time at George's hardware store across the street. She is always pleasant, has a smile, and come-to-Jesus looks. I know that is why Jonesy keeps her around. Grace is not much to look at anymore, and her manner is about as sour as last weeks blue plate special. The only reason his wife tolerates Misty is because she works hard and Grace doesn't want to work at all.

I'm eight years older than the girl and I had ignored her at first, except for a sneak look at her legs when she passed or a shot down her blouse when she bent over. That's what started the trouble, but hell, I hadn't done anything that any other normal man hadn't done, including Jonesy. He took every opportunity he could to brush past her in the narrow aisle behind the counter or to put his arms around her to "help" with the heavy dishes she was carrying.

I'll admit I'm not pretty. Hair is a bit too long for most people's tastes and I can, and do, go several days without a shave. I work hard at the lumber mill, and my clothes are neither new nor clean, but that's about par for Prairie Pines. An old lumber mill with a lot of old worn-out lumbermen, the residue of a high desert town that has seen better days. I'm also not old school in town. I arrived on the highway when I was twenty-two, looking for a job and a place to get off the road awhile. That was four years ago. Misty wasn't even in high school then, and I wasn't aware she existed. That changed when she started working for Jonesy.

There is only one other place to eat, a steakhouse plus cocktail lounge that caters to the occasional tourist and the few businessmen who can afford it. Most of the time, I fix dinner at my place and eat with the cat. Cougar doesn't mind my blue-collar looks and manners and we get along fine. But about once a week, I need to see and hear someone besides the cat and the fellows at the mill. Jonesy's food and Misty's looks are required respites from the cold cabin and its isolation three miles from town.

Closing the front door of the cabin, no need to lock it, I climb into the beat-up and bruised pick-up, a twenty-year old Ford with a rusted chassis and threadbare tires. It is hard to tell what the color had been, disguised by numerous patches of primer and unfinished attempts to repaint it. The door clangs with a metallic reverberation that suggests the hinges are at their functional limits, but it starts easily enough, and I wind my way down the gravel road and onto the highway toward town. It is Saturday night but you wouldn't know it from the streets or the traffic. The diner usually stays open until nine, giving way to the cocktail lounge and the bowling alley that pushes it to twelve or two, depending on business. It is six thirty and just beginning to get dark as I kill the engine in front of the Pines Stop and Eat. Only one other car is in the lot. Jonesy and Misty usually park around the back, although Misty often walks from her house, about a mile away.

I'm prepared to play bad, to create a disturbance Jonesy won't soon forget. Misty is usually off by four on Saturdays—I don't want her to witness my tantrum. I did hope there would be more customers, providing me a suitable audience for the performance. When I enter, I sense immediately that everything is different. By now there should have been a crowd and decorations on the wall, all of the accompaniments of the proposed anniversary celebration. There is no sign of Grace or Jonesy, but Misty is there, waiting on the only customers, a middle-aged man and woman at one of the five booths along the left wall. She gives me a smile as I sit at the counter near the door, my usual place. I might be a social pariah, but I can still "stop and eat" there during business hours.

"Be right with you, Jason," she says over her shoulder, hurrying to the kitchen window. Ryan is on duty at the grill. He is part-time, filling in when Grace or Jonesy are off somewhere.

I look around. The restaurant is quiet, unusually so. I think about putting some coin in the jukebox, a nostalgic artifact from the real diner days. Jonesy has a thing about that, the old days. Must have been when he was really something instead of just thinking he was. Misty strolls down the counter and props her elbows in front of me, her face not more than six inches from mine.

"What gives, Misty? How come you're here? Where are the lovely Missus Jones and her illustrious husband?"

"Gracie collapsed early this afternoon and he's at home with her. He left me in charge, but I'm fixin' to close up in a few minutes, soon as they leave." She nods toward the booth. "Of course, I'll get you what you want, Jason." She looks intently in my face and I lower my head, unable to meet her eyes.

"Guess I kinda made a fool of myself last week, huh?" I'm hoping she'll say something to dismiss my bad behavior, to blow it off like it was nothing, which I am pretty sure it was.

She smiles and stands straight. "I guess Mr. Jones doesn't want any competition, but its okay. You've never been anything other than polite to me, a gentleman, and I appreciate it. What can I getcha?"

"A few minutes, huh? Is your cook still here?"

"He's washing up, but I can rustle you up a sandwich or a bowl of chili, maybe some fries."

"How about a sandwich to go. Grilled ham and cheese?"

"Got'cha, be right up."

There goes the grandiose plan to piss off Jonesy. I forget to ask further about Grace. I don't much care for her, but I don't wish her anything terrible. Jonesy is different. If he drops dead in the street tomorrow I will be a happier man. The early closure also means I'll be returning to the cabin before I had planned, another night with the cat, maybe a book. Someday I'll have to get a television or some other way to entertain myself.

The couple gets up, leaves some money on their table, and walks out without glancing my way. Ryan steps out of the kitchen, says goodnight to Misty, and goes out the back way. Misty slips my sandwich into the microwave. Another Saturday evening in Prairie Pines, and it isn't quite seven. Whoopee doo.

I walk to the jukebox, drop a quarter, and play "Somebody to Love" by Queen. The piano intro starts as Misty comes out of the kitchen with a paper bag and a couple of napkins.

"That's one of my favorites," she says, handing me the bag. When she gives me the napkins, my hand touches hers and lingers an extra second or two. "Going back to your cabin?"

"Yeah. Not a whole lot of choices around town and the drinks over at Blackie's are a bit out of my price range. Even on a Saturday night there are very few there I know or care to know."

"You have a cat, dont'cha?"

I nod, wondering how she knows that. I don't remember mentioning it to her, but someone else could have told her. What else does she know about me?

"I like cats. I feel safe with guys who have cats. Seems like they're different than most guys."

"Yeah? In what way?"

"More sensitive, easier to talk to. Guys with cats listen to you. They're patient." She tells me this as if she is an experienced woman of the world, someone who has known many men, with or without cats. I doubt this.

"Hmm. Cats are not much in the way of companions, not like dogs. I had a dog once, never wanted to leave my side. Cougar is okay, but he's not overflowing with warmth, and he's a lousy conversationalist."

"Jason, you can say no if you want to, I'll understand and this is probably not very bright of me…"

"What is it, Misty?" I look at her carefully as she takes her apron off and throws it on the counter. Her eyes are bright, lighting up a plain but not unattractive face, awash in freckles. Her light brown hair is tied back, but she reaches back and pulls a pin, letting it fall to her shoulders.

"I thought maybe you—and your cat—would like some company for a change. You got anything to drink or any games we can play? How about some music to dance to?"

"Uh, Misty, I don't have any games, except for a deck of cards. Do you play gin rummy? As for drinks, you're underage and I can't provide you anything stronger than a Coke, but I have that in the fridge. And all I got for music is a radio, which in this town don't pick up much."

"Sounds great, best offer I have had in, well, a long time. Wait for me while I lock up?" She turns toward the kitchen.

"Misty?"

She looks back, smiling like a kid on her birthday. "Yeah, Jason?"

"How about two coffees? Two coffees to go."

GHOST BIRDS

Love and competition are not strangers. Lovers may attract rivals, requiring one to choose between partners and outcomes with uncertain consequences. Unpredictability is an attribute that promises excitement and competition stokes the ego's need for validation. But rivals are supposed to obey the rules of engagement, aren't they?

White, fast and feathered, appearing without warning and disappearing just as suddenly. They are here and then they are not. Silent, lacking a song or call, ghostly flapping wings signal their presence, as if they belong somewhere else and only appear in my world when it suits them, attracting my attention for some purpose I can't yet imagine. Apparently, I'm the only one who can see them, so I started calling them ghost birds. My personal Harvey the rabbit, but you're not old enough to remember him.

My girlfriend is sitting with me, having a morning-after cup of the good stuff, a Colombian brew, watching songbirds land on the patio deck, scrounging for crumbs. We're sloppy eaters and I'm sure they and their friends are grateful for what we leave behind. The gathering consists of the usual assortment of sparrows and a couple of juncos going about the usual hopping and pecking business. The flash of white wings heralds the arrival of my mysterious visitors. They are about the size of small doves, which I initially had mistaken them for, but they aren't doves. These are streaks, flash—land—flash, gone again. I discern a dark beak and very black eyes, as if they lack pupils, just deep dark orbs, big dilated ones like the kind one expects on night flyers. I mention them and Gillian looks at me with her mouth slightly open.

"What?" she says, as if I had announced the arrival of leprechauns.

"Don't what me," I reply, smiling as if she is putting me on. "Didn't you see the white birds? You were looking right at them."

"I don't see any white birds, do you?"

"Not now, they're already gone. How could you miss them? They landed right in front of us." The other birds are still hopping around, pecking at and retrieving bread-crumbs and other garbage.

Easy to ignore a single incident—maybe she didn't see them, a momentary distraction. It happens. However, on several other occasions, the birds came and went, not so quickly that a normal person with ordinary awareness wouldn't notice, but they didn't linger. I couldn't point to them and say, see, there they are. Right on that branch or on that park bench. Now they're gone. Each time, with dif-ferent people and in different settings, the same result. I see them, others don't. At first it was an annoyance, you know, one of those minor irritations that doesn't command your full attention. Nothing to get excited or write home about, as my dad used to say. I never wanted to make a big deal about it, especially with Gillian.

I am trying very hard to get somewhere with her, besides sleeping over and an occasional romp. I like her and we seem to be compatible on most things. However, I'm uneasy about those sure-you-see-it looks she gives me when I mention the ghost birds. Gillian is very down to earth, the practical type that doesn't believe in ghosts, UFOs, alien Elvis, or the Holy Trinity. She is about shopping lists, sensible but tight-fitting clothing, and economy cars. Well, one out of three ain't bad.

When I'm alone, the birds seem more important, consequential visitors if you will. That's the problem. What consequences? Is this an imaginary prank, an alcohol-induced vision, however fleeting? No feeling of dread or even vague foreboding accompanies the appearances. But they are consistent—the spread white wings displaying the extended flight feathers, the short rounded tail, and the black eyes. They aren't bright laundry-clean white, more of a sullied white, not beige or tan, but as if they need to molt or had rolled around in the dirt. I guess even ghost birds can get grungy flying from place to place. Flying must be magical, I decide, even for birds. It would be for me. I think about it more and more, lifting off the ground and willing myself somewhere else, without notice, asking for permission, or long TSA lines. Just go. Maybe there are other people on the ghost bird itinerary. I'm afraid to ask. No problem, they just visit—we don't talk.

It's Sunday morning. Gillian and I linger in bed, reluctant to plan anything, including breakfast. The curtains are open, and a bright sunny spring day blasts into the room, eradicating the last vestiges of slumber and sexual intentions. Gillian looks at me with that shall-we-get-up expression, one mixed with inevitable duty and we've had enough of this. She is facing me and I'm looking over her shoulder as the white bird flies into the window. It doesn't collide and there is no thump, it merely flies up against the pane, outstretched wings and feet grasping at the smooth surface.

Gillian sees my eyes widen and she turns toward the window. "What?" I gulp but don't answer. The bird is still there but she doesn't see it or pretends she doesn't see it. The bird stays longer than it ever has, a full ten seconds or so. Gillian turns back to me. "Seeing things again?" she asks, putting her hand over mine, like a mother calming a spooked child.

"No," I say. "It was nothing, just the sun in my eyes." The bird is gone and we get up and search for our hastily discarded clothes. When the passion comes, it waits for no man or pants. Getting dressed again is not as urgent.

MY FRIEND AUSTIN IS AN ORNITHOLOGIST. NOT A PRO-fessional, but a very dedicated bird watcher, a member of Audubon, and a frequent hiker with others of his kind, his flock, he says. They add to their life lists and always get excited when something new is seen in the vicinity. He has been to many countries, particularly in the tropics, and he has a few thousand birds on his list, many of them documented by his own photographs. He is very proud of that list and his photo albums, and we are looking at it one day when I finally get the nerve to ask him about my white birds.

Describe them, he says, and I do. Austin is puzzled by the black eyes and beak. He asks a series of questions. Does it look like an owl? An egret? A tern? No to all three. I know what owls, egrets, and terns look like, I think. He grabs a couple of field guides to see if they might be strays from somewhere else. Then he consults some larger tomes, the expensive kind that the pros use. No luck. He asks me to take a picture of them if they return. Strange, that thought had never occurred to me. I have a couple of cameras, including a nice digital SLR. I usually keep a small digital camera, about the size of a cell phone, handy for a candid or two. I tease Gilliam about her being a porn star on You-Tube someday, but her sense of humor is not as developed as mine.

I tell Austin I'll try a photo but I warn him the would-be subjects appear and leave quickly and don't seem inclined to pose. I admire them for that, never a captive be. I also don't want to try for a shot while Gillian is around. Then I think about the outcome. Do I really want my ghost in a camera? Suppose, very likely, there isn't any image of a bird. Then what? Of course the same question, only stranger still, would result if a bird does appear in all of its digital glory. I haven't told Austin about my ability to observe what others can't. I don't need another *what*.

***

A QUIET AFTERNOON AT HOME BY MYSELF. I HAVE TEM-porarily replaced Gillian for a triple shot of *Tres Mujeres,* one of my favorite rums. The cameras are ready, and I sit in a far corner of the patio under a tree, trying unsuccessfully to blend into the suburban yard. Crumbs have already attracted the small beaked ones, the normal ones, and I sip slowly, determined to get the photo, get drunk, or—prefer-ably—both. The smaller camera, easier to aim and shoot, sits in my lap, pointed toward the patio. I'm not sure why I believe they will appear there, or anywhere for that matter, but I have seen them on the tiles or on the metal table three times before. The camera has a zoom, but I probably won't bother with it. I can always blow up a quick snapshot later.

I'm more concerned about getting something, anything, for Austin to inspect.

A slight breeze rustles the leaves overhead. It is a very pleasant evening, and the rum is beginning to expand that inner warm spot, spreading from the gut outward. I am soaring with heavy eyelids, and I'm just about on the verge of not giving a damn whether my white phantoms show, when they do.

Three. In front of me. One is on the left arm of my chair, about a foot from my left hand. He appears to be looking at my watch. The second one is on the lawn between my extended legs. One swift scissor kick and it would be dead meat, but I'm neither inclined nor prepared for athletic maneuvers. The third bird is the problem. It is in my lap. It has one foot on my camera. I stare at the bird and it stares back, head cocked to one side. I am holding my breath, so I let it out slowly, trying not to move. For the first time they seem to be waiting, as if giving me the privilege of the next move. The irony of my useless camera, so close and so inaccessible, forces me to smile. I need a drink more than ever, but my right hand remains motionless, and the rum waits along with the rest of us. I click my tongue softly, and all of the birds raise and lower their heads, a small bobble to reward me for my patience. Sure.

The phone rings inside the house and the sound through the open patio door disrupts the tableau of our impasse. The birds disappear. They don't fly away. They disappear as if they never existed. Did they? I look at my watch. I have been sipping my drink for over an hour. I am not drunk. I am not confused and I'm no longer sleepy. A dream? I am still holding the glass of precious liquor over the edge of the chair. If I had been asleep, it would now be watering the lawn and providing endless pleasure to earthworms and other crawlies. The phone rings three more times before the answering machine kicks in to let the caller, a telemarketer, know I'm indisposed. Cradling both cameras, I finish the drink and walk back into house.

No photos, no evidence, just my word about another incident in the intermittent saga of the ghost birds. If one of them had pooped on my pants or on the lawn, I might have had something to analyze. What kinda shit is this, Austin? Instead, all I had was me—an analysis I wasn't terribly keen on. Gillian was due from work in about an hour. I needed a lukewarm shower and a hot cup of strong coffee.

I WAS ABOUT TO GIVE UP ANY ATTEMPT TO PHOTOGRAPH the white ones when blind luck, that most fickle female, intervened. I had just finished recharging and installing the camera battery when one of the birds landed outside the closed patio door. An outdoor light provided enough illumination to see the creature clearly. I stared at it for a few seconds before realizing the camera was ready, in my hands, and all I had to do was aim and press the button. I did and the bird was still there, peering into the house as if ready to enter and make an inspection. I aimed and took another photo, then a third. The last one caught it leaving the ground, wings outstretched. Flight is less unsettling than disappearance, something I can relate to. I peered into the yard from the glass door but there was no trace of the visitor.

The image of my last shot was on the view screen. There was a flash of white light across the frozen outline of the door and the background of patio and yard. Damn, they're fast, I thought, no details of the blur were visible. It might as well have been a white cloth flapping across the door. I anxiously backed up to view the first two shots. The door and patio were evident and there was the bird, I guess. It was also a white glow, with a vague avian shape. I imagined a head and a slender body and barely discerned an impression of legs and a stubby tail, but no beak or eyes. It resembled a miniature Halloween ghost, demarcated only by the shape of some thing under a sheet.

Staring at the two photos, first one then the other, I couldn't believe the results. Everything else was in focus and well exposed. The white blurs provided minimal credence to my perception of something. I wasn't dreaming, making it up, or going crazy. Was I? But what could Austin or Gillian or anyone else make of it? Nothing. That was all I had—nothing, an unexplained artifact on an ordinary photo of a glass door. It might get me on the nightly news, but not because I had discovered a new species of bird.

Gillian entered as I slipped into shorts and sandals, my formal wear for around the house on a Friday evening. She must have sensed something had happened. Some women have an uncanny knack for that sort of thing, and the talent was highly developed in my girlfriend. I had become habituated to her what's-going-on look and had even managed to assume a deceptive mask of casual indifference when needed. Not this time. My troubling thoughts betrayed me and her look turned into a this-requires-an answer question.

"Jack, what did you do today? Anything interesting?" She said it casually, like the start of any routine how-was-your-day, but I know she was on full alert and the usual bullshit wouldn't do.

I was in the thesis stage of my graduate degree in western U.S. history, and days could go by without leaving the house. Me, my computer, and a glass of rum, ho-ho. She wanted me to get out more, walk around the block, ride a bike, go shopping (did I mention she liked to shop?). I always feigned lack of time and purposeful intent, had to get the job done, the paper submitted, and on with the rest of our meaningful lives. No time for blurry bird pictures.

She threw her purse and coat over the couch and stepped into my arms for our customary welcome home smooch. It was more than a kiss and less than the prelude to the real naughty bits, as the British would say, but we never hesitated to endure the ceremony for the good things it brought out in us. You smell good, she said, referring to the still soapy residue around my ears. She backed up, arms on my shoulders, looking into my eyes. It was a serious look that brooked no nonsense, no half-truths. "Something happened, didn't it?"

I motioned her to the couch and produced the three photos I had printed from the computer. She looked at each of them, first in rapid succession, then slowly, as if trying to make sense of what I'm showing her. I didn't say a word as I watched her expression, trying to determine what she was thinking. I knew what she was thinking.

"What are these, Jack? I see the patio door, but what are these white blurs?" She asked it matter-of-factly, without judgment or emotional tags.

I told her she was correct, they were indeed photos of the patio door. The white blurs? Something was there, I told her, but I wasn't sure what. She continued to stare, waiting for more. Then I told her what I had seen, the earlier incident with the three birds that disappeared, and my discussion with Austin. I reminded her of the day I had seen them and she hadn't, and I told her about the numerous other times.

She remained silent for a minute, absorbing what I had admitted. Is it what she suspected? She must have known I was not trying to be funny or deliberately strange, even though she had always thought me a little weird. I could smell the friction from her brain gears grinding, trying to frame the next piece of conversation in a rational but non-confrontational manner. Her hand covered mine with her familiar gesture, either of difficulty or affection. I wasn't sure which this was.

"So you are still seeing these…these birds, Jack?" I nodded. "What does Austin think about them?" I told her he couldn't identify them and they didn't fit with any of the birds he knew or had information about. He had suggested taking a photograph and today was the first chance I had to do so. The results, as we both saw, were less than enlightening. She wanted to know if I ever dreamt about them, and I denied it and explained why I didn't think I had been asleep when the three birds appeared.

She reminded me she couldn't see them even when they were visible to me, and I confirmed others were also unable to see them. But, I persisted: something was there. How else could you explain the blur on the photos? The blurs corresponded to what I saw, even the third shot of the bird flying.

She looked at me and stood up. "I need to change," she said and asked me to pour us two glasses of wine. "I need my own glass," she joked, trying to lighten the moment. We often started weekends with a glass or two of wine, but tonight the taste of the vine held additional currency.

There were no more birds for over a month. I was about ready to shrug it all off, one of those sweet mysteries of life that never yields an answer. Gillian didn't mention it again and I told Austin I was unable to get a photograph. To my relief and disappointment, it was over and I was ready to get on with more practical affairs. The thesis was in its final edit, and Gillian and I were discussing a European holiday to be followed by a formal engagement. It was a pleasant if not entirely exciting future. I suppose all bachelors confront prenuptial misgivings. That and the emotional letdown from completing the long-awaited academic finale had me in a bluish-gray funk. Not the kind requiring a bottle, but one that led to quiet mediation about flying, soaring through the air to someplace else, a destination I had never been or imagined. It had long been my unrequited fantasy, but time and money, as always, were the things that kept me grounded. And Gillian, she kept me grounded, but not in an unkind way. Quotes from Jonathan Livingston Seagull about flying and freedom came to mind at these times, but that was also a long time ago.

The black-eyed white bird with the stick in its mouth was an unexpected and unwelcomed intrusion into the orderly schedule of summer priorities. It wasn't actually a stick. It was a cigarillo, a small cylinder of some substance wrapped in brown papers. It looked like tobacco, dark brown and ground fine, more like hash than marijuana. The bird met me at the mailbox across the street from our house. It perched on top of it as I was approaching, sitting patiently until I stopped three feet in front of the box. It showed no fear as I stood there, taking in every detail. The coat seemed cleaner, not as dingy. The eyes were just as dark, bright and unfathomable, as I remembered. The beak was entirely black and it held the cylinder carefully before placing it between its feet in one graceful bow. Our eyes met and held for at least a quarter of a minute. Then, with a slow, graceful motion, it lifted from the box, made an aerial turn and dip, swinging to my left. Rising slowly, unhurried, it climbed and disappeared into a cloudless sky. My gaze returned to the cylinder, and I stepped forward, bending to smell and inspect it before picking it up. There was no odor I could detect. The unmarked paper was wrapped tightly, professionally, around the contents. It looked very much like a cigarillo, blunt and open at one end and tapered at the other. I placed it carefully in my shirt pocket, retrieved the mail, and returned to the house.

Gillian was fixing lunch in the kitchen and I handed her the mail. Most of it was advertising, and she looked through it with the usual comment, is that all? No, I replied, and produced the cigarillo. Her eyes lit up with amusement, and she asked me if that was a new service from the post office or did we have a neighborhood salesman.

"I found it on top of the mailbox," I said.

"Well, Jack, surely you're not going to smoke it, are you? We don't know what might be in it. Could be poison for all we know."

"Of course not," I assured her. I rarely smoked pot and then only if it was from a trusted source. I wasn't sure what a white bird with black eyes was distributing, but I decided I would keep that part of it to myself. I mumbled something about turning it over to the police in case it was dangerous and left the kitchen. I put it in the lower side drawer of my computer desk and forgot about it for the next three weeks.

THE THESIS HAD BEEN SUBMITTED, I HAD TENTATIVELY accepted a part-time teaching post at a local community college, and Gillian and I booked our dream trip to Europe. Life had purpose, expectations, and obligations, leaving little room for half-formed regrets or unanswerable questions about mysterious avian visions and visits.

Needing to replace blank checks in my bankbook, I opened the bottom drawer of the computer desk. There it was, lying to the side, inviting another episode of inquiry and speculation. What was it? Why was it brought to me? Who was the messenger, and what was it trying to communicate? I tried to forget, but could no longer think of this affair as a random, casual chain of events. For some reason known only to my avian companion, I have been designated as the recipient of this dubious present. Gillian was at work, and I was relaxing in the short summer interlude between full time school and gainful employment.

I stared at the cylinder for about a minute, reviewing all of the good and sensible reasons why I should throw it away and never look back. Unfortunately, the bird had left me with an equally compelling set of reasons not to dispose of it. Uniqueness and association with the ghost birds were paramount. I could never rest easy if I didn't investigate the nature of the gift, for a gift it was, beak-delivered to my mailbox for my use by a creature only I was privileged to see. It was crazy either way, but flashes of childhood fantasies, of magic closets and mirrored portals to improbable places, overcame any impulse to dispose of the strange cylinder. I was also intrigued by the messenger's departure. It clearly flew away, like any normal bird would. What had changed?

I held it in front of me and once again noted the lack of a distinct odor. I put the blunt end to my tongue but a brief taste revealed nothing. I decided a glass of rum and the backyard should accompany the grand experiment. I poured the drink, obtained a book of matches, walked outside, and straddled my favorite lawn chair. A few overhead clouds puffed by here and there on a gentle breeze, and the day was pleasantly warm. After a long sip, I sat back and lit the cigarillo. Taking a shallow drag, I waited for any unexpected or adverse effects. It was a mild smoke and still unidentifiable. Another sip, another drag, a bit deeper and longer this time. A few sparrows landed near the patio but the yard was clean. Sorry guys, I said to them, maybe tomorrow.

The afternoon wore on and the drink was gone, the last embers of the cigarillo barely alight. Shadows had reached the patio doors, and I knew Gillian would be home soon. I looked toward the bushes forming our back property line. Five white birds, all with identical black eyes and beaks stared at me. I smiled at them. Hello guys, welcome back, I said, happy to see my friends once again. I laughed and bobbed my head. Thanks for the cigar. Got any more of these? The absurdity of it all surfaced, unbidden, as the birds walked slowly across the lawn toward me, heads bobbing slightly as they strutted.

Gillian walked from the living room to the back patio door. It was standing open so she knew Jack had to be somewhere in the house or in the yard. She glanced outside and noticed an empty glass beside the lawn chair. She didn't notice the small white feather nearby. A bottle of rum, about half full, sat on the kitchen sink. She walked through the two-bedroom house, calling his name, but there was no answer. Puzzled, she changed clothes and walked into the back yard and looked around the sides of the house.

Later that evening, she called a few of his friends but no one had seen him recently. She talked to Austin and she asked him if he had any additional information about Jack's birds. He didn't. She spent a restless night trying to determine if his disappearance was her fault. He seemed satisfied, happy his thesis was done, thankful for a teaching position at the college, and they had Europe and a wedding in their near future. Was it the wedding? She thought again about his obsession with the ghost birds and his occasional fancies about flight and freedom. Was that what this was all about? Were the birds an escape clause, his passport to… what? Where have you gone Jack? Do you just need a night or a few days away? Couldn't you have left a note and told me not to worry, you'll be back?

Three days later, she filed a missing persons report with the police. She could tell them very little and decided not to mention anything about birds. They assured her it wasn't unusual for someone making an important transition in life to leave suddenly and cut all ties. They noted in their report the couple was unmarried. Unless she had evidence or suspicion of foul play, they would not pursue it further. She didn't so they asked her to notify them if Jack turned up.

He never did.

———◆———

UNDER THE PORCH

Love is a glorious feeling—there is nothing like it. Until you have to say goodbye, to leave it in the rear view mirror or whisper a final farewell. Sometimes it leaves you and there's not a damn thing you can do about it. People and all other animals share a common mortal destiny, but people left behind continue on, remembering and cherishing the departed.

t was time, his time. Cougi was an indoor/outdoor cat, eighteen years old. Like many old-timers, human or cat, he had his share of medical problems: diabetes and incipient kidney failure. A few attempts ensued to prolong his life, renal dialysis, intramuscular shots of insulin, but now he refused to eat and didn't want his usual caresses. We were keeping him indoors during treatment, but he waited patiently by the glass sliding doors of the kitchen, watching birds in the yard, mewing softly when we came near. It didn't take an expert in animal behavior to understand what he wanted.

"Should we let him out? Would he be okay?" Alice asked as she sipped a cup of coffee in the dining room. We had watched Cougi with growing uneasiness for the past two weeks. We had accepted the inevitable—he wasn't going to get younger or better.

"We might not see him again," I said. "He might just disappear and we won't know where he is or what has happened. Cats do that."

"But that's what he seems to want, to go out, to be there. If he is going to die, shouldn't he be able to do it surrounded by the smells of plants and the sounds of his feathered friends?"

I chuckled. Cougi's "feathered friends" were welcome companions indeed, the ever present repast for a hungry predator. He had brought more than one home, depositing a slow sparrow or hapless junco on the back porch. Unlike many cats, he ate most of what he caught. He wouldn't be catching another one. He still twitched and mewed when they flew by or landed on the steps, but he had neither the speed nor the strength to launch an effective attack.

Alice and I had discussed numerous times the issue of death with dignity, the need for self-determination to face the final journey. My mother had passed on the year before and to the end she had insisted on no hospital, no tubes, no strange faces paid to offer false comfort. She wanted to die in the apartment she had spent the last thirty-five years in, surrounded by her books, photographs, and old records. Like Cougi, she didn't eat during the last two days, sipping only some warm chocolate milk. We said our goodbyes and waited. She got her wish and when the day came, actually a week of quiet vigil, she left peacefully.

We made a promise, Alice and I. We would respect each other's wishes when the time came. I fully expected I would be first. Women usually outlast men and I was several years older. She didn't like that, being left behind. Twenty years of marriage will do that and it had been twenty good years, full of love, adventures, and appreciation. "I hope we go at the same time," she would say, "not soon, of course, but when we do, I want us to be together." We never finished the conversation about how or what, leaving the circumstances unspoken and undecided, quietly agreeing that an unanticipated accident would be best.

I was already in my seventies and the specter of death was no longer an academic issue of the remote future. I was still in good health, but I had witnessed enough terminal events of friends and relatives to satisfy me that my mother was right. I wanted to go quietly, my way. What I couldn't decide was whether it should be alone or with family at my side. I entertained romantic visions of marching off into a rainforest, disappearing with only a brief note to my wife and children to say goodbye and to inform them I had "gone to kiss the jaguar." They knew what that meant. A different fantasy had me walking into the surf from a favorite beach and swimming out to sea. I agreed with mother—no hospital, no tubes, no strange faces.

I got up from the table and walked to the glass door. Cougi looked up at me expectantly, a short swish of his tail. I reached down and scratched him behind the ears and he reacted as usual, twisting his head to meet my fingers, behind his ears, under his chin. Alice held onto her cup, trying to be brave but the wetness on her cheek betrayed her. I looked at her once and opened the door.

It was a fine spring morning and Cougi sniffed the air before stepping forward, unhurried, onto the wooden porch, his first outside visit in several days. He walked down the steps and onto the scruffy lawn that bordered the side of our house. Beyond the grass was a broad fringe of overgrown grasses and small bushes that served as a refuge for birds and other small animals. Cougi entered the greenery and briefly disappeared. Alice and I watched him from the door but didn't make an effort to follow.

That evening I walked around the house and found Cougi. He was under the porch, in a dark corner, against the concrete foundation wall. I crawled to him and stroked his head and neck and he licked my hand. He was weaker but still responsive. I went inside and returned with his water dish and some food, just in case. He licked at the water but ignored the food. I talked to him a few minutes, and when my eyes became blurry I went into the house.

Alice was on the couch reading a magazine. She knew what I had been doing. "Do you want to see him?" I asked her. Alice looked up from her magazine and moved her head slowly back and forth.

"I can't…I just can't. Is he okay?"

"He's fine. He lived like a cat and he will go out like a cat, on his terms, where he wants and when he wants. He has water and food. I'll check on him in the morning."

She nodded and went back to her magazine. Tears were running down her cheeks, but I decided to walk away, to leave her with her grief.

I retrieved Cougi the next morning and buried him among the tall grasses and bushes in which he liked to hunt. Alice watched me dig a shallow hole, wrap him in a degradable paper sack, and lower him to his final place. I replaced the dirt, knowing that within a few weeks, weeds would obscure the site. We mumbled a few incoherent words, held each other for several minutes, and walked back to the house arm in arm. Promises fulfilled, promises to keep. Someday, maybe I'll crawl under the porch.

I AM NOT
A WELL-QUALIFIED
BUYER

Some people seem to have all the luck, the Midas touch in all they do. Love and fortune follow them, and they can select the path to happiness and prosperity. Others are less prepared, less qualified to meet the challenges of the game of life.

Visiting my doctor is never fun. I know, it's not supposed to be; it is necessary—something you do because you have no choice, unless you are one of those. Not a hypochondriac, but a medicophil (I made that up), a person crazy in love with the smell of alcohol, the hypodermic's sting, and believing that a grave prognosis is akin to a date for a Saturday night horror movie. You know if you are one. I am not, but I keep having these headaches. Maybe they are migraines, maybe staying up too late, maybe a brain tumor. I don't know, but worse, my doctor doesn't either. He schedules me for MRIs, enzyme studies, EEGs, a neurology consult, sleep studies, and recommends I take two magenta-colored pills each day. I ask him about side effects. They might make you drowsy, he answers. They could upset my stomach, cause diarrhea, stimulate suicidal thoughts, result in an incurable skin disease, increase my risk for seventeen different types of cancer, and give me dry mouth. He says this without a trace of humor. As I said, not a fun guy.

Nodding, I take the written prescription and put it in my shirt pocket. Dry mouth isn't so bad. I tell him a cold highball will cure that. He looks at me curiously, not understanding. He is much younger than me, too young to have graduated from medical school, but a nice looking framed certificate on the wall tells everyone he did. I tell him a highball is a mixed drink, usually whiskey and ginger in my case. I am always happy to help educate the educated. He patiently tells me alcohol will only make dry mouth worse and it may be what is causing my headaches in the first place. Beware: headaches may result in forced sobriety—it would make a great slogan over my bed.

Leaving the office, my old pickup truck awaits me in the far corner of the parking lot. No one wants to park next to it, probably in the belief that years of dirt, rust, and dents are contagious and will infect their shiny luxury sedans and SUVs. It was new when I bought it, eighteen years ago. I was a man then, smoking unfiltered Camels, wearing a *Playboy*-recommended wardrobe, and driving a man's truck, one that would guarantee my macho-ness (don't bother to Google it) for a long time, but apparently not for eighteen years. Can't afford cigarettes and *Playboy* anymore.

My cellphone rings as I open the door and climb behind the wheel. Convenient things, keeping me connected. I can play the stock market, a variety of adult and not-so adult games, book rooms and flights, and stay on top of my social world. I have never flown in my life and I don't need a computer to get the kinds of rooms where I occasionally stay. However, I have two followers on Facebook and my account has only been open for seven months. Maybe this is one of them, and I eagerly answer the call. One reception bar. The voice cuts in and out, and I can't tell if it is my sweet aunt in Cincinnati, my first-ever like, or someone in Myanmar. The line goes dead, and I look at the phone for another minute, wondering if he-she-it will call back. They don't. The phone is smart and it's expensive. Without it I don't have a life. Gotta keep something going for me, right?

My truck starts on the third try, and I rumble out of the lot in a cloud of black smoke. The outside smells like an oil refinery, and the inside smells like last week's lunch gone bad. Probably some of it slipped beneath the seat. I need to fix the muffler and get some tires. A local garage will exchange all of the fluids, give me new wipers, balance and align the wheels, check brakes, even fix the muffler. If I wasn't renting, maybe I could get a third mortgage or find some other collateral. I offered them a credit card, but the bill would have exceeded my credit limit and those sharp-eyed bastards read the expiration date on the card. I let them keep it and drove away in an especially magnificent cloud of oily smoke. Rings, I need rings.

⁍⁌

"No money down, your bad credit is good with us. Come in now and pick out the new vehicle of your dreams." It was the third time in two hours of beer and football that the shouting local announcement blazed across my fifteen-year old television. We'll take anything in trade, they promised, even if you have to push it onto the lot.

What did I have to lose? And I didn't have to push—I drive my red Ford and its omniscient black fog onto the lot and step out to face a young overweight guy in a sport coat and dark shades.

I'm ready to pick up my dream, I inform him, pickup for pickup. I indicate my eighteen-year old companion and he looks at it with a smile. He shakes my hand and tells me I've come to the right place. A slap on the back and we walk down an aisle of new trucks. Crew cabs, electronic marvels, cameras that can tell me when to stop, connectivity to the entire universe, and all of it can be mine. I can get that macho feeling back, even if I no longer smoke. George becomes my best friend as we stroll and shop. He knows what I want and he shows it to me, all of it, the shiny knobs, the central dashboard screen, cruise controls, and the twenty thousand horsepower engine that can conquer Mount Everest. The Corinthian leather and tortoiseshell side panels are also nice touches. I make a subtle humorous reference to wanting some rocket launchers, a la James Bond, for clearing highway congestion. George answers me with a straight face: anything can be arranged for a price. I believe him.

My dream truck is big, black, and beautiful. They must have put twenty-seven coats of wax on it. The chrome gleams like a dentist's mirror and it smells of raw, unabashed newness. No one has ever dumped a chiliburger on the floor, no one has gotten sick in it, and there are no dents or scrapes inside or out. George stands back a step so I can indulge my fantasy, embrace it like an octopus engulfing dinner. All traces of a headache have vanished. I look at my new friend and he smiles, not the big happy-to-see-me smile of greeting, but the quiet encouragement of someone who has entered my soul and sampled my dreams. George leaves the keys in the ignition. He believes in me.

We sit in the office. It isn't large or fancy. The furnishings are modest but comfortable. My chair has a straight back, encouraging me to lean forward and pay attention as George shuffles through some forms and obtains the preliminary information—name, address, etc. I proudly tell him I am connected on social media and bring out my cell phone to provide further evidence. He smiles at that and frowns only slightly when I tell him I rent. I am anxious to hear the total price and what my monthly payments will be. I know I will need to drink more beer and fewer cocktails and probably will only be able to eat two, maybe one, meal a day, but it seems like a small price to pay for a new outlook on life. The truck sits outside George's window, the keys in it, ready to roll. I keep looking over my shoulder at the magnificent vehicle. I am only a few signatures from driving away and becoming an instant sensation in my working class neighborhood.

The next few questions force me to sit up straighter. George is all business as he asks me about collateral, credit scores, bank references, and other financial matters. The bank references are easy—I don't have any. My paychecks are cashed, for a small fee, at the Cash 'N Carry next to the liquor store. But I happily inform George that the owner has known me for more than ten years.

"The owner of the liquor store?" asks George.

"Him too. I've known both for a long time." I sit back and smile.

After George explains what he means by collateral, I realize neither my rare beer can collection nor the promise my sweet aunt had made to leave me a little something when she dies will qualify.

"What about the no money down and no credit needed?" I ask. I didn't have bad credit—I didn't have hardly any credit, which George confirmed when he tried to get a score. I decide not to mention my expired credit card, which I don't have anyway.

"Bad credit is usually better than no credit," he explains. "Any business references at all?"

"No, I'm a dayshift worker at the door assembly plant, owe no one anything." I don't have a savings account, but I used to have a checking account. That was quite some time ago, but better not mention the bouncy checks. I do have a few hundred dollars in penny stocks, which I relate with the hopes it serves as a financial resource. George is not as enthusiastic about it as I am.

"Well," George begins, clearing his throat two times. "You probably couldn't read the small print, most people don't," he laughs, "but the no-money-down actually applies to well-qualified buyers." He pauses and gives me time to let the words register.

I stare at him as if I had met those requirements, but he shakes his head and sadly tells me the only way I can qualify is to demonstrate the ability to meet the monthly payments. He writes the APR on a piece of paper followed by the monthly rate. It reads $687.13. He doesn't say anything, just holds the paper in front of me. My monthly take home is $817.94, enough to live on without the truck purchase, but far short of giving up a meal a day. I stare at him in disbelief for another minute, and he remains silent. He turns off his computer, folds his hands on his chest and sits back, waiting for my next move. The clock behind him says 6:10, and I suspect it is time for him to go home.

I turn once again to look at the truck. The keys are dangling from the ignition. I can't see them but I know they are there. I rise from my chair and mumble something incoherent. I'm not sure what I said, but George seems to understand perfectly. He shakes my hand and tells me he is sorry, sincerely sorry. I walk out onto the lot and get in my red pickup. As I leave the lot in a dark cloud of exhaust, I glance one last time at the black dream truck in the rear view mirror. George is getting in it. I wonder if he is going to drive it home. They do that, you know.

Reaching into my shirt pocket to retrieve a cigarette, I remember there are none. It's been two years since I quit but the habit lingers. Instead, my hand closes around the prescription for the purple pain pills. I decide to stop at the drugstore. I can feel another headache on the horizon and the need for a VO ginger with ice. Maybe someone will call.

THE OMAHA TWO-STEP

Love can show up in strange places and at unexpected times.
Most often, we don't initially recognize it as love. It comes unbidden
but not unwelcome, and only needs to be recognized as a departure from
the usual rough and tumble dance of life.

Henry turns off the television, has a last sip of a beer from a can sitting too long and well past too warm. He looks at the empty can and throws it at the screen, missing it by three feet. He stomps into the bedroom, not waiting until midnight, not caring if it ever comes. Let the whole fucking thing end right now, he mumbles, and crashes onto the bed, not bothering to undress.

It's been that way ever since the divorce. Even a last-minute shot at reconciliation, a hasty phone call to attempt a year-end get-together, fails big time. Has someone new, she says, not bothering to disguise the smug satisfaction in being able to deny him a chance at a comeback. Not that he hasn't tried a few shots—about every six months, but all with the turn down, the quick insincere sorry, the dial tone ringing in his ear. Turning to an office worker he barely knows but suspects isn't popular enough to land a holiday date, he waits for her at a downtown restaurant, sitting with a few cocktails for two hours, but no show. The few friends he could claim have other destinations, other plans that don't include him. Without a party, without a place, the television is his only companion. His last semi-coherent thought is about getting a dog. Within minutes he is snoring, oblivious to the rising din outside his apartment window, the buildup to another New Year's Eve celebration.

CHERYL SITS BEHIND THE WHEEL OF HER '58 CHEVY AT the drive-in, trying to watch a double feature. In her lap is a big tub of popcorn, half finished. An unopened bottle of sparkling wine sits on the floor of the passenger's seat. She is crying, tears flowing freely, unable to focus on the screen. Time for a New Year's Eve toast, even though an hour of the old year remains. She lifts the bottle and unwinds the wire retainer. After a few back and forth tugs, the cork comes out with a loud pop, followed by a gush of warm bubbly that douses her from head to blouse. Her hair is dark and long and now it is stringy and hanging down in front of her face, temporarily covering red eyes and wet cheeks. She takes a swig of the wine and suppresses a shudder. It doesn't go with an earlier soda, but it will have to do.

Looking around she sees only a few cars present in the lot. Most have steamy windows. There must be better places to be tonight, she thinks. She puts down the bottle and removes her wet blouse. Sitting in her bra, she once again tries to concentrate on the film. She glances out the driver's window—no one notices, no one cares. Better things for others to do than pay attention to a sobbing, soaked woman. This is the bottom level, the basement of her loneliness. The only thing that keeps her at the movie is the thought of returning home to an empty, dark apartment.

CHERYL IS IN THE NIGHTCLUB WITH HER FRIEND, A woman her age from work. The two divorcees are watching the band, sharing some casual conversation about men and how disturbing some of them seem to be. Their collective experience with the opposite sex, inside or outside of marriage, has not been exemplary. They start their second round of cocktails and begin to relax to the music. Cheryl's friend Lois is tapping her feet, and her shoulders sway to the country and western beat. Lois is overdressed for the modest bar and dance floor, but Cheryl wears the same unremarkable clothes she wore earlier that day for work. She tries to forget New Year's at the drive-in two weeks earlier.

Henry sits at the bar behind them, watching the crowd and the mating game as guys approach girls, older ladies, occasionally other guys. Some come to the tables just to talk, to dance, to buy a round of drinks, or to convince someone to go somewhere. Your place or mine? Some are married, some are not. Some want to be, some do not. Henry is drinking his third blackjack and Coke, about to embrace the first stage of nightclub courage and lose his usual reticence. That often occurs at about one o'clock, an hour before closing, and by then it is too late to score. He watches the two women in front of him, deciding the one with the blond curly hair and snazzy dress might be a possibility. He might be able to manage a fast dance, but slow ones only highlight his clumsiness. Better yet to talk, buy a drink or two, and convince her to leave with him. The other one, with the long dark hair and somber face, is for some other lonesome fool. Henry prefers blondes.

He puts his glass down and stands up to start his approach, trying to appear casual. Another guy slips in front of him, touches his target on the shoulder. He bends down close to her. She smiles, nods, and walks onto the dance floor with the intruder. Henry is caught between the table and his safety chair at the bar. He looks around quickly but no one seems to be watching. He wants to return to the bar and get another drink, to rethink the tactics of the game. Henry likes games and believes he is a player.

Instead, he walks over to Cheryl and asks her if he can talk to her. She looks up at him and nods ever so slightly, but it is an affirmative. She hasn't refused, hasn't sent him crawling away in humiliation. He smiles and sits down next to her, his hands fumbling under the table. He looks at her and she looks back, neither smiling nor grimacing, but waiting to see what comes next. That's a problem for Henry, especially before one o'clock. What comes next?

"Can I buy you a drink?" he asks, apparently oblivious to the full glass in front of her.

"Not yet, I just started this one," she says, not unkindly but still wary. She looks out at the dance floor and catches the eye of her friend. Her friend smiles back, relieved that someone is talking to her. "Do you dance?" she says hopefully.

"Yeah, sometimes. You know, if it's got a beat and not too slow." He pauses, trying to assess what and how much to tell her. "I need to have a drink or two before I can get out there."

She takes a sip of hers while he catches the attention of a waitress and orders his fourth cocktail. "My name's Cheryl," she says, after the waitress leaves.

"Oh, yeah, uh, hi, Cheryl." He looks at her, but seems distracted, as if he didn't expect to be sitting at her table.

"So, you got a name or is it a big government secret?"

It is hard to tell if she is being mischievous or sarcastic. Her tone is neutral, but Henry decides it is too late to back off and too soon to judge. He recovers quickly. "Uh, sorry, my name is Henry. Some call me Hank, but I still prefer Henry." He starts to hold out his hand, but it seems awkward and he doesn't want to hit her glass, so he quickly puts his hands back under the table. She notices and picks up her glass for another quick sip.

"Henry it is then. What did you order?"

"Jack Daniels. Blackjack and Coke. It's what I usually drink," he says, not sure whether it is cool or not. She appears to be drinking a margarita, but without the salty rim.

The number ends and Lois and her partner come back to the table. They sit down and Lois tells them, "This is Bert. He's a salesman, from out of town." Bert raises his hand to order and gives Cheryl and Henry a big salesman-type smile.

"Howdy," he says.

Cheryl nods and announces, "Henry, this is my friend Lois and, well, Bert the salesman."

Henry looks at Lois and Bert. The salesman is sitting close beside her, like they have known each other much longer than one dance. "I'm Henry," he says, almost apologetically, as if he doesn't belong in their company.

"What do you sell?" Cheryl asks Bert.

"Well pumps and accessories. I travel around a three state area: Nebraska, Iowa, and South Dakota, mostly small towns with family farms." He states this as if reading a script for the umpteenth time, a simple litany that says everything one needs to know about who he is and what he does.

"Fascinating," says Henry, failing to keep the sarcasm out of his voice. "You must meet a lot of interesting people."

He isn't going to forgive Bert for derailing his plans to play for the blonde.

The waitress brings Henry's drink and takes Bert's order, a glass of merlot. What kind of guy drinks merlot in a cheap motel bar while trying to pick up a dame? Henry cannot believe it but says nothing. Lois notices the slight smirk as Henry leans back against his chair and hoists the whiskey in front of him.

Bert immediately takes over the conversation, asking Cheryl and Lois what they do. Insurance clerks, they answer, working for Liberty Mutual. Lived in Omaha all of your lives? No, Lois is from Lincoln and Cheryl is from Council Bluffs, across the river. Really been around the world, huh girls, interjects Henry, trying to be funny. The three of them stare back without comment and Bert begins anew. What is there to do around here, besides drink and dance, he asks the women. Bowling, they answer. We both belong to a bowling league, on a team sponsored by our agency. Oh, you get to wear those cute bowling shirts with the clever logos, teases Bert, leaning toward Lois, arms touching from elbow to wrist. They laugh as Henry finishes half his drink, wondering whether to remain and order another or to leave and cut his losses.

Cheryl looks at her friend's arm lying beside the salesman's. How easy it is for her, she thinks. One dance and fifteen minutes and they are like old friends. She glances at Henry but he is looking behind him at the bar. Someone has taken his previous stool and his options list is now smaller. There is always the front door, but he decides to stick it out, to see what Bert will do. If the salesman takes off somewhere with Lois, well, maybe Cheryl isn't the worst thing that could happen. Better yet, if he decides to go with Cheryl, it would leave Lois alone.

A fast number starts and Henry gulps down the last of his drink. Inspired by the warmth of Mr. Daniels, he turns to Lois and says, "Would you like to try something on the floor?" Oops, he hadn't quite meant for it to sound so crude and their look sobers him a notch. Bert smiles and raises his glass toward Henry, as if giving him a backhanded compliment. Lois quickly takes charge.

"How about Cheryl? She'd probably enjoy it and I'm still catching my breath from the last one." She looks hopefully at her friend, but Cheryl sits stiff and straight, holding her glass as if it were the last lifeline to the Titanic.

"Ah, sure, yeah, how about it Cheryl, would you like to dance?" Henry stands, almost hitting the table and knocking over the drinks in his eagerness to make amends. Bert can contain himself no longer, putting his head in his arms and laughing out loud, shoulders shaking. Lois keeps staring at Cheryl, trying to silently encourage her, to take Henry somewhere, anywhere.

Cheryl puts down her drink and stands. She is almost an inch taller than Henry, something he hadn't realized until that moment. She reaches out, takes his hand, and leads him onto the dance floor without looking back at him or the table.

"Whoa, there's a couple of fun kids," says Bert, facing Lois, one hand on his glass of wine and one hand resting softly on her free hand. She looks at the hand but doesn't withdraw it.

"She's been through a couple of tough times and she's shy. I don't think Henry is going to be any good for her, but it won't hurt to dance. Maybe it'll attract some other guys."

Bert looks at them on the floor. Cheryl seems relaxed but Henry is ungraceful, as if trying to force the rhythm.

"She has a nice figure and she'd be better looking if she did something with her hair. Is she some kind of hippie or what?" He doesn't remark on the contrast between the clothes of the two women, but he checks it off mentally, a practiced element of his salesman training.

Lois looks at Cheryl, nods, and turns back to the salesman. "Yeah, she could probably use a make-over, physically and mentally. I just wish she could find someone who would appreciate her, try to understand her. She's really a great girl—she can be a lotta fun with the right people."

"I'm a lotta fun with the right people. Are you righteous?" Bert's eye contact is direct and intense.

The double meaning doesn't escape Lois and she withdraws her hand to pick up her daiquiri. She sips it slowly, looking down at the table as Bert scans her face, trying to assess her reaction. A disturbance from the back of the room draws everyone's attention. A man is standing up at a corner table, fists clinched and shouting at another guy sitting near him. The bartender starts towards them, but the standing guy waves him away and sits.

"Happens in here all the time, not the greatest or most sophisticated clientele," remarks Lois.

"Present company excluded, I hope," he says with a laugh. Bert sits back in his chair and draws a pack of cigarettes from his pocket. "Okay if I smoke?"

The room's yellowish lights are almost obscured by the thick haze. Lois glances around her and back to Bert. "Would hardly make any difference in here, would it?"

He lights up, offers a cigarette to Lois, she shakes it off, and he takes a long drag, a man completely in control of his situation. Until Henry and Cheryl return. The number isn't over but Henry is panting and Cheryl looks frustrated.

"He almost fell on me," she quietly tells Lois as she sits down and reaches for her drink. It is almost gone and Bert asks her if she would like another. Henry sits and says nothing, hands under the table, head down.

Cheryl looks at Henry, then smiles at Bert. "Sure, lime margarita and no salt." She slides the empty glass to her left.

Henry looks up and sees the waitress approach. "Another Jack and Coke, darlin.'" He tries to brighten the mood and notices that Lois also has an almost empty glass. He points at it but before he can say anything, Bert tells the waitress to bring another daiquiri and merlot.

The salesman pulls out a wallet and lays a fifty on the table. The bulging wallet indicates there is more where that came from. Lois casts an eye toward Cheryl, but she is watching the band. Lois smiles at Bert. "You must be a pretty successful salesman. I'm sure you could afford a better place than this."

"What is a nice, good-looking, prosperous young man doing in a place like this? Sometimes you find gems in unlikely places." He flashes an award-winning, sales-boosting smile at both of the ladies.

Henry starts to respond but thinks better of it. This is not going well at all and the front door is rising among his options for action. He studies Bert, his clothes, his posture, his hands. The salesman's hands are on the table, holding a cigarette, caressing a wine glass, always visible but calm, his fingernails trimmed and clean. Henry looks down at his lap. His nails are broken with traces of embedded dark matter, his hands have callouses from manual labor. No callouses on mister hotshot's hands, probably never did an honest day's work in his life, Henry thinks.

The band plays a medium slow number, a country waltz

or two-step, whatever you prefer. Cheryl looks at Henry, as if willing to give him a chance to redeem himself, but he ignores her and stares at something on the other side of the room. Bert puts his cigarette out, not half-finished, and motions for Lois to join him again on the hardwood floor. She glances once at Henry, puts her hand on Cheryl's arm and tells her she'll see her in a couple of minutes.

As Lois and Bert dance gracefully around the floor in the traditional circular motions, Henry watches them. He clears his throat and looks at Cheryl. "The Omaha two-step, he's got it down to a science, doesn't he?"

"Pardon?" She turns to face him, her elbows on the table, fingers locked in front of her.

"The two-step. Step one, fall all over yourself laughing, buying drinks, showing off with money. Second step, get the bitch in bed and bang her lights out. Simple dance, simple moves." There is no humor in his words or face. His arms are crossed, hugging himself, withdrawing further into another night of darkness.

"At least he has something to show. I don't know where you're from or what you think of Omaha or of Lois and me, but we are not what you think we are. You can take your two-step and…"

"Peace, peace, hell, I'm sorry. I didn't mean to insult you or your friend, I was merely commenting on the mating habits of the out-of-town salesman, a well-known predator in these parts." Henry's hands are raised above his head and for the first time his expression seems soft and contrite. He leans forward as if to cement a pending truce, a cessation of the hostilities he realizes he brought to the table. "Give me a chance to apologize." He pulls out his wallet, not as thick as the salesman's, and places a twenty on the table. "I'll get your drink, if you'll let me."

Cheryl visibly relaxes and leans back. She gives him a slight smile and tells him that would be nice. The waitress brings the round of drinks, and Henry pays for all of them, retrieving an additional ten dollars to cover the charges and tip. He sighs and picks up his whiskey. "I need to start drinking something that lasts longer," he jokes, looking at the other three glasses. Are those any good?" He nods at her margarita.

"Never had one? Really?" She pushes the glass toward him. "Try it."

"I've had tequila, you know, the shot, salt and lemon thing, but never with all the juice." He picks up the glass carefully and takes a dainty sip, makes an exaggerated lip smack, then a second small sip. He pushes the glass back to Cheryl. "Not bad. I'd probably want the salty edge, though."

He laughs for the first time and Cheryl joins him as Bert and Lois return to the table. The fifty is still in front of Bert's chair. The salesman raises an eyebrow at Cheryl and she shrugs, quietly mentioning that Henry covered the round.

"Well thanks, old man," says Bert, holding out his hand, as jovial as ever.

Henry grasps it briefly and mumbles a "my pleasure" but immediately turns his attention back to Cheryl. She sits closer to him and Lois notices the dramatic change in mood. She wonders what has happened during the few minutes she was on the dance floor, but chalks it up to a minor miracle for the social outlook of her friend.

The next hour passes pleasantly as the four talk and consume two more rounds, each time including a margarita for Henry. No one has to work the next day, but Lois and Bert inform the other two that they'll turn in for the night. They leave together. Henry represses further remarks about two-steps. Cheryl asks him if he would like to go bowling some time.

"Haven't done that since I was a kid," he says. "But if I can try a new drink, I can guess I can try to hit some pins with a three-holed ball." He looks at her hopefully, a bit drunk but finally relaxed.

"At least you know the ball has three holes. It's a start." She is smiling and Henry finds that she is a lot better looking than he first thought, possibly more attractive than her friend. And, it's one o'clock. He won't be too late tonight, even if they don't do the two-step. There is always the Omaha tango, a more demanding and complex dance, but one that speaks of exotic encounters and lingering romance.

RECEPTION

Does it taste like a fine pinot from the Willamette Valley? No, it tastes like recycled pulp fiction from the 1950s, complete with a got'cha punch line. So it goes. I love this stuff.

He stood straight and tall, official and competent, the stereotypical icon of the public relations professional.

"This is why selection is critical. We have not found a way to eliminate or lessen the recovery time. Doctor Stanfield will be committed to the designated time for about six hours. By necessity, we are also committed to the same interval."

The speaker glanced about the room for the next question. A hand shot up to his right, and a young woman rose.

"If the historical record is missing or unclear, such as in the current venture, doesn't that represent a significant and unnecessary risk?" Her manner was smooth and assertive. She had been present at the first departure, armed with the same questions, the same skepticism. An unmistakable challenge flashed in her eyes as they met his.

"Miss Dardean, welcome back…uh, I think." Shifting chairs and a low murmur of laughter rose from the audience. "As I remember, you raised similar doubts about the last trip and yet your televid report pronounced the mission 'a remarkable achievement and a resounding success.' Am I quoting you correctly?" he asked with a boyish, near flirtatious, smile perfected from years of practice interacting with the press.

She answered without hesitation, "Mr. Trudeau, my congratulations on your memory. If mine serves me as well, preparations by your corporation for the last voyage engaged a staff of several hundred researchers for the better part of a decade. There was little left to chance and we were assured that…"

"That is correct," he interrupted, turning toward the center of the group and shifting his voice into a professorial baritone. "Transtemporal Limited has consistently promoted the view that the first trip was to function as a confirmation of theoretical calculations and to prepare the way for the expedition we are launching today."

She was still standing, shifting slightly to one foot, her arms folded across her chest. One hand clutched an electronic clipboard. "That first destination was a well-documented minor event in the recent past. There were no unknown hazards. My questions then concerned the acknowledged unknowns of introducing a new technology."

"And your point is?" he asked without attempting to hide his irritation. She showed no sign of yielding the floor.

"My point is that your research staff knew exactly when and where to target the visit because records were precise and verifiable. There were no surprises and…" she paused to look around at the other media representatives, "…so there were no unexpected consequences. Only the application of the technology had to be determined. Your present operation, by your own admission, is visiting a time and place in which events are poorly understood, especially by *your* staff. I have expressed my concern with your corporation's itinerary a number of times. My research on this period indicates that…"

"Your research is not relevant to the current project," he interrupted in a commanding voice and paused. He continued in a controlled tone, "We've heard this before, Miss Dardean."

Putting an icy emphasis on her name, no one present misunderstood his tone of dismissal. Her face was frozen as she slowly took her seat amidst a sea of murmurs and nodding heads. The other members of the media exchanged comments about the anticipated demonstration while others voiced hushed approvals of Trudeau's skill in dealing with disruptions.

Trudeau recovered his public relations facade and nodded in apparent agreement, visibly relaxed. "Miss Dardean is correct in that we lack a few details about the actual event that occurred at the proposed target. But *that* is the very reason for selecting this particular destination. We *do* know an event took place and it was apparently associated with a major breakthrough in energy production. We can only speculate on the reasons why this discovery and other events related to it were systematically erased from historical records of that time and later."

Dardean coughed, but Trudeau continued, "I don't have to reiterate the expense involved. All of you have copies of the financial statements, and our engineers have already briefed you on the amount of energy consumption required for each trip. The costs in resources are staggering, even for an institute as large as this one." He smiled again, letting the implications settle with his audience. "We are forced to leverage our research by finding answers that could impact further energy acquisition and exploitation. The past may have clues to events or discoveries that will directly benefit our current research as well as provide new—or old—energy resources for all of society."

"Mainly for the benefit of Transtemporal and their shareholders," interjected Dardean.

"Miss Dardean, in spite of your press credentials, you are rapidly assuming the status of persona non grata. Do I make myself clear?"

"Perfectly, Mr. Trudeau," she replied in a resigned monotone.

Another hand went up, this time from an older man seated in front.

"Yes, Arnie?" acknowledged Trudeau, returning to friendlier faces.

"Has any progress been made on isolating the observation crew from the traveler? Will we still be in direct contact with Stanfield when he arrives at the target?"

"Good question, Arnie." Once again the speaker stiffened and assumed an authoritative posture. "A few of you weren't with us last time, and therefore the relationship between us and the traveler…uh, Doctor Stanfield, will seem strange at first. Think of it as a series of bubbles. We will be in the observation lab and it, along with the rest of our world, is one bubble, existing in a moment of time, our present. The target destination will be another bubble of time. Between these two bubbles—and the only link between them—is Dr. Stanfield's bubble. His bubble contacts the surface of the two bubbles representing separate times and places. Through his link we, that is our world, contacts and shares the environment of the targeted time and place. We generate his linking bubble, and we must maintain it as a stable connection for several hours. Our observation target is unaware of our connection and cannot be affected by us. However, within the lab and within our linking bubble, we receive and enjoy all of the energy-based sensory modalities of their world, including light and dark, the effects of warm or cold weather, and we hear the sounds in their environment, as if we had a microphone present. In short, we share anything that represents a transfer of energy."

"Isn't that also the reason why all of us have been immunized against infectious diseases of that era?" asked another reporter.

"No, we don't believe that matter, even individual molecules, penetrates the bubble barriers. That is why we can't detect odors or taste anything—these senses require molecular contacts. So we will be entirely safe from biological organisms, but the Public Health Commission insisted on these precautions and we weren't in a political position to argue with them."

"Is that also why we can't actually collect anything solid from the past, like artifacts or treasure?" asked one of the new reporters from the back.

Trudeau smiled, as he always did when that question arose. "Yes, we cannot extract anything from the past. We can only observe in a passive manner. For example, we can see and hear, but we cannot touch anything and that is just as well because no one has solved the so-called time paradox."

The speaker looked around at the audience but there were no questions. Almost everyone had heard of the time paradox, the idea that a time traveler from the future might disrupt that future if he or she changed something in the past. The classic example, often cited, involved a person going into the past and shooting his father before he was conceived. No one knew what the consequences of tampering with the past would be, but the current technology didn't permit it so it remained a game for party time philosophers. The triple bubble technology, as the press had dubbed it, was more like a remote video camera than the usual concept of physical time travel.

"We are ready to enter the lab," Trudeau declared. "Please assume your assigned seats. The bubbles have aligned and we will be ready to make connection within about an hour. All events during the next six hours will be continuously recorded and made available to you in a variety of formats, so you can sit back and enjoy the show. Refreshments and bathroom facilities are available within the laboratory." He smiled again and led them into the small amphitheater attached to the lab.

A large wrap-around screen dominated two-thirds of the circular room, facing several rows of high-backed cushioned chairs. An electronic banner above the screen was divided vertically into three panels. The top panel displayed the current time and the elapsed time for bubble connection. A second panel displayed the date and time for the target location. The final panel displayed the target site's geographical location in latitude, longitude, and elevation.

The audience quickly settled in, and Trudeau turned to face the reporters. All but one seat was filled. Puzzled, he looked down at the seating chart in front of him. Dardean. She hadn't entered the room with the others. He looked back at the exit. It was already sealed and wouldn't be opened until six hours from now. It was her loss and good riddance, he thought, turning back to the screen.

The panels flashed information as the main viewing screen displayed an urban industrial setting.

PANEL A: CURRENT TIME AND DATE
    Time: 0943 PST   Date: 05 January 2067
    Elapsed Time: 01:17:51 Counting

PANEL B: TARGET TIME AND DATE
    Time: 0600 Local   Date: 06 August 1945

PANEL C: TARGET LOCATION AND IDENTITY
    Lat: 34.385203°N   Long: 132.455293°E
    Elevation: 331 meters, AMSL
    Identification: Hiroshima, Empire of Japan

Tamara Dardean finished the final draft of her report and closed the transmission cover to send it to her news service. She was sitting in a subterranean restaurant located twenty miles from Transtemporal Limited. She picked at her salad and sipped on a glass of Chenin Blanc.

Too bad about the institute, she thought, *I might have even enjoyed working for Transtemporal.* Her double doctorate in media communications and twentieth century history would have been a good match for their research department. Although she regretted the destruction of the institute, the nearby town, and the loss of several press colleagues, her conscience was clear. Despite repeated warnings both public and private, they had ignored her. She wasn't sure what had happened in the target place on that date, but it must have been significant. Most of the twentieth century was well documented, in writing, in photographs, films, and monuments. Oddly, all traces of this specific time and place, contemporary or retroactive, were missing, as if someone or something had deliberately excised a piece of the past. She was one of the few researchers that not only found it intriguing but alarming.

Unfortunately, she had to miss the historical period she had spent so much of her life trying to investigate. It would have been a window to the past, a rare chance to view history in the making. The thunderous sound, blinding light and massive shockwaves from Transtemporal Limited an hour after her departure provided a possible explanation for why the event had been systematically kept secret. The reception in the laboratory must have been brilliant.

HEALTH FAIR

Love your self, body, and mind, reads the first commandment of survival and self-preservation. Sometimes we need a little help with that.

feel good. Not great, not outstanding or exceptional, but a solid, respectable good. The kind of good that reminds me life is all right and I am doing better than I have a reasonable right to expect. I'm neither shy nor modest about my expectations. My wife will verify that in a New York-minute. She has lived with my impatience, my ambition, and my occasional scams for seventeen years. At fifty-eight and a few months, I have ventured well into middle-age land but I'm still a few miles and a few years short from being one of those. You know, one of those AARP seniors, the modern maturity set, the are-you-ready-to-consider-early-retirement folk with white hair, crappy skin, and arthritic pains that mark you as a downhill slider, never again to reach the summit of prowess and potential. No, I'm not there yet and I feel good.

Jennifer suggested we stop in at the local hospital health fair, an annual event in our community. I am initially bemused. I had my semiannual checkup four years ago and everything was close to normal. I'm not taking any medications, unless you count an occasional aspirin or vitamin pill. I can still do a couple of pushups, when I'm in the mood, touch my toes, and run out to the mailbox for the morning paper. Not bad, right? Besides, I am all too familiar with much of the medical economics game. I spent some time in medical administration, and I know first hand about the pressure on doctors to order unnecessary laboratory tests and medical imaging studies. The pharmaceutical economy is a scam and scandal of enormous proportions, and I don't want any part of it. To paraphrase a well-traveled blues song, the very thing that makes them rich makes me poor.

But Jennifer wants to check her blood pressure, cholesterol, and talk to someone about mammograms, pap smears, and other female stuff, so I say okay, I'll go with her, hold the hand of my forty-two year old wife and give her the reassurance my marriage contract said I would. She tries to convince me our age difference means there is a shadow, albeit a very small one, that creates some concern for her about my health and survivability. She doesn't exactly put it in those words, but I know what she is thinking about and so I tell her I will also let them run a few simple tests on me. Reassurance and comradeship, that's all.

The fair is being held in the high school gymnasium, and it is packed with exhibitors and health-conscious visitors. A number of the stations consist of tables and chairs where blood can be drawn for simple blood tests. Nurses and nursing assistants, some from the local college, are present at other stations to take vital signs or conduct surveys on everything from diet and nutrition to lifestyle choices and family history. Other booths and tables are more commercial in nature, offering various health plans, air evacuation and emergency response services, or representing recreational activities, such as hiking clubs, tai chi, and weight loss groups. Support groups for people with various diseases are also well represented. Anyone want to join the prostate club?

We check in at the door, pick up tote bags to carry give-aways and brochures and start down the first aisle. I walk with the confidence of a man who should be somewhere else. But Jennifer needs this and I need her, so I smile and we stop at the first table on our right: weight and body mass.

We sign a list with our names and email address and step up to be weighed and measured. Jennifer is in the green BMI zone, good weight for her height and age. She has always sported a good figure and her numbers are right where they should be. I am in the yellow zone—overweight but not obese. A few inches too much around the middle, jokes the young woman with the tape measure. Jennifer nods in agreement.

Hey, I'm not obese. Just need to work it off, maybe a beer or two less a week, I tell her. Nothing to worry about, I feel great. More of me to love. Healthy for men my age. A sign of prosperity, according to nineteenth century standards. Jennifer's look tells me I have said enough.

The blood pressure station is next. Jennifer sits down first and extends her arm. The young woman smiles at her, writes down her name on a sheet, and places the cuff around her left arm. It is an old-fashioned device that requires a stethoscope to listen for changes in arterial pulse.

It might be a bit high, Jennifer tells her. I tend to worry about things and I sometimes feel like I have pressure in my head.

We'll see, the girl responds and quickly pumps it up. She releases the pressure as she listens. When the cuff deflates completely, she looks up at my wife, smiles again, removes the cuff and writes down the numbers.

Very good, 124 over 74, right where you want it to be. She hands a card with the measurements on it to Jennifer. Jennifer stands and walks behind the chair as I take her place.

No problem here, I think, and extend my arm. She repeats the procedure, writing down my name and inflating the cuff. After it deflates, she looks up at me and asks me if she can repeat it, just to be sure. I agree, recognizing she is young and probably still learning to take pressure readings. After the second reading, she removes the cuff and writes down the numbers on a card and hands it to me.

She looks into my eyes and asks me, Mr. Bradshaw, how long have you had an elevated blood pressure?

Elevated? There must be some mistake. I've never had an elevated pressure, I tell her. I read the card: 154/98.

Her eyes don't leave mine, as if she is searching for signs of a false declaration. Umm, well, it's elevated now. When you are finished with the vital signs section, you might want to talk to one of the health advisors over in the far corner. She points to the far right section of the gym, between the basketball net and bleachers.

I stand and thank her. Has to be a mistake, but I don't want to make a scene or embarrass her, so I'll just let it go. Jennifer, however, remains there with her hands folded in front, that age-old posture that says I'm not satisfied and you have some explaining to do.

What was it? She asks, blocking the aisle.

Just a bit elevated, high normal, you know, I answer, trying to step past her. Probably from the excitement of all of these medical people around. Besides, she was a very attractive...

What was it? A little more determined, that voice and stance.

I kiss her on the forehead. On to the next station, love, it's all good. And your b.p., by the way, is great. I say it like she has just won an award at the county fair for the best marmalade.

Still not appeased is my love, but we walk hand-in-hand to the next station: pulse and temperature. Another young woman, not quite as attractive, but eager to do her part. There are two chairs and we sit. She takes our temperature from behind our ears and quickly reads our pulse. Two more cards with our results—Jennifer and I are boringly normal. I show her my card with I-told-you-so smugness. See, I tell her, no problems.

Your pulse is just a bit high, but not bad, my wife says as we walk toward the next examining area.

Yeah, she wasn't quite as exciting as the first one, I remark, ever the light-hearted one. Jennifer is used to these kinds of comments. She knows I look and assess, but never act on the information. She is safe because I am not inclined to wander, only wonder. I tell her it keeps me young and isn't that what she really wants? She agrees and indulges me, her old man.

The first exam result is now forgotten as we sit down for the cardiac and respiratory evaluations. A woman, probably in her late thirties, is in charge and I see on her name tag that she is a nurse practitioner. No mistakes here, I think, now we have some people who have the experience to pro-vide the right results. I sit straight and loosen my shirt so she can listen to my chest. Jennifer sits behind a modesty curtain, but I am out there for all of the world, or at least the gymnasium, to view and appreciate. It's not an Adonis body, but it's reasonable for the wear and tear it has received.

She listens and moves the cup around to different parts of my chest. Behind me, she listens to my lungs as I take in several deep breathes. She steps back in front of me and fills out another card. Before handing it to me, she asks if I am under the care of a physician. My first reaction is that this is a rare example of medical humor, a bit of fun in a non-critical care environment. She probably says that to all the middle-aged men, just to get a rise, to break the monotony of doing the same task hundreds of times in a single day. But, there is no smile, no indication this is a bit of harmless banter.

What? I say. I can't think of anything more astute or medical. I'm suddenly aware my shoulders have sagged forward, my mouth is open, and I must look like an idiot. I straighten up and tuck in my shirt.

Mr. Bradshaw, I can detect a slight murmur in your heart. Nothing to be alarmed about, but I think you should follow up on it. You can actually get an EKG here and now and we can forward that to your physician. The EKG is at station 18. Oh, and your lungs sound fine. She hands me a card. On it she has stamped "EKG" and initialed it. She remarks they don't do this for everyone, but if they find something out of the ordinary, they like to follow up now because they know some people just don't get around to it. She smiles, finally, as if she knows I am one of those pro-crastinators who last visited a doctor four years ago.

I thank her and stand up as Jennifer comes out from behind the curtain, beaming as if she has won another marmalade award.

How's it going, big boy? She asks, putting her arm through mine. Ready for the next station?

I look up the aisle and see the banner that announces Laboratory Testing. Good, I think, maybe Jennifer's cholesterol will be higher than mine. We walk to a table, sign in, and take seats to wait for blood drawing. Jennifer goes first and I see it is done from a capillary finger prick, just a few drops. This is for hemoglobin, glucose, and cholesterol.

I'm pretty sure the first two will be normal for both of us, but Jennifer is passionate about enchiladas and anything with sour cream, so there is hope. No, I don't want her to be really abnormal, but just a bit higher than mine. I don't mention the EKG or the health consultation yet. Maybe I won't need to.

I'm called and sit down in front of a young guy. His nametag indicates he is a clinical laboratory technician and he is employed by the hospital. He asks me if I am fasting, and I tell him no, I ate two hours earlier. Perfect, he says, and notes it on a card. He chooses one of my offered fingers, sticks it, and draws a few drops of blood into a thin glass tube. He hands me a cotton ball and tells me to come back in thirty minutes to get the results.

Jennifer and I have finished most of the physical exams. One left to go, respiratory function. We sit down, blow into a plastic bag, and they measure our lung capacity. Jennifer watches mine and hears the respiratory tech pronounce my result as good, for my age. I look up at her, but this time with relief rather than smugness. I seem to have lost some of my self-assurance during the rounds in the gymnasium, and I still have the follow-ups to face. I'm desperately trying to concoct a way to finish my health check without Jennifer knowing.

The rest of the exhibits are informational or sales efforts: products, organizations, and community activities to promote a healthy lifestyle. We stroll, stop, talk, and pick up pens, pins, pamphlets, and other promotional items. Thirty minutes have gone by and it's time to get our lab results. I look forward to this moment, the chance to even the playing field, the opportunity to justify my older but just-as-healthy standing in the family.

We present our cards and a lab clerk writes down our respective results. We thank her and step back to compare numbers. We each have normal hemoglobin values, hers a bit lower as a woman, but both of us well within the expected range. Her glucose is 133, normal for two hours after eating. Mine is 159. Not dangerously elevated, but a bit higher than one wants to see. The lab's normal values are printed next to each result. Her cholesterol is 192. One ninety-two! How can that be? She is not overweight and she is moderately active, but all that sour cream and those other hearty lipid-heavy meals. One ninety-two? I look at mine: 268! I can't believe this. Did they switch our blood samples? Four years ago, my cholesterol was in the low 200s. My diet hasn't changed dramatically, so what gives? One advantage occurs from this result. Jennifer sees it and doesn't say much, but her furrowed brow and lack of overt amusement tells me I now have a perfect excuse to see the health consultant.

It'll only take a few minutes, I tell her, and I can ask her about diet and some other things. My sweet wife immediately agrees and tells me she wants to go back to one of the booths and talk to someone about mammograms and ultrasound procedures for diagnosing breast cancer. Her mother had breast cancer and it is a continuing subject of concern for Jennifer. I tell her I will meet her back at the entrance in about twenty minutes, longer if I have to wait to talk with someone. We part and I go directly to Station 18, looking back to make sure she isn't watching. She isn't.

A man about my age takes my card with the bright red EKG stamp (I wish they would use a more soothing color, green, or blue) and motions me to a table behind a curtain. He asks me a few questions—my name, physician's name, some history about any chest pains, family heart history, any recent illnesses. I remove my shirt and he spots me with a cold (sorry for that) jelly and attaches the EKG leads. This is only a preliminary EKG, he tells me. They might need to follow up with a more complete and accurate one as well as a stress test. I smile at him and tell him, no problem, I was already beginning to feel some stress. I glance at my watch. Ten minutes gone already. I have to hope Jennifer doesn't come looking for me.

The test is completed in another five minutes and I am on my way with a note and caution to follow up with my physician. Nothing to be alarmed about, he says, but do follow up. No alarm here, I think, as the ringing bells sing loudly and persistently while I make my way to the consulting area. Twenty minutes, but at least I am where I said I would be so if Jennifer finds me, no problem. I try to relax as I wait my turn to talk with one of the two people behind desks engaged in conversations with others.

One of the attendees having a consultation is a woman who looks to be in her seventies. Probably a lot of problems there, might take some time. I'm in good shape, nothing to worry about, as I attempt unsuccessfully to drown out the clanging bells. The other "patient" is a young, very pregnant woman. She gets up first and the woman behind the desk signals me to approach. Another nurse practitioner. I give her my cards and she turns to a computer screen. I can see my name and the results of the day's visit are posted and she is looking these over carefully.

Mr. Bradshaw, I see your last visit to a doctor was four years ago. Is this the usual schedule you keep with regard to medical exams? She says this with a somber expression of disapproval, as if I have violated a community code of ethics or had displayed reckless disregard for others. I have never driven while intoxicated, and I've never refused vaccinations for infectious diseases.

I'm in perfect…well, near perfect health, I tell her. No need to overtax the health care system if nothing's wrong, right? I look at her, hoping to get an indication she appreciates my clever word play. She doesn't.

Mr. Bradshaw, your blood pressure indicates you are borderline hypertensive, you are overweight, and your cholesterol tells us you may be a good candidate for statins. Before I can defend or interrupt, she pushes on, hitting me with my biggest vulnerability. And, I see that you have a heart murmur and an abnormal electrocardiogram. Do you understand what I am telling you?

Yes I do. I used to be a hospital administrator—an assistant director in personnel. I am sadly mistaken in thinking this pronouncement will establish a sympathetic bond between us.

She isn't being hostile, but she isn't sugar and spice either. Not my expectations of tender loving care. I feel trapped and unprepared for the attack. Not the unanticipated results in themselves, but the sudden and vicious assault on my well-being and on the confidence I felt when I entered the gymnasium. Doesn't anyone understand? I am here to counter the slight paranoia of my wife. This is for her sake, damn it, not mine. I am only an innocent bystander, a passive onlooker who can smile and nod towards the other attendees. Aspirin and an occasional vitamin pill, that's me.

My hands are folded in my lap as I answer her. I'll follow up with Doctor Hargrove. I'll make an appointment this week.

Good. That's the right thing to do, Mr. Bradshaw. She writes a few things on the computer, hits a button, and hands me the print out. Take these with you when you see him. Good luck and good health, Mr. Bradshaw. Finally, a smile as she folds her hands in front of her. It is, however, the condescending smile of someone who has indulged a lesser creature, permitting them a courtesy they likely did not deserve. She offers one last bit of professional courtesy. Any questions I can answer for you?

No, I'm all set. Thank you, I mumble mechanically, the appropriate thing to say at the moment, nearly drowned out by the bells and sirens. I walk away from the consulting area to reunite with Jennifer, my sweet and healthy wife, waiting at the entrance.

As we walk out the door, the health fair banner hangs above and across the triple gymnasium doors. It's not fair at all. I feel a lot less healthy than when I entered.

DOOR-TO-DOOR

Love doesn't always involve intimates, present or proposed. Sometimes it represents a less substantial target—a vague, generalized appreciation for the liberty and integrity of others. More important, it requires the same regard for oneself.

Never again. Never will I put myself through that kind of crap for twice the money. The ad looked promising, especially to someone who had just left a minimum wage factory job with bleeding hands and an aching back. This one required slacks, coat and tie, but I could do that. And, as I was only too well aware, there weren't a lot of other options at the moment.

MONDAY, DAY ONE: THE INTERVIEW

It was hot as hell outside, a typical Sacramento midsummer day. The fans and air conditioning blasted cold air in the small hotel conference room, providing momentary relief. White shirts, thin ties, and cheap suits sat around the polished table. I couldn't afford a suit, but I had an off-the-rack sport jacket and the requisite, sixties-fashionable, thin tie. Dressed for success, I told myself. Not yet eighteen and fresh out of high school, I was the youngest in the room. There were others in their late teens and early twenties, all looking for a job, all needing money and some sense of validation. We were all respondents to the newspaper ad for "educational consultants."

There were seven newbies among us. They had never sold anything, not even a newspaper. Two others, a bit older, had tried other sales gigs. One sold appliances at Sears and the other spent a few months on a used car lot. Neither had been successful. That will all change, we were told, because we have the products and we have the methods. Do what we say and you'll be pulling down all the money you will ever want or need. I didn't believe it for one minute, and I'm pretty sure that none of the other prospective trainees bought it either, but the ad promised us two weeks' salary if we qualified to work for Global Book Encyclopedias. Wear a coat and tie, show up for an interview, and be prepared to be amazed. Well, two out of three ain't bad. Now my task was to convince them to take me on, to at least give me the two weeks' salary I badly needed.

Global Book was represented by Mister Stewart (just call me Dave), the District Sales Manager. He was the local boss and would make the hiring decisions. Three of his employees, each a field manager, sat on either side of him, across the table from the would-be trainees. Coffee and doughnuts were available for everyone. We would have preferred bourbon, laughed good old Dave, but that's for after you bring in some contracts. He looked at me and a couple of the others. Probably would have to settle for sodas for some of you, he said. They all got a big laugh out of this.

Now it was time for the interview, a group process with the four of them asking us questions, sometimes confronting us as a group, at other times four-on-one. It was a freewheeling session, between slurps of coffee and mouthfuls of Crispy Cremes. We began to relax and I was feeling encouraged about the chances of being picked. They asked us about our attitudes and abilities to meet people, to project ourselves as trustworthy and serious educational consultants. Dave made each of us introduce himself, talk directly to him in a relaxed, confident manner. The other three nodded in agreement as we talked, except once. The former used car salesman stumbled and mumbled and couldn't meet Dave's piercing glance. Even with smiles and encouragement, he couldn't deliver a simple introduction. I finished three years of drama in high school, a talker. Role-playing came easy. It was a game and it didn't take me long to figure out the rules.

We described our hobbies, a favorite pet, and what we had studied in school. A few of the guys had gone to college—one had graduated with a degree in English. When I mentioned drama and my experience in several plays, one of the field managers said I should do well. Dave gave us a brief summary of Global, their mission to provide everyone with educational resources in their own home, and why owning an affordable set of encyclopedias should be the goal of every parent's aspirations for their children. We nodded in agreement. Anything for two weeks' employment.

The meeting started at nine and the "interview" ended at eleven. Time for a whiz break, Dave said and stood, pointing down the hall toward the restrooms. He asked us to wait in chairs outside of the conference room as they made a decision on each of us. At eleven fifteen, we were sitting, talking about the interview and what we thought our chances were. Some were relaxed, others clearly not. I was somewhere in between, hopeful but not confident. The conference room door opened, and Glen, one of the field managers, called the former appliance salesman to enter. He did and the door closed. Two minutes later, he stepped out, smiled at us, and said he would see us later that afternoon.

Glen called one of the others, a guy about nineteen who seemed friendly and eager to work for Global Book. Only a couple of minutes passed before he also stepped out and told us he would return after lunch. Good luck, he told us with a cheerful smile, and walked down the hall. Glen pointed to the used car salesman, smiled, and said he was next up at bat. It was four minutes before he exited and there was no smile, no words. He put his hands in his pockets and shuffled quickly down the hallway, head low. Glen looked at me and said it was my turn.

Up to then, I had relaxed, thinking that perhaps all of us would make the team, but the departure of the car guy sucked that out of me. I was short on job prospects and had no way to pay for college. Hanging around with my friends all summer, trying to score with the girls at the drive-ins and find another party somewhere, was no longer an objective. I knew I was the youngest and least experienced and the most expendable. I followed Glen into the room and sat down opposite the four of them. Just me on my side of the highly polished table.

William, Dave began or can I call you Bill or Willy? I told him Willy was okay, although adults in my family had always used my formal name. Willy, we'd like to have you be part of our team. Do you want to be successful and to fill an important role in bringing education to the homes in our community? Dave sat back after making a sweeping gesture with outstretched arms, embracing our community.

Yes sir, I assured him. Good, he replied. But, it will mean sacrifice, hard work, and persistence. Not everyone immediately sees the value of an educational consultant. You will need to convince them they need you. You need to convince yourself they need you. Now, before we let you go to lunch, any questions?

I had thought of a couple while we were waiting. I was curious about the lack of women, either among the trainees or among the employees. I asked him. Dave smiled (always a big face-splitting grin, as if he was getting ready to swallow something huge) and told me there are females working at the corporate headquarters, but that fieldwork was left to the men. You'll understand in a few days, he said with a conspiratorial wink. Are there other field consultants? I asked. Oh, yes, you'll meet them later this week. We will assign each of you to field teams, and there will be successful consultants to help guide you and give you tips towards your success.

I thanked him, we stood, and he shook my hand, telling me he would see me at one thirty to begin our training. I walked out the door and gave a friendly nod to the others waiting, then strolled down the hallway as if I had just taken a bow after the third act.

THE TRAINEES, AS WE ARE NOW CALLED, HAVE BEEN reduced from nine to five. We sit in the conference room facing a portable screen. Behind us is a slide projector. In front of us are glasses of water and tablets with pencils. We sit for the best part of four hours as Dave, and occasionally one of the field managers, lectures on GBE, as we now refer to the company. They present the GBE proud history and current market breadth. Statistics and colored graphs fly by. From time to time we are given handouts so we don't have to write down a lot of boring numbers. Dave is still swallowing big things.

After a twenty-minute break to stretch and take care of other urgent business, we learn about the job itself, our role in providing education to the masses and how we go about the daily business of consultation. We are each assigned to one of the field managers. Ricky, one of the other younger hopefuls, and I will be with Glen. I like Glen. He dresses well, talks intelligently, and seems to take his job seriously. I feel like I could do worse.

We are told each day starts at nine thirty in the same conference room. This will only last for two weeks, the time of our training period. We will continue to discuss consulting techniques and meet for inspirational sessions. For example, each morning, we will celebrate the consultants who have successfully placed encyclopedias in homes the previous day. There is nothing like success to stimulate more success—your success, he emphasizes, making sure we understand. We do.

And what about the salary, asks Ricky. I'm glad he asked. I haven't gone to lunch because I have only a dollar in my pocket. I would save that for a soda later. Oh yes, your trainee salary. Good question, Ricky. Dave with the big gestures and big smile paces the table in front of us, looks down at his feet as he passes by each of us. We will all receive our pay at the end of the two weeks, with two conditions. First, we must stick it out for two weeks. No quitters, he says. Quitters don't get paid. At the end of today we will each sign a trainee contract indicating we understand this. The second condition? Each trainee will need to produce a signed contract with a client for an encyclopedia placement.

The contract will be subject to verification by corporate headquarters. But, guess what? Not only will the contract validate our trainee payment, but we will also receive a fifty dollar placement commission, for that one and for every other one we write. Can't expect you guys to do all that work for nothing, can we? Big grin, almost a laugh.

This is the first mention of an actual commission payment. The word "sales" has not been mentioned at all, but now Dave tells us we are not salesmen. In fact, nobody is selling anyone anything. If we were selling them, the encyclopedias would actually sell themselves, they are so valuable and well produced. They are beauties, aren't they? Knowing smiles and nods of approval from the field managers. Dave has example volumes for us to look at. He also has a presentation board, a flat that displays the spines of all thirty volumes in the set. The bindings are handsome, important looking.

At first, I am puzzled, then troubled, by the conditions. The two-week thing I get, it is a reasonable requirement that we complete the training. We are provided with daily transportation and also lunch. Morning meeting, lunch, then out to the field, each day until the training period is finished. After that, no free lunches (big smile), but the field managers and their team will still gather each day at one to select a new suburban area to visit for placements. Be prepared to work evenings, sometimes until after dark, he warns us. Successful consultants can write five or six contracts a week. Actually, there is no limit on what you can do. He leaves it to us to figure out what fifty dollars times a number of contracts will buy us in 1960.

Before leaving, Dave pulls out five briefcases and gives one (lends one, he corrects) to each of us. In each briefcase there is a sample volume and a flat of the spines to show to our prospective clients. There are also tablets and printed contracts, as well as some additional handouts with advice for the field consultants. We are told to study the materials and to return prepared, prepared for success. Now I have something to show my mother and my friends, tangible evidence I have a job. From a dollar in my pocket and a cheap sports coat to a leather briefcase. I leave the conference room with a slight swagger, anxious for the next day.

TUESDAY, DAY TWO: TRAINING

THE NEXT DAY I LEARN A NEW WORD, AT LEAST NEW FOR me and in a new context. Dave tells us it is the most important word we will use with regards to our careers. The word is "close." Not close as in nearby or close as in shut the door behind you, but close as in don't leave anyone's house without a signed placement contract. This is called writing, as in presenting the contract and getting the head of the house, the financially responsible member, to sign it. When the consultant signs it and puts it safely in the briefcase, the deal is closed and the contract is written. Dave holds up a crisp fifty-dollar bill. "Understand?" he asks, looking in turn at each of us to acknowledge that we see and understand the obvious.

A lot of questions follow, about what if they won't sign a contract (then they don't receive the benefits of our educational products), what if the contract falls through at corporate headquarters (then you, that is the consultant who wrote the contract, don't get the paper with the picture of U.S. Grant on it), et cetera. During this time I finally realize this is very much like selling, like being a salesman selling books at people's houses. Vacuum cleaner salesmen come to mind and I remember my dad's advice about never opening or even answering the door when the man on the porch has a briefcase or a vacuum cleaner in hand. For the first time, I understand that "educational consultant" equals door-to-door salesman. I raise my hand and provide my new insight for the benefit of the room.

No, no, no, we are not selling books. Didn't you read the contract and the materials in your briefcase? Can anyone tell Willy here why we aren't selling books? The field managers say nothing and finally one of the other trainees speaks out, looking back and forth at me and at Dave, who smiles encouragingly. The answer is delivered in a monotone, a statement that invites neither refutation nor further questioning. We are placing educational products in homes. The contract specifies that the first volume is delivered free and that subsequent volumes are available at a very low monthly fee, mostly to cover handling and mailing costs. After the fifth volume is paid for, Global Books will provide a handsome wood bookcase in which to proudly display the set in the client's living room. The contract never mentions a purchase price or total amount, only the monthly service fee for providing the next volume.

The display criteria are very important, Dave tells us. Homes are not public libraries, and clients shouldn't be expected to share their resources with everyone in the neighborhood. But once neighbors and other friends and relatives see the set in all of its fashionable and prestigious glory, they will want a set of their own. It's the American suburban dream, we are told, but that isn't even the most important aspect of what we are doing. It's the children, the young raw minds of the early readers, the grade schoolers that have questions that mom and dad can't possibly answer. And where is the school or public library? When is it available and how far away? Children, and adults, can be easily frustrated when they can't get an answer or satisfy their thirst for knowledge at their own convenience. Furthermore, any family that refers a new prospect to GBE will receive a free, bonus yearbook to keep their encyclopedias up to date.

I think about this, the times when I wanted to explore some topic or get additional material on a homework assignment. My dad's reading was usually confined to the daily newspaper and *Readers Digest Condensed Books*. My mother was happy with cookbooks and western romance pulps. I acknowledge the need and the value, and Dave assures me it is a good question and that we should all be ready for similar questions from clients. Read the material, he reminds me.

Lunch is brought in, and we spend the rest of the afternoon talking about the next day's assignments, some legal aspects of contracts, and about the psychology of parents and how they can be helped to understand what we are offering. I leave that evening feeling like a crusader about to embark on the holy quest. I hope I am worthy.

WEDNESDAY, DAY THREE: FIRST DAY IN THE FIELD

IT IS OUR THIRD DAY AT GBE, AND AT NINE WE MEET some of the other consultants. Besides Ricky and me, there will be a man in his early thirties, Scott Richards, who will accompany us. This is Glen's field team. Normally, he tells us, there is only one trainee on a team. Since there are only four to a car, we will only have Scott and Glen to give us additional help in the field. Glen tells us that in a couple of weeks we won't be trainees, and he'll have a fully competent team again. Ricky asks him what happens if we don't get a contract before the end of the following week. I have the same question but don't ask it, not wanting to project weakness or lack of confidence.

Hey, no pressure, Dave says, that sometimes happens, even to the best of us. At the end of two weeks, you'll be working on commission only. Remember? No free meals. When you get your contract, you get paid, whenever. Then Dave looks at Ricky, this time without a trace of compassion or amusement. However, he explains to all of us, GBE can't carry non-producers. If you are making a sincere effort to do the job, we'll work with you. We've invested in you, right? Your success is our success. Then he explains how the field managers (I look at Glen) and the district managers (he points to himself) earn their income. The field managers receive a twenty-five dollar bonus from each set placed by a member of their team. The district manager receives a twenty dollar bonus for every successful contract written by any field team in his district. That's why the management team can't afford to entertain weak consultants. Occasionally, the managers will try to write their own contracts, especially if things are slow or they are breaking in a new batch of trainees. We eat lunch, once again catered sandwiches and cake, and prepare for the field. After a few words of encouragement and a hand-grasping ritual in the center of the room, a bonding rite to be repeated everyday, we grab our briefcases and head for Glen's car. It is two thirty.

A beautiful day highlights our trip to the suburbs north of Sacramento. The area has developed and expanded during the past ten years, and much of it is low to medium-priced tract housing, endless rows of me-too residences with the look-alike patches of front lawn and a token ornamental tree not yet ready to provide shade. Glen has a map of the area, and he has selected a section for us to visit. He assigns Ricky and I each to a four-block strip, both sides of the street, comprising almost a hundred houses that represent my first venture. It is three thirty. You won't get to all of them today, he says, unless no one is home or you're really having a bad day. A full presentation can take anywhere from fifteen minutes to half an hour, so unless we are super efficient, we can probably only expect to close three or four deals in the time allotted. He says this with a hopeful smile, but neither Ricky nor I believe it. We'd be thrilled to write just one contract.

Glen parks the car. He tells Ricky and I to leave our briefcases in the car because we will be observers on our first consultation. Glen pairs with me and Scott takes Ricky. We walk in different directions. Glen swings his briefcase and walks like he has just closed a dozen sales that day. He tells me to say nothing and observe everything. He and I walk up to a pink stucco house with a low open porch, and Glen rings the bell. About fifteen seconds later, a woman appearing to be in her early thirties answers the door. Glen greets her with a warm smile, introduces us, and delivers his opening spiel about education and the great opportunity that Global Books is about to bestow on her family. After every two or three sentences, he smiles and asks her if that isn't great news, or how about that, or something similar, followed by an affirmative nod of his head. She is transfixed, staring at his smile, hanging on every word, looking at the briefcase. She answers his questions about her children, their ages, and their hobbies. She invites us in, and we enter a small living room with modest furniture. A television faces a sofa and two easy chairs. There is no bookcase.

Glen launches into the presentation, displaying the flats and handing her the sample volume, the one that will be hers free if she accepts the generous offer to provide her with a beautiful bookcase full of magnificent volumes of knowledge. He never talks for more than a minute without pausing to coax an affirmative response from the young housewife. She is convinced and is handed a contract. Glen quietly asks her if she and her husband rent or own the house and if she can sign legally for the offer. They own and she can, to which Glen smiles and takes her through the formalities. Twenty minutes later, he is shaking her hand, congratulating her on a decision that will change the lives of her three children. The completed set will be the pride of the entire family.

We step outside and move down the street toward our car. We see Ricky and Scott also walking up the street. Good to go, says Scott with a grin and Glen turns to Ricky and I. That's all there is to it, he says. We get in the car and drive a few miles to a different housing tract, but one that looks very much like the one we just left. He drops Ricky and me off at a corner and has each of us walk in opposite directions. Glen tells us to memorize the corner and he'll pick us up at seven thirty. If you are not there, I'll assume you're writing something up. I'll return at eight for a final sweep. If you're not there then, call a cab, and we'll reimburse you. Now grab your briefcases and go write up your first deal. The car moves off as Ricky and I step away from the corner to begin our consulting careers.

I smile with more confidence than I feel and walk toward the first house off of the corner. Four hours. The thought occurs to me to find a park somewhere close by and relax. Suddenly, the rah-rah and camaraderie of the conference room is far away, and I am just a seventeen year-old high school graduate without a clue. You'll make mistakes, Dave had said, especially your first couple of days. Don't worry about it—just give it your best shot. Pretend like you're in a play and the script says you will come out on top. A hand on the shoulder and a firm look in his eyes, sending his only son into battle. I guess that's his job.

The first house is a blue and white structure that looks like almost every other house on the street, except for color. All are pastels with white trim, an attached garage, and a small front porch with overhang. This one, number 401, has two flowerpots hanging from the eaves. I memorize the number so I can make it back to my pick-up corner. In a few steps, I am ringing the doorbell. It will be mostly housewives at this time, we were told. That's good. It's the mothers who will be my focus, even when the father is present. Fathers worry about money, mothers worry about their children. I wait. I ring again, and I can hear something inside. No one comes and after a few more seconds I'm back on the sidewalk, moving quickly to its neighbor, 405. The house is identical except for orientation—the garage is on the right instead of left. Also, same result, no answer.

On to 409, again with a left garage. This one is done in lime green and has a different type of trellis across the porch. I ring and wait. I can hear footsteps approach and the door opens. She is probably in her mid-thirties, pleasant looking but not gorgeous. The screen door remains closed and she asks me if she can help me. I launch into my opening presentation.

"Good afternoon, ma'am. My name is William Rutledge, and I am an educational consultant for Global Educational

Services, the publisher of Global Educational Books. This afternoon I am visiting with select homes in your neighborhood to determine if you or one of your neighbors might qualify to be the recipient of a special reference program we are initiating." My opener is delivered flawlessly, following hours of practice the night before. I know how to do this. Her eyes follow me up and down, coming to rest on the briefcase in my left hand.

"What kind of program?" She asks.

Ah, that first all-important step, bingo! She asked me a question, giving me a chance to elaborate.

"Please allow me to elaborate. I have in my briefcase something you will truly find a marvel, something that can change your life, and your children's lives…"

"I don't have any children. My husband and I, well we just haven't been blessed yet."

I can't see her that well through the screen, but she might have tears. Her voice is a bit shaky and I'm caught off guard. I need to say something, anything to keep the moment going.

"I'm sure it's only a matter of time, ma'am, just got to keep giving it that old college try, you know?" I smile but it probably isn't very convincing.

"I doubt if you're old enough to be in college." She shuts the door without further words.

I am stunned. What did I do wrong? Was it something I said or didn't say? I stare at the closed door for another moment before turning and walking back to the street. She seemed so nice. I was right at the inside move, the time to cross the threshold and enter her sanctum, according to the training. They had a name for everything, each part of the presentation and for different types of settings and client assemblies. So much for quick results. The next two houses produce no answers. I think I see someone flash across a window at the second one, but I'm not sure. I check my tie, still straight. I'm beginning to perspire under a hot sun on a concrete platform with little available shade and no effective breeze. The briefcase is heavier than when I started and my new shoes, nicely polished, are not as comfortable as they had seemed that morning.

The door at the fifth house opens. A man stands there, shorter than myself, with balding hair and a cigarette held in his right hand.

"What can I do for ya?" he says. He doesn't sound like he wants to do anything for me or even to discuss it. But I launch into my opener and get as far as my name before he interrupts. "Don't give a damn about your name. What'd ya want? I'm busy"

Sorry, I tell him, sorry to interrupt what you were doing. Perhaps I can come back some other time at your convenience? I don't really intend to come back, unless he looks like a closer, which he doesn't, but we have been taught to maintain our professional demeanor throughout and to indicate we are interested in serving everyone, and always at their chosen time and place.

"Don't bother, I don't want what you got in there," he says, and steps back inside. The door stays open and I walk away. Five down and ninety-five (?) to go. It is only three forty-five and the park idea sounds better with each step. Unfortunately, I didn't see the map and I have no idea where a park or a school might be. Trudging to the next house, number 421, I resolve to put it behind me, to move forward with fresh resolve and good spirit. Dave and Glen were both pretty clear about this. You don't give a rat's ass

about the no-niks, they said. One contract will wipe twenty
or thirty of them away without a trace. You only care about
the yes-I-will folks. Forget the rest. Yeah, forget them and
the ones that don't answer. They will be denied the pleasure
of having one of the best educational resources in the world.

By five-thirty, cars are driving by and pulling into drive-
ways. Hubbies returning home from work, a slight shift
in strategy called for when presenting to a couple. I keep
looking for torture tools—swings, slides, and sandboxes in a
side yard or glimpse of a back yard—indications of children.
Glen told us that closing rates were two to three times more
successful when torture tools are present. Parents that invest
big bucks on their own private backyard park are not going
to hesitate to provide a few bucks for their kid's education.
And, says Glen, don't ever use "torture tools" in front of the
parents—that's our little joke, hah-hah.

I look at my watch as I try each house. At most, there is
no answer. Those that do come to the door usually tell me
they are not interested or simply to go away and not bother
them. I begin to marvel at how lucky Glen was when we
visited the first house together. Just need more practice, I tell
myself, after the twentieth house is a no show. I keep count
of the attempts as a perverse marker of my incompetence,
a testimony to my growing sense of failure as an educational consultant. Now I walk and knock in order to get to
seven-thirty pickup time. Hope has all but fled of making
a presentation, much less of writing a contract.

At house number twenty-three, on the first side of the
fourth block of my allotment, a man in his late twenties
answers the door and doesn't immediately dismiss me. But,
he isn't fooled. Door-to-door is it, he asks, looking me up
and down. I start to explain about consulting and education

but he smiles and interrupts me with a grin. Helluva of a way to make a living. I tried it myself a couple of years ago, selling cleaning products, he tells me. Once again, I try to refute the salesman label, but he cuts that short by asking me if I need a drink of water or iced tea. Damned hot out there and that stuff you're dragging around in that suit probably doesn't help. He holds the screen door open for me and I follow him to the kitchen. He pours and hands me a glass of ice water, which I gratefully take and consume in a flash. I hand him back the glass and whisper thanks. No sale here, he says, but good luck. You'll need it. I leave the house in a daze, thankful for his hospitality and friendliness.

It is almost seven-thirty when I arrive back at the pickup corner. Ricky looks like I feel, wrung out by the heat and strung out by the lack of appreciation or enthusiasm from our would-be clients. We confirm our failures to Scott and Glen when we enter the car. Neither are surprised, and Glen tells us that it would be actually unusual for a trainee to close on his first day. Has anyone ever done it, I venture. No one in our lifetime, laughs Scott, as if it was all a big joke. Tomorrow is another day, a better day, right, boys? Glen is always happy.

THURSDAY, DAY FOUR: ANOTHER MEETING, ANOTHER FIELD DAY

THE NINE O'CLOCK MEETING STARTS OUT SOMBER. As foretold, none of the trainees wrote a contract the day before. Oddly, each of the field managers accompanied by a trainee did close, and they proudly display their signed forms for us to read. They are glowing with smug satisfaction as we stew in the frustration and uncertainty of yesterday's efforts.

Dave says nothing for a few minutes, but he makes sure everyone has coffee and doughnuts. Today, the sweet roll selection is fancier and more colorful, in sharp contrast to the mood.

Only one day, a few hours, Dave begins. Nothing to worry about. You'll be writing like pros in no time. He walks around the room, asking each of us for comments, observations, what went wrong and right. I mention the ice water. See, Willy at least got into a house and talked to someone. Felt good, huh, Willy? Ricky had spent ten minutes talking to a woman on the porch, but she wouldn't let him into the house. From about eleven on, we receive additional words of advice on how to break down resistance, how to counter a list of objections to our presentation. By lunchtime, Dave has us pumped up once again, smiling and praising our determination and pulling a fifty-dollar bill from his wallet and waving it as he jumps up and down like a demented cheerleader.

Wild isn't he? Glen is sitting next to me and offers his comment as if confiding in me but loud enough for several to hear. A few others join Glen in admiring the spirit of the moment and, by the time the food arrives, we are participating in cheers and slogans designed to motivate and move us into the field for another day of educational consultation.

This time, Glen and Scott simply drop us off at the same place, to complete our circuit on the other side of the street. I wonder where they go when they leave us, asks Ricky. I don't have an answer so we move off in our respective directions, trying to retain some of the morning magic and cheer.

It doesn't take long for the magic to disappear. At the third house, I run into my first hostile encounter. It is an older man, a huge guy in his forties or fifties, wearing a stained t-shirt and jeans. He looks very blue collar, like he works in a factory or garage and he isn't having any of my gab. He opens the door and yells at me to get the fuck away from his house. I don't say a word. Backing up, holding my briefcase in front of me with both hands, I mumble something like okay or yes sir, I'm not sure exactly what. He steps onto the porch, his fists clenched, jaw sticking toward me like he is about to throw a punch. I stumble backwards off the porch step, barely managing to keep my feet as I back down the walkway to the street. And don't ever come back here, you little son of a bitch. It is loud enough for any neighbor to hear, but there is no one else in sight. I walk quickly up the street, passing the next two houses without stopping.

I want more than anything to go home at that moment. If not home, then a drive-in, a park, anyplace but the housing tract with its miserable people. I am trembling, on the verge of tears. This response had not been covered in our meetings. I finally approach another house and I'm relieved when there is no answer. The afternoon and evening unfold like the day before, a few uninterested people at the door, no invites, no ice water. I arrive at the pickup corner fifteen minutes early. Ricky comes on time and he can see I am not a happy businessman. I tell him about my encounter. What would you have done if he had swung at you, he asks. Left the damned briefcase with him and fled for my life, I tell him. At that we both laugh and Glen is there with the car. He listens to my tale without any attempt at levity, then informs me I did the right thing and that it does happen, although not often. He asks me if I'm okay, and I tell him I think so. I don't mention that I am ready to forget the whole enterprise, and it wouldn't take much to quit then and there.

I probably don't need to mention it. Glen understands more than I think he does. It isn't his first rodeo.

FRIDAY, DAY FIVE: CELEBRATION

FRIDAYS CAME WITH SPECIAL RECOGNITION FOR THE consultants who had written during the week. Their names were announced, and they were presented with certificates and checks. All of the field managers received money, to the applause of the assembled group. None of the trainees had been successful, although the appliance salesman had almost closed on a placement. It fell through at the last minute when the husband rejected the terms in the contract. The before-lunch pep talks were enhanced by the payments and recognition, and we were told to emulate the field managers, ask questions, think about what we were doing right and wrong. No one mentioned my nasty encounter to the group, but Dave drew me aside and indicated he had heard and sympathized. There are always a few assholes out there, he said, his hand on my shoulder, giving me the son and dad routine. Do you want us to go to his place and beat the crap out of him? He said it with a serious face and when he saw my eyes dilate, he cracked up and walked away, shaking his head.

THE AFTERNOON HOUSE VISITS START OUT LIKE MOST days, no answer and a few polite but disinterested people at their doors. It is just after six o'clock when I approach a white stucco house with a dark brown frame, one of the few houses that look distinctly different from the ones next to it. I am feeling discouraged again, only prepared to make a half-hearted effort for my introduction.

The main door is open and only a screen door stands between me and the living room. I can see people moving around, so I knock on the door frame instead of using the bell. A teen girl, appearing just a bit younger or about the same age as me, steps up to the screen and says hi. She is the first young person, other than one or two small children, that has answered the door during my week of visits. I say hi and launch into my intro. An older man, her father, comes to the door and stands beside her as I continue.

Come on in and let's see what you have, he says, and he holds the screen door open so I can enter. His wife stands in the middle of the room. When I enter, she walks to the television, and turns it off. The girl disappears into a dining room and kitchen to the left.

My mind is racing, trying to get ready for the presentation phase, my first opportunity to deliver it in the real world. Have a seat, the man tells me and points to an overstuffed sofa with a coffee table in front. The woman expresses her concern that it is a hot evening and I must be thirsty. I affirm this and she walks into the kitchen. The man sits in an easy chair across from me and indicates he is ready to listen to what I have to say. I am suspicious. Must be a slow night on television, I think, but what the hell. I'll try to be amusing. I give him the sample volume and start my routine, extolling the benefits of a major reference work with easy access. He carefully examines the book as I talk. I attempt to emulate Glen's technique of pausing and asking my prospect to respond. He looks up at me and says that this must be an expensive set of books, from the look and feel of them. How many volumes, he asks. I pull the flat from the briefcase and toss it on the floor as we had been taught to do, so it opens to reveal the thirty volumes with matching spines as they would appear in the bookcase. The mother and daughter return from the kitchen and the girl hands me a large glass of cola with ice. I look at her and smile. I hadn't asked for a Coke. You must have read my mind, I tell her, grateful for the drink I was all but addicted to.

The mother sits down in a different chair, but the daughter takes a place next to me on the sofa. She is dressed modestly, in a below-the-knee patterned dress. Her hair is brownish-blonde fixed in a ponytail. She wears no makeup and she isn't beautiful, but she isn't unattractive. She has a down-home wholesomeness about her and her parents reflect a casual, neighborly friendliness.

The three of them listen attentively to my presentation, asking a few questions for clarification. I become more excited as I realize that I am on the threshold of writing a contract. I tell them about the free first volume, the book-case, and the low monthly purchase plan—no objections are voiced. The girl keeps looking at me and the mother keeps looking at her daughter. She apparently has no brothers or sisters and she, like myself, has just graduated from high school. This isn't the ideal family profile for an encyclopedia placement, but their interest seems genuine.

The daughter takes my empty glass and asks me if I would like some more. Also, we have some pecan pie I made this afternoon. She says that with obvious pride, and her mother tells me that Darla is a great cook, that I really should try some of her pie. The father nods and everyone, including myself, is in agreement. Eating pie and drinking Coke provides a much better way to kill Friday evening than knocking on more doors. Darla brings me another drink and a big hunk of pie.

In between bites, I retrieve a contract and give it to the father. He indicates they would need to discuss it and give it some thought. Can you come back here on Sunday, he asks. If you can make it for dinner, we might have a better answer for you then. Dinner? I didn't work on weekends and I didn't have a car or a driver's license. The opportunity to close seems very real and I don't want to pass on my first chance. A homemade dinner (Darla can really cook up a meal to feast on, according to her mother) was also appealing, but how to take advantage of it? I hesitate and then explain. I am only seventeen, don't have a car, and I need to conclude the business during a weekday. If not tonight, then some day the following week. I know that would occur only if I can talk Glen into bringing me to the house before my scheduled route.

The father and mother look at their daughter, then at me. Perhaps some other time, he says. Do you have a card? I did not. We only received cards if and after we finished training. The father stands up, shakes my hand, and thanks me for coming by. We'll think about it, he says. The mother and daughter are silent as I repack my case, put the contract back, and follow the man to the door. I look back and the daughter gives me a smile and a wave of her hand. It is the last time I see her or them.

The rest of the evening passes quietly with no new hopes, but somehow I feel relaxed and at peace. The respite has been a good one and my faith in people has been restored. When I tell Glen and Scott about my dinner invitation, they both grin and congratulate me on a nice try. One of the perks we mentioned, says Glen with a wink. Ricky had also had a better evening, but without a write-up. They drop us off at the downtown office, reminding us to be sharp and ready at nine on Monday.

MONDAY, DAY SIX

I spent most of the weekend reliving the highs and lows of the previous week. Most of it was not dramatic: doors that didn't open, apathy when they did. Only two times was there anger and only one of those came as a threat. Darla and her family had been the other extreme, but unfortunately I couldn't take advantage of it. I didn't know if they were potential clients or whether their main interest was in me as a possible friend for their daughter. The steady referral to her cooking and her availability for dinner seemed to indicate the latter, but their ardor seemed to cool after I told them my age and that I was without wheels. She was probably hoping for someone with potential and better established in a promising business. Suit, tie, polished shoes, and a briefcase don't necessarily equate to success.

***

The second week starts off like most of the first week, although there are two changes. The five trainees decrease to four and GBE is getting ready to run another ad to recruit additional personnel. There is also a subtle but noticeable undercurrent to the sales meetings. First of all, they are now referred to as sales—the pretense of consultation is all but dropped. There is also a reminder there will be no compensation until a placement closes, including final acceptance by GBE corporate headquarters. Other than lunch, it means we are still working on our own dime. I don't know about the others, but it was a very thin coin.

The afternoon brings us to a new neighborhood. It appears a bit more affluent, nicer houses and yards, many with expensive sets of torture tools. Despite the upturn in the surroundings, the results are all too familiar. Polite, but no thank you. I am no closer to writing a contract than on the first night.

That evening, after we arrive at the downtown office, Ricky tells me he is leaving. This is his last day. I ask him if he has informed Dave or Glen. Glen, he says, I won't see Dave—no reason to. Why, I ask, why not stick it out the next four days and try to earn the two weeks' pay. I remind him that contracts can be written—we saw our field team do it the first night.

That's the problem, he tells me in a quiet voice, his head lowered. I found out from someone who once worked for GBE how that works.

I don't say a word, waiting for him to continue.

It was all a setup, a show for the suckers…us.

What? What are you talking about?

He looks into my eyes and the sad story spills out. A friend of mine worked for them, he says, and I asked him last night about how easy it had been for the managers. My friend laughed and told me they had taken us to a place where the so-called prospects have been paid in advance to accept and sign a contract. The sale doesn't actually take place. He even told me where they took us. They've been using the same four or five places for the past three years.

I am stunned and angry. It makes sense, however. The continuing deception, the misleading terminology, the generous deal in which we never mention the total cost of the purchase. There are two sets of victims: the clients and the trainees. Undoubtedly, some individuals did sell and collect money, but most of it was a pyramid scheme. The managers make their money mostly through the salesmen they supervise. I leave Ricky at a bus stop and walk the three miles home lost in deep thought. It still made sense to try and collect the promised salary in the next four days, but I now know this is anything but a career. Regardless of what happens, this would be my last week.

TUESDAY, DAY SEVEN: FINALE

ANOTHER SALES MEETING, PEP TALK, AND A LUNCH. Now there are three trainees, including me. Glen indicates that only two cars would go out and the appliance salesman would be with Scott. Glen keeps looking at me, trying to encourage me. I can't completely hide my mood, but I say nothing about what Ricky had related. A new set of trainees were to be interviewed on Thursday.

Glen drops me off at three thirty, and I start my route. After knocking on several doors with little encouragement, I come to a small, poorly maintained house on a corner. The lawn has not been mowed recently and the front needs to be painted. A tricycle is turned upside down on the porch and a couple of toys are scattered in the side yard. No torture tools, but kids are in evidence. I step up and ring the doorbell. Footsteps approach and a young woman, perhaps in her middle twenties, opens the door. She is friendly and after I introduce myself, she invites me in.

She is wearing a chemise, a bag-like dress that emphasizes her hips. Her hair is wet, as if she has just emerged from a shower. I apologize for possibly disturbing her, but she disregards it. We sit down and I start my presentation. In between my comments, I learn that Sarah Ferndale has recently been divorced and has three kids, aged six, four, and less than two. I can hear the youngest one shouting in a back bedroom. I hand her the sample book and she seems impressed. The flat showing the bookcase draws a smile and she indicates that it would be a great asset for her oldest daughter who would be entering the first grade. By the time she acquires all of the volumes, her daughter would be in the third grade.

She is ready to place an order so I pull a contract from the briefcase and begin filling it out, including personal and financial references. She has a bank account for checking but no savings. That isn't my main concern—that's something GBE would evaluate. Her six-year-old enters the room and sees the displays. She looks at some of the color plates and smiles at her mother. This is going better than I expected and I know that I can finally close on a contract and collect my two weeks' salary. All that is left is her signature. And a question.

With the pen in her hand, she asks me if the first book is really free. I tell her yes, that in fact, she is holding it. We give the purchasers the first books so there is no delay or second thoughts. We had extra copies in the car if we wrote additional contracts on the same day. And the others? I told her they would come once a month and all she had to pay was shipping and handling. Of course, I tell her with a smile, you do have to agree to display the books prominently once we send you the bookcase. It is also free, except for shipping and handling. We want you to show these proudly to your neighbors, all part of our educational mission.

I almost choke on this last instruction. She bends over the contract. How much did you say the shipping and handling charges come to? I watch her as she looks up from the contract she has just signed.

Currently, they come to $26.98 per volume or per month, I tell her, as casually as I can. She sits up on the couch.

With the bookcase, doesn't that come to over $800? It doesn't take her any time to calculate it, as if there was an adding machine inside her head. I nod. How could I deny it? Few people bothered to figure the total. We were in the land of time payments; nobody ever paid full price up front for big purchases. Not our nobodies—we depended on spreading the pain over a two and a half year period.

She sits there and looks at me. She puts the pen down. I don't have a job right now, she says. I have some welfare coming in, and my husband is supposed to pay child support but it hasn't started yet. I will have to wait on this. She turns to her daughter. We can get this for you later, I promise.

I am numb. Not because I have just lost a sale; I know now that her finances would never make it past corporate. The feeling comes from knowing that she really wanted this for her children, that if she had the resources she would have gladly sacrificed other things to get it and—she couldn't. I look around at her shabby furniture, bare floors, at her daughter's torn dress.

I reach over, pick up the contract, and tear it up. I give her a big smile. Not for you at this time, I say. Your daughters will do just fine. Feed them, clothe them, keep them in school. I feel much older than seventeen as I put the torn contract and my display materials back in my briefcase. Tears were running down the side of her face as she leads me to the door. She takes my left hand in both of her hands and thanks me for understanding. I thank her for helping me understand something more critical.

I still have two hours before my pickup time. There is a bus stop and bench on the chosen corner, and I sit down and wait, ignoring the comings and goings of buses and their passengers. When Glen pulls up, he is alone. I throw my briefcase in the back and climb in after it.

How did it go he asks over the front seat as he drives toward downtown. I had a signed contract I answer. Great, way to go Willy, you just earned your way out of trainee status. Dave thought you'd make it.

I didn't make it, I say. I tore up the contract. She didn't have a pot to pee in, and there was no way she would have passed by corporate.

His face falls. He starts to tell me that I should have sent it on anyway and let GBE make the final decision. He must see the nasty glare I'm giving him through the rearview mirror, because he shuts up and doesn't say another word to me as we drive back to town.

See you tomorrow? He asks half-heartedly as I get out of the car. I leave my briefcase in the back seat.

Not a chance. Not tomorrow, not ever. I slam the door and walk away, head high for the first time in nine days.

AFTERWORD

LOVE CAN BE, AND OFTEN IS, ELUSIVE. AT TIMES we believe it is something solid, a thing we can hold in our hands, examine, and describe in detail. It is real, predictable, and at our beck and call. Neurobiologists, physiological psychologists, and anthropologists attempt to describe the emotional repertoire of love and romance in terms of chemical transmitters and neural circuits, conditioned responses, and cultural contexts. How convenient to be in such control.

The reality is far different. Love, either in scientific explanations or in the musings of poetry and prose, is a nearly indefinable condition. It is subjective, to say the least, a product of an individual's relationship with others and also with one's self. Hard to quantify, difficult to reproduce, sometimes unattainable for those who need it most, yet love can raise its beautiful head at times and in places we least expect. Love can be expressed at people, animals, other objects of nature, and inanimate creations. Like a talented actor on an ever-changing stage, it manifests itself in an infinite variety of guises. No two performances are exactly the same, and no outcome can be predicted with certainty. How lucky is that?

ACKNOWLEDGMENTS

THE AUTHOR GRATEFULLY ACKNOWLEDGES THE FOL-
lowing for their critiques and comments on various
versions of the stories included in this volume: John
and Eva Lund, Leo Dubray, William Cook, Lee French,
and Alla Powers. My thanks to Roslyn McFarland
for the cover illustration—she nailed it! My editor at
Luminare Press, Patricia Marshall, and her publishing
staff (Claire Flint Last, Melissa Thomas, Kim Harper-
Kennedy, and Jamie Passaro) are the dream team every
writer wishes for. I was inspired to write some of these
stories by real people and real events. Without naming
or embarrassing you, thank you for being a part of my
real life and my imaginary universe.

ABOUT THE AUTHOR

LAWRENCE W. POWERS IS A RETIRED UNIVERSITY professor living in Eastern Oregon. He writes fiction under the name of L. Wade Powers. His first novel, *The Home*, was published in 2017. Luminare Press published a short story collection, *The Party House*, in 2019. Several of his short stories and a poem have appeared in anthologies. A third novel, *New Albion Sunset*, is in preparation and based on the presence of Francis Drake in the Pacific Northwest. Powers has served as a contributing editor for the *Journal of the Shaw Historical Library* and as the creative nonfiction editor of *Timberline Review*, a literary journal based in Portland. His critical essay on Steinbeck's *The Winter of Our Discontent* was published in the *Steinbeck Review*.

www.ingramcontent.com/pod-product-compliance
Lightning Source LLC
Chambersburg PA
CBHW032053050726

47590CB00001B/256